Ahead of Her Time:
The 1920s Woman

Ahead of Her Time: The 1920s Woman

Genevieve Smith

Copyright © 2005 by Genevieve Smith.

ISBN 10:   Softcover   1-4257-1903-1

ISBN 13:   Softcover   978-1-4257-1903-6

All rights reserved. No part of this book may be reproduced or transmitted in any form or by any means, electronic or mechanical, including photocopying, recording, or by any information storage and retrieval system, without permission in writing from the copyright owner.

This is a work of fiction. Names, characters, places and incidents either are the product of the author's imagination or are used fictitiously, and any resemblance to any actual persons, living or dead, events, or locales is entirely coincidental.

This book was printed in the United States of America.

To order additional copies of this book, contact:
Xlibris Corporation
1-888-795-4274
www.Xlibris.com
Orders@Xlibris.com

32075

For my angel daughter, Donna, with all my love

Chapter 1

Mary Dunmore pressed a handkerchief over her mouth, trying to stifle the sobs in her throat. She struggled to blink away the tears in her eyes. Ben's casket rested on a walnut buffet, hugging the parlor wall. Tom had spent hours in the cellar. The parts of the box had to be shaped and joined before they were stained and waxed, becoming lustrous like the strand of pearls that his wife wore.

Tom snuggled his arm around Mary and drew her close. "I did the best I could, sweetheart." The words soft spoken instead of his usual firmness.

Tears spilled down her cheeks. "I know. It's fine."

She dabbed at her face with the back of her hand, then leaned down and pressed her lips against Ben's pale cheek. Still trying to comprehend that he was actually gone, felled by the flu that had been raging in West Park for weeks. Mary had tended him like an angel, hovering over with cool cloths and gentle hands, but the virus had done its due, squeezing the life out of their little boy who had been a magnet of energy.

She reached in the pocket of her dress and felt Ben's gold ring, pulling it out and slipping it on his finger. He had loved that ring. It was never worn when he was digging in the dirt for buried treasure or building a sand castle edged by a moat. He wore the ring when he went to Sunday School or birthday parties. Highlights of his short life.

The air was filled with the sweetness of the yellow roses nestled at the foot of the casket. Ferns provided a feathery backdrop for the baskets of flowers. She moved to the end of the buffet and peered at the visitors' book. Gertie Schumaker, her best friend, was first on the list. A single page, filled with the names of those who had dared to come to the door, anguished looks on their faces and faltering voices of condolence. Some wore gauze masks. Others brought food or flowers and handed them in before scurrying away. A few dared to enter, glanced quickly at Ben, scribbled their names in the book and left. The obituary that had appeared in the Gazette was pasted inside the front cover.

DUNMORE—On Sunday, Feb. 23, 1920, at 6 p.m., Benjamin T., beloved son of Thomas B. and Mary Dunmore (nee McGuffy), aged 3 years 6 months. Funeral services will be held at the parent's residence, 1200 Twelfth St., West Park, McKees Rocks, Wednesday afternoon, Feb. 25.

Tom patted her shoulder. "I'll go get Lily now."

Mary's gaze turned to the Bible, resting behind the guest book. The name, Thomas Benjamin Dunmore, printed in gold letters on the leather cover. Tom had been reluctant when the salesman came to the door, showing off the HOLY BIBLE, published by The National Publishing Company in Philadelphia. But she persuaded him to place an order and pay in installments. Somehow she'd figure a way to cut back on what she spent to put food on the table. The thought needled that the words in the Bible might unravel the reason why Ben had to die when he had barely begun to live. Only a few weeks ago, before his deep cough and the blood-tinged froth in his mouth took hold, Ben had been pedaling his tricycle around the boardwalk, circling the house as fast as his sturdy little legs would go.

Tom came through the arched doorway with Lily, their five-year old in a dress Mary had made. Long-sleeved, pale rayon with ecru lace on the bodice. Lily's tawny hair brightened by a pink bow pinned to the top of her head. She was their first child to come down with the flu, then pneumonia in February. But Lily was on the road to getting better when Ben took the flu and was whisked away in only two days.

"You look very pretty," said Mary, leading Lily by the hand to the casket.

Lily stood motionless, her eyes focused on Ben, taking in his long lashes and his lips that held a faint smile, his brown hair with a wave brushed back from his high forehead. She stood stiffly. "It's like he's asleep, Mother. Is he gonna wake up soon?"

"Ben's awake in Heaven now," murmured Mary.

A handful of friends came for the service and settled in the metal chairs that had been delivered and put in place by Howard Honeycutt, the funeral director whose parlor rested on Chartiers Avenue, a busy thoroughfare in the Rocks. Reverend Dryer arrived, a short man with an unlined face, dark eyes, and a smile lit up by his gold tooth. He had christened Lily and Benjamin two years ago in this very room. Gertie Schumaker served as sponsor. Tom was at work in the railroad yard by Island Avenue and didn't cater to baptisms and the like.

When the Reverend nodded, Mary and Tom took their places on the homespun-covered settee. Lily sat between them with hands clasped, a gold bracelet dangling on her arm, her buttoned leather shoes smoothing back and forth on the carpet.

Emma Sulzer played *Jesus Loves Me* on the Meister piano before Reverend Dryer began to speak, his voice easing forth like honey from a pitcher. Mary sat in numbness, eyeing Ben's casket, the minister's words drifting overhead, a storm cloud ready to burst. Later, no matter how hard Mary tried, she could recall nothing about the Reverend's message except the 23rd Psalm that he recited before everyone joined in the Lord's Prayer.

The afternoon sun cast a glow through the muslin curtains at the casement windows as they prepared to leave for Ben's burial in Mount Calvary, a cemetery nestled on a hillside that spread its arms wide. Friends huddled at the front door while Mary and Tom headed to the hall for their coats and hats.

Lily edged to the casket, glancing furtively at Honeycutt as he folded up the chairs in a hurry and put them in a stack. Quickly she bent down, slipped the ring off Ben's finger and hid it in the pocket of her dress.

Chapter 2

The next morning Mary and Tom rose to a chilly bedroom, the windows frosted over by the breath of a new-fallen snow. Tom peered through the foggy panes as Mary pulled her woolen house gown from the hanger and headed to the bathroom.

"I have to go back to work today," muttered Tom, reaching for his heavy pants and suspenders, strung over the Colonial chair in the corner.

While Tom was shaving the stubble from his face, Mary hurried to Lily's room and peeked in. She was still asleep, Grandma's patchwork quilt pulled high over her head. Mary decided to let Lily sleep a while longer. She turned to Ben's room and hesitated, recalling how he always balled himself up and settled on his stomach. Opening the door, one look at the empty bed twisted her stomach into a rock-hard knot and the tears came. She pulled the door tight, trying to shut out her pain, and headed for the stairs.

At the landing she stood still and took a deep breath, holding onto the smooth banister to steady herself. Remembering the time Ben had slid down the railing and jumped off onto the floor . . . and the time he'd taken the roll of toilet paper and trailed it down the steps 'til the tissue ran out and only cardboard remained. Mary grimaced, the picture looming . . . Tom's picking up the leather strop that smoothed his straight-edged razor and whipping Ben's bare behind 'til it turned fiery red. The remembrance still overwhelmed her with helplessness.

"That's what my father would have done," Tom had roared when she flung recriminations at him.

Mary hurried to the kitchen, choking back her anger and forcing herself to focus on breakfast. The only thing she craved in the mornings was rolled oats with milk and brown sugar and a cup of hot tea. Three years ago, after rationing began, the sugar allowance was reduced to two pounds per person per month. She gave up the heaping spoonful of sugar on her oatmeal in hopes that the soldiers would get it. No need to worry about having enough sugar now. The bin in the Hoosier kitchen cabinet was filled to the brim.

While putting on her apron, a memory floated. She and Tom had married in 1910 and began to work painstakingly. Tom at the Pittsburgh & Lake Erie Railroad. Mary at the A&P Tea Company. They stowed away every penny for building their dream house, but she quit her job after Lily was born in 1914, the same year Germany declared war on Russia and France.

Mary shuddered. The Germans started sinking U.S. merchant ships in 1917, causing the United States to declare war on Germany. She and Tom moved into their two-story brick bungalow in West Park, Pittsburgh's first urban park. The house boasted a cellar, fireplace, three bedrooms, two porches, and a yard big enough for flowers and two youngsters.

She had to admit that they were lucky. The World War brought plenty of heartache to the town, but Tom kept his job at the P&LE. He was a fireman, feeding and tending the fires of locomotives, jokingly called Iron Horses by the old timers. The Island Avenue Yard was a gathering point for cars to and from local industries. The cars were assembled and classified in the yard that was always congested, but Tom loved his work, feeling a surge of power as he stoked the fire and watched the red hot flames leap into life.

He went to work in the afternoon. It was close to midnight before he got home. In winter's rain or snow or summer's sun and heat, he walked from Island Avenue through the dark tunnel to Broadway and finally to 1200 Twelfth Street. Mary was always waiting with a hearty meal and a loving touch. They went to bed at 1 a.m. when most folks were already tucked away. Mary rose early to tend the children while Tom enjoyed his sleep 'til later in the morning.

She moved to the kitchen window and opened it, reaching into the box that hung outside where they kept perishables cold in the winter. After pulling out a package of sausage, she filled the coffee pot, set it on the gas stove and began to make patties. They were put in an iron skillet, along with slices of cornmeal mush she'd made during the week. Two eggs, fried sunny side up, topped off Tom's breakfast.

He came through the kitchen door, tall and lean, his rugged arms holding the newspaper and the milk that had been delivered on the front porch. Sitting down at the table, the faded blue of his work shirt mirrored the blue of his eyes. "I called to tell them I'm on the list for today. What are you gonna do, sweetheart?"

She bit her lip. "Haven't given it a thought. There's always plenty of work. I'll think about that later." Turning to the stove, she stirred oats into the pan filled with boiling water.

"If you need something from the store, I can go down street for you." Tom's voice bordered on gentleness. She shivered, imagining how it would be to face friends who'd be asking about Ben, but she knew Tom would be up to the task. He'd give them a clipped answer that would stifle further questions. Picking up the plate filled with food, she set it in front of him and poured his coffee.

"I don't need a thing, Tom. Nothing. There's plenty here to eat. Everyone brought us so much food I don't know when we'll ever finish it."

After filling a bowl with oats sprinkled with sugar, she set it on the table and sank into her chair. Instantly she was overcome with thoughts of Ben, wishing that he was in his highchair beside her, kicking his feet happily against the wooden legs, banging his silver spoon on the plate to make music as he ate. A speck of relief rippled . . . Tom had stored the highchair out of sight in the cellar, yet she ached for the feel of Ben's highchair by her arm.

She swallowed over the lump in her throat and struggled to regain her composure. "I wish Lily would get stronger. She seems so fragile. Her color isn't a bit good since she's had the flu."

"Don't fret, Mary." Tom leaned back in his chair and peered at her, his heavy brows forming a furrow between his eyes. "She'll pick up in good time. Maybe you ought to give her cod liver oil. I heard the druggist say that's real fine to pep up the blood."

"I don't know." Staring at the bowl of cereal, she suddenly felt an impulse to heave. Ben had loved oats and lapped it up dog fashion every morning of the world.

"Lily starts school this fall," said Tom, spreading butter on his mush and forking a bite toward his mouth. "She ought to be in the best of health. She'll be around a lot of kids and can catch germs."

Mary shook her head. "I'd have to ask Dr. Winter before I gave her anything."

Tom cast a determined look. "I want to make sure we're doing all we need to. Call the doctor this morning and see what she says."

Mary nodded and took a sip of her tea. Reluctantly she got up and stood at the back door window, gazing out at the sparrows, scratching the porch for the bread crumbs she scattered outside every day.

"You haven't eaten. Come back to the table," urged Tom as he spread out the newspaper on the table. "I don't want you to get down sick."

"I'm not hungry," she murmured, gazing at the trees coated with snow and the icicles streaming from the gutter on the back porch. All she could think about was Ben lying under an ice-cold blanket at Mount Calvary.

She heard Lily coming down the stairs, every step evenly paced. It reminded her of how different Ben was, darting and leaping over the steps two at a time, bubbling with laughter all the way down. Tom said he'd have to varnish the stairs again because of all the wear and tear that boy put on them.

Mary prodded herself to turn from the window and smile as Lily came through the door. "Good morning, sweetie. I hope you slept well."

"Yeah, but I got kinda cold." Lily's voice sounded froggy.

Tom pulled the stool close to his chair. "It was in the 20s last night. Yes sir-ee, winter time, Lily. Maybe you need an extra blanket on your bed. Mother will see to it. Come sit beside me and have your breakfast. That'll warm you up real good."

Lily climbed on the stool while Mary reached for the Baker's box stored on the shelf over the stove. "I'll fix your cocoa and toast while you have your oats."

Tom patted Lily's shoulder. "This would be a good day to play in the cellar with your dolls and all that furniture I made for you. It's too cold to go in the yard."

Lily shook her head hard. "I don't wanna play with dolls, Daddy."

Mary eyed her child, wishing that she'd been blessed with Ben's easy-going disposition. "Daddy made all that nice doll furniture for you. You ought to play with it, Lily. Pretty soon you'll be in school and won't have any time for dolls."

"You said you'd give me a piano lesson, Mother." Lily's words were defiant.

Mary buttered the toast and laid it on Lily's plate. "Not today, honey. There's too much to do. I'll give you a lesson later."

Lily's voice spiked. "Today. I want my lesson today. You promised."

Tom scratched his head. "Mother's worn out now. Wait 'til she's up to snuff."

Lily drooped. Mary set her cup of cocoa on the table.

Pushing his paper aside, Tom glanced at his railroad pocket watch, then reached for the pack of cigarette papers and the tin of Velvet Tobacco. Lily eyed him, instantly enchanted while he sprinkled tobacco on a thin paper and rolled it up to form a cigarette.

"Think I'll go down street this morning. I want to talk to the druggist about something."

Lily perked up. "I'll go with you, Daddy. Can I? Can I?"

"Finish your breakfast, child." He paused, a wrinkle skipping over his high forehead. A glimmer as he gazed at Lily. "You'll have to wrap up real good. It's cold as Christmas this morning."

Mary looked at Tom. "Lily's wool cap and scarf will keep her nice and warm. Don't let her stay outside too long."

Lily squirmed around on the stool and faced her dad. "Can I get candy at the drug store? Those red watermelon slices with sugar all over?"

Tom lit his cigarette and leaned back contentedly. "Eat your breakfast, Lily. I'm gonna have a smoke before we leave. Maybe we'll see about buying candy later."

Mary picked up her bowl, carried it to the counter, and scraped the oats into the pan where she kept scraps for the birds. She winced, thinking she'd never take another bite of oats as long as she lived.

Chapter 3

It was March, almost a month since the funeral. There wasn't a moment that Mary didn't have Ben in mind. She hadn't set foot in his room or even cracked the door open again. Not even once.

Sitting in front of her dressing table, Mary stared in the mirror. She was spiritless, the lack of vitality written not only on her face but in every movement of her slender body. Picking up the brush, she swept it aimlessly through her dark hair, letting it drift around her shoulders like a shawl. She reached for the pins in a bowl, gathering her long tresses, carefully forming a knot and fastening it at the back of her head with one pin after another. Finally, she pressed a mother-of-pearl comb into her scalp above the twist.

Lily appeared in the doorway of the bedroom. "I'm ready for my lesson. Hurry up, Mother."

"I'm coming, honey." Mary sighed as she rose from her bench at the dressing table. She'd never had a piano lesson and was learning how to play by studying the book so she could teach Lily. Progress was being made, but she wished they could afford lessons from a teacher who had studied at music school. That couldn't happen. It was hard enough making payments on the Meister that she'd coaxed Tom into buying. He didn't give a hoot about playing the upright piano or even listening to any music. He simply wanted to read his newspaper in peace.

Downstairs, the parlor was colder than usual with snowflakes fluttering outside, piling up at the bottoms of the windows. For a moment, she considered turning on the gas logs in the fireplace but changed her mind. The effort seemed more than she could bear at the moment. Besides, that would run the heat bill up higher, and she was intent upon saving every penny. She sank down on the bench beside Lily. *Teaching Little Fingers to Play* was already open to the page titled *Rain on the Roof*.

Lily giggled. "There's snow outside. I'm inside, playing about rain."

Mary frowned. "The snow will make it harder for your daddy to walk home from work tonight. I wish we had an auto."

"We'll have one some day, won't we?" Lily's words expectant.

"Maybe a long time from now. One of those fine Fords. Right now, let's get to work on your lesson." Mary pointed to the signature. "It's four-four time, Lily. Remember, four counts to each measure. The quarter note gets one count. That's the black note with the stem."

"The keys make me shiver," snickered Lily as she began to play.

After her lesson was over, Lily was enjoying sugar cookies and milk in the kitchen when Mary stepped out on the front porch to get the mail. Her spirit sailed when she spied the letter from her brother, Andrew McGuffy, stationed in the Army in Texas. Quickly she returned to the kitchen where she could relish everything that Andy had to tell her. He didn't write often, but his letters were always long, newsy ones. It was a momentous event to receive a soldier's letter after the War with Germany had ended. On the tail of life-threatening combat, a soldier struggled in an effort to return to some kind of normalcy.

Mary admired Andy's beautiful penmanship and regretted that she hadn't been able to graduate from high school like her brother and become an educated woman. Being the oldest child in a family with six children—three girls and three boys—meant there was much work to be done and very little money. Her father worked from dawn to dusk on the farm when the weather obliged and helped out in the only grocery store in town whenever he could.

Schooling was meager in the pint-sized Ohio town where she grew up. The school bell rang loud and clear, not only to begin the day but to end it. She walked a quarter-mile on a dirt road that turned into a mud pie on rainy days. At school, she shared a bench with three other students and kept a slate, notepad and dog-eared book close at hand. The teacher fed coal to a potbellied stove in the center of the room. In the winter, the water froze in the pail with a dipper, sitting by the door. Going to the bathroom meant hustling outside and dashing across a field to a smelly shed with bad words chalked all over the wall. Lunch was homemade bread with jelly or peanut butter tucked inside and maybe an apple, stashed in the corner of her book sack. Still, school was the brightest light in her life. She cried when she finished sixth grade and class ended. From then on, she read every book she could get her hands and eyes on.

Born ten years later than Mary, her brother, Andrew McGuffy, was blessed to be the youngest child in the family. During his growing-up, he attended a grammar school that flaunted desks, bathrooms and a furnace. Then he went to a spanking new high school that became a bridge to an Army career. He loved writing and wanted to work for a newspaper, but after the Germans sank the liner Lusitania with a submarine in 1915 and began sinking Allied ships during the World War, he joined the service as soon as he graduated in 1916. Later at Camp Gordon, Georgia, he became a member of the 82nd Infantry Division, nicknamed "All-Americans" since the men came from all 48 states.

Mary went to the cupboard and handed Lily another cookie. "I have a long letter to read from Uncle Andy. It'll be almost like he's visiting us. I hope you'll get to see him one of these days. Be quiet while I read, sweetie."

15 March 20

Dearest Mary:

I appreciated your letter and was deeply grieved to learn about Ben's death from the flu. I know how much he meant to you and Tom—Lily, too, of course. I cherish the pictures you sent me since he was born and have put them in an album with his name in gold on the cover.

I read in the paper that the flu virus started at Camp Funston, Kansas and underwent a mutation there. Then the soldiers carried it to the European front where outbreaks were reported as far east as Poland. A second mutation occurred on the front, making the virus even more deadly. They called it the Spanish Flu because Spain's media coverage spread the word. By 1918, the virus was attacking the population in the States. Worldwide, millions died, both young and old. There weren't enough doctors or medical supplies. They had no cure. Hospital tent camps were put up to care for the sick and dying. In four years, the World War killed millions. In only six months, the flu killed millions, including civilians.

Time has sped by since I boarded an army carrier in 1918 with the 82nd Infantry Division. We sat, stood, and slept on our kit bags piled on the deck. We hung over the rail, gawking at all the food and medical supplies being toted on board. Nobody would say when we were leaving because the German U-boats were lying in wait if they found out.

Finally the order came, "All men below!" and we knew we were leaving. We slipped out to sea in the dark and dropped anchor five miles away. By the time daylight dawned, there were other vessels around us. They were flying the flags of the Red Cross, Belgian Relief, Spanish, and Dutch. Other transports arrived and cast anchor. In a short while, everybody set sail for France. At that time, we had no idea where in the world we were headed.

It's been a while since I was one of those "Doughboys" in France, fighting the German Imperial Army. We fought in three major campaigns and did our part to defeat the enemy. Pershing never believed in the slow warfare of the Allied armies. They used bayonets and gas masks and hid in trenches. Often they risked death by scurrying across big fields and thick woods. Pershing was determined that the Americans were going to fight independently. He trained his men for rapid, driving warfare. When our planes were overhead during reconnaissance, the German anti-aircraft batteries shot at them, intent upon destruction. We got our share of shrapnel bursts, but I never saw one of our planes hit by a shell.

Well, Mary, that's enough of my running off at the mouth. I do have some good news though. I'm leaving Camp Travis in Texas and going to First Officers' Training Camp at Fort Riley in Kansas. I've been accepted and have made up my mind to follow an Army career. I'm certain that's what I want to do with my life now.

I've been dating a nurse, Amanda Roberts. She's a graduate nurse, registered by the State Board of Examiners and enrolled in the Red Cross Nursing Service. Amanda is eligible for service in war hospitals at home and abroad. This relationship may end like a shot out of a gun, but for now I'm enjoying her friendship. She's not one of those untrained women who became a "nurse" out of the goodness of her heart but is likely to make a mistake that causes irreparable loss to a soldier. I know of one case where a wounded lieutenant lost his leg because a "nurse" got him out of bed when he should never have been moved.

I must close now and write Mom. She'll want to know where I'm headed. Then I have to start packing. Again, I'm deeply sorry that you've lost Ben, and I know you are suffering mightily these days. I only wish there was something I could do to ease your pain. Please give Tom and Lily my best wishes. I regret not being with you at this sad time, but it is simply impossible.

Love,
Andy

Mary folded the letter carefully and tucked it in the envelope.

"What did Uncle Andy write?" asked Lily, eyeing her pensively.

Mary wiped a tear away. "He wanted us to know that he was very sorry about Ben and wished he could be here with us."

"Why can't he, Mother?"

"He's going to stay in the Army. Have a career as a soldier."

"What's a career?"

"It's what a person wants to do with his life."

Lily was puzzled. "You mean like Daddy works on the railroad?"

Mary nodded. "That's right, Lily."

"Do you have a career?"

Mary turned pensive. "No. I don't have a career. I'm only a housewife. I take care of you and your daddy and this home, Lily."

Chapter 4

Lily was practicing her piano lesson in the parlor while Mary packed Tom's lunchbox in the kitchen. A ham sandwich, devil's food cake and coffee in a thermos to relish during his break. Mary was gleeful. Soon Gertie Schumaker would arrive to spend some time. Her best friend and confidante to whom she could spill anything, no matter how bad.

Tom relaxed at the table, enjoying his smoke and the feel of a freshly ironed work shirt. "Have you begun to clean out Ben's room yet?" he wanted to know.

"No. I'll get around to it later." She snapped his lunchbox shut, wishing he'd stop asking her that. "When the weather turns warm. It's too cold upstairs now, Tom."

"I can paint the room any color you want. Wouldn't you like that?"

"No." Her answer knife-sharp. "The blue's fine. Leave it like it is."

Tom cleared his throat huskily.

Mary frowned. "You shouldn't smoke so much. It's giving you a bad cough."

"I'm fine and dandy, sweetheart." A questioning look caught his face. "You ought to pack up Ben's things, Mary. It's been awhile now. I've got plenty of boxes you can use. I'll store them in the cellar where they won't be in your way. Then you can fix the room any way you like."

"Not now, Tom. Stop pestering me."

Silence swirled between them. Lily's piano scales drifted through the open door, filling the void. Disgruntled, he ground his cigarette stub in the ashtray, got up and shoved his chair in place. "Maybe we'll have another boy some day."

Her heart missed a beat. "I have to go help Lily now." She hung her apron on the hook by the stove and hurried away.

After Tom left for work Gertie Schumaker arrived, her naturally-curly red hair fastened behind her ears with gold combs, her green eyes alive with anticipation. She gave Lily a bear hug, then wrapped her arms around Mary.

Gertie handed Lily a package. "Here's something to keep you busy, doll."

Lily peeked in the bag and pulled out a coloring book and a box of crayons. She beamed. "Thanks, Gertie. I'll color a picture for you." Lily headed for her bedroom upstairs.

Gertie turned to Mary. "I'm sorry I haven't seen you more since the funeral, but I've been covered up. I decided I was coming by after school today no matter what."

"I understand. I don't know how you can teach and cook and keep house, too."

"My house isn't neat as a pin, Mary." Gertie tittered. "I let the dust gather 'til it's an inch thick. Pete doesn't mind. He spends most of his time at the office, poring over all those cases he has. People suing people for all kinds of crazy reasons."

"It must be grand to have a lawyer husband who works in the daytime. Tom and I go to bed in the wee hours. He's only here for 6 o'clock supper on his days off."

Gertie patted Mary's shoulder. "Sometimes Pete works late at night when he has a big case pending. Anyway, things might change for you some day. I know you've had a horrible winter, but you've gotten through it, bless you. Spring's here now, and you have this wonderful house to putter around in."

"I'm not so crazy about this house anymore, Gertie." Mary headed toward the kitchen. "Come on. Let's have some tea and cake that I baked this morning."

"I shouldn't." Gertie pointed to her waist. "It's grown an inch since I ate all those Christmas goodies." She took a seat at the table while the refreshments were served. She squinted at Mary. "What exactly did you mean when you said you weren't crazy about the house?"

Mary shuddered. "Everything reminds me of Ben. I can't get him out of my mind, can't go in his room. I haven't even put his things away."

"That's tough, hon. Real tough. I imagine you're going to need much more time. It hasn't been long, you know. It'll probably take quite a while."

"Tom's hankering for me to pack up Ben's belongings and store them in the cellar, but I can't stand to do that." Mary paused. "Said he'd paint the room again."

Gertie took a bite of cake. "Um. Delicious. Your baking's the best, believe me." She eyed Mary carefully. "I'd help you pack Ben's things if you wanted me to."

Mary sat down. "I can't stand the thought of going in his room."

"How about Lily?"

"I told her never to go in there."

"Why?"

"It doesn't seem right, her poking around in there, rummaging through his belongings. He never liked her to fool with his toys. Especially those little cars he loved."

"How's Lily doing?"

"She seems like herself. Happier even. She gets more attention from Tom now. He used to spend a lot of time keeping up with Ben and his antics. I'm trying to teach Lily to play the piano. Imagine that. I don't know how to play, but I'm giving her lessons."

"That's swell, Mary. I'd give you some pointers if I knew how, but I don't know how either. I've been teaching my girls to type on Coronas and transcribe from the Dictaphone. I have to teach myself about the Dictaphone. Of course, my teacher's degree from the college helped, but when new equipment arrives you have to figure it out yourself before you can show anyone how it works."

"You're lucky you went to college, Gertie. I didn't get to go to high school." A shadow slipped over Mary. "There's no way I can get educated now that I'm married. I'll always be uneducated."

"Look at it this way, hon. When Lily goes to school, you'll have time to work on whatever interests you. You're lucky you can have babies. I can't have any, but I'm a teacher and I do plenty of mothering. That fills a big void in my life."

Mary sighed. "I wish you could have an operation to set things right, but the doctor told you that's impossible."

"I know. I'm lucky I can teach school."

Mary sat up straight and scratched the back of her neck. "I can't believe that Lily will be in first grade in September. I hope she gets a good teacher like you."

"She'll like school. And you'll be free to do anything you want."

Mary's eyes suddenly took on a sparkle. She left her chair and yanked up her skirt. "I'll be a flapper like those girls I see in Collier's magazine. Wear those dresses that come way above the knees and do the Charleston like this." She twisted her legs in and out and swung her heels sharply outward on each step while Gertie enjoyed a belly laugh.

Mary stopped dancing. She grabbed Tom's cigarette stub out of the ashtray and pretended she was puffing. "I'll smoke. Have all the drinks I want. Be like a man!"

"Good heavens, I can't picture you doing any of that stuff. Besides, there's prohibition. You'd have to buy your whiskey from a bootlegger. Then you'd get arrested. Your name would be in big headlines." Gertie flung her arms in the air. "Mary Dunmore Jailed for Boozing. Just think how embarrassed you'd be!"

"No," snapped Mary, a smirk on her face. "I'd be dead. Tom would kill me."

Gertie grinned while Mary threw away the stub. "I don't have to worry. You'd never do those outlandish things. They really get wild at their parties from what I read in the paper. Some of them are a disgrace, but that'll change. Pretty soon they'll go back to being prim and proper like ladies are supposed to be."

"Those girls helped a bunch while the war was going on, Gertie. They raised money. Gave things to the soldiers' families. I know that women at my church sent letters, licked envelopes until their tongues were sore and made phone calls. Did everything they could to help the war effort. I only stayed home, ran the house, and took care of my family."

"That's what you were supposed to do, Mary."

"Maybe so, but I wish I could have done something to help in the war." She brightened. "I just had a wonderful letter from Andy. He's going to stay in the Army and go to First Officers' Training Camp. He'll have a career while I'm doing housework."

Gertie sipped her tea. "Andy must have liked being in the War. President Wilson was a victim as much as those men who fought and died on the battlefield. He'll never recover from his awful paralytic stroke. Probably brought on by his struggle to win two-thirds approval by the Senate to adopt the Peace Treaty."

"Tom says Wilson's chance of getting everything he wanted in the Treaty and the League of Nations was wrecked because too many Republicans were in Congress and voted against his ideas."

Sadness flitted over Gertie. "That's true. Everyone expected him to resign after his stroke, but he hasn't. He stays in bed most of the time except when papers have to be signed. His wife helps him do that."

"I wish women could vote," muttered Mary. "We deserve to be in the voting booth. By darn, women should have as much say as men do about running the country."

Gertie clapped her hands. "Pete keeps me up to snuff on women's rights. I admire Jeanette Rankin, a Republican from Montana. She was the first woman to be elected to Congress and began to serve in 1917. She voted against our participation in the War. When it started, a woman suffrage amendment was submitted to the House of Representatives. Pete says it'll become law pretty soon and women will be allowed to vote. Then you'll have to decide whether you're going to be a Republican or a Democrat, Mary."

"Tom's a Democrat. That's what I'll have to be."

"No." Gertie was forceful. "You can be whatever you want to be."

Mary frowned. "Seems like everything important has two sides. Tom told me Grandpa Dunmore was in the Civil War. He fought on the Union side because he had a farm in western Virginia. There were awful disputes in the state about slavery. When the Confederate troops fired on Fort Sumter in Charleston Harbor, it started the Civil War. People in Virginia had to choose sides. The counties in the west where Grandpa lived formed a new state. They called it West Virginia."

Gertie nodded. "My grandpa owned a tobacco plantation in Virginia. His house looked like a palace. It had pillars and a big porch that wrapped all the way around it. The Negroes worked the fields . . . loaded the tobacco in barrels they called hogsheads. Grandpa's horses pulled them to the wharf where they were shipped to the customers."

"Was he on the Union side?"

"No. He was a Confederate."

"There you have it again, Gertie. Two sides—Confederate and Union."

Gertie snickered. "Mother's Day will be here soon. The second Sunday in May. Mark your calendar, Mary, and remind Tom to buy you a present. If it will make you feel any better, there aren't two sides in this case. We don't have a Father's Day."

"Seems like there ought to be."

"It takes two to make a family," chirped Gertie, carrying the cups to the sink. "Maybe there'll be a Father's Day. Let's go see what Lily's doing."

They climbed the stairs. At the top, Mary stood dead still. The door to Ben's room was open wide.

"Lily knows she's not allowed in Ben's room," murmured Mary. She walked to the door and looked in. Lily sat on the bed, running Ben's little cars back and forth over the spread. She took one glance at her mother, jumped down and ran out of the room.

Gertie trailed Lily down the steps while Mary stood transfixed, gazing at the cars. Slowly she walked out, tears streaming, and shut the door tight.

Chapter 5

Mary eyed Lily, hoping it was a day when she was in a get-along mood. "I have to do the laundry, honey. Bring your book and crayons that Gertie gave you. You can color pretty pictures while I work."

As they went down the cellar steps, Mary recalled the aftermath of finding Lily in Ben's room. Telling Lily in stinging tones that she'd been naughty and should never go in there again. Gertie had stood stiffly, zipping her mouth shut while Lily sobbed and tears ran down her cheeks.

Then Gertie left in a hurry, mumbling, "I'll call you."

Mary still hadn't gotten the nerve to tell Tom about the episode. She worried about his reaction. Gnawed by the fear he'd tell her that she was wrong to keep Lily out of Ben's room and should let her roam through his things as she pleased.

When they reached the foot of the steps, Lily plopped in a chair in her playhouse and tossed her book on the floor. "I don't wanna color now. I can play with Ben's cars. I'll run them around here on my table. Have a real good race."

Mary shook her head. Lily didn't seem to miss Ben, only craved his toys.

"Why can't I? Why, Mother? Why?"

The "why" boggled Mary. "Because they're Ben's and belong in his room, Lily." Anxious to escape the conflict, Mary dashed to the other side of the cellar, opened the chute and bent down to sort the dirty clothes that flooded onto the concrete floor. Her heart was pounding. She wondered if life at 1200 Twelfth Street would ever be day-to-day normal or pleasant again.

Small windows on both sides of the basement invited meager light, fine for doing the wash when the day was sunshiny, but it was raining now. Distraught, Mary left the piles of clothes and went over to the Maytag, yanking the overhead cord to turn on the light that Tom had installed. A streak of comfort . . . Tom had given her the washer for Christmas. It boasted a multi-motor and a swinging reversible wringer. No more scrubbing clothes on a washboard until her hands were raw. No more wringing wet clothes that made her wrists throb.

Lily wandered over to the Maytag. "I wanna wash clothes."

Mary swallowed hard. "It's not safe, Lily. You might get hurt. I have to boil water in the big pot on the stove over there and soak Daddy's work clothes to make them come clean. I don't want you near that hot water or the wringer. Go play with your dolls. Then you can hand me the pins when I'm hanging the clothes on the line."

"I'm not gonna play with dolls," grumbled Lily. She turned away and started toward the other side of the basement . . . to Tom's sturdy workbench and the rows of shelves stacked high with his tools, materials, notes, and sketches of future projects. The area was off limits to everybody in the world except Tom.

"I wanna see Daddy's stuff. His hammer . . . and that big thing." She pointed to the shiny saw hanging on the wall.

"You know Daddy doesn't allow anybody around his workbench, Lily. Not me. Not even a mouse can touch his tools."

Lily turned listless. "When'll Daddy be back?"

"He's gone down street. He'll be home pretty soon, honey."

Mary watched as Lily meandered back to her table. Tom had spent hours fashioning her playhouse before Ben came into the world. A kitchen, dinette, parlor, and bedroom displayed his talent for woodworking. But Lily spent only a thimbleful of time playing house, even though Santa had brought gold-rimmed dishes for the china cabinet, crocheted pillows to put on the couch, and an ironing board to use in the kitchen. Instead of staying in the cellar, Lily spent time in her bedroom, ignoring her dolls and talking to Miss Cat and Mr. Pup as though they were people who lived and breathed in West Park.

Lily stopped walking abruptly when she reached the formidable coal furnace stationed across from her playhouse. She studied for a minute. "I wanna see in the coal cellar, Mother."

"Goodness no, Lily. You'd get all sooty. Might catch a cold. Nothing but dirty old coal's in there."

Mary blinked, realizing that she was telling a lie. She had persuaded Tom to store Ben's highchair and his trike and homemade wagon in the coal cellar. No way she could bear to see Lily riding those wheels around the yard, reminding her for days on end that Ben was gone.

Suddenly the side door at the top of the steps opened and Tom came in, his arms clutching brown paper bags. Lily squealed and rushed up the stairway to greet him. Mary breathed a mite easier. She was frazzled with coping.

Mary hung the last shirt on the line in the cellar, switched off the light and climbed the steps. Tom sat at the kitchen table, so engrossed in the newspaper he didn't even glance at her or utter a word. Lily was putting Miss Cat and Mr. Pup in the chair, intent on telling them, "You have to know how to set a table after you get married."

"Cats don't marry dogs, Lily," remarked Mary, gazing at the counter covered with bags. "I'll fix lunch as soon as I put away the groceries."

"The flour and sugar go downstairs," said Tom, his attention still caught by the newspaper. "I'll take them to the cellar later."

She turned to Tom. "I'm glad you're off work today. Maybe we can go somewhere for a change. I'd really like that, hon." She began to unload cans in the cupboard, thinking Tom was smart to buy food on sale and store it in the basement. She never had to worry about running out of anything except bread or milk. In a pinch, she could make biscuits or use the canned milk that was always on hand.

"What's so interesting in the news?" she asked.

He looked up, a smile on his face. "What do you know? We're gonna have a radio station in Pittsburgh pretty soon. Yes sir-ee. Westinghouse Radio Station KDKA."

Mary stowed the last can in the cupboard and shut the door. "Are you sure?"

"The story's right here in the paper. It says in the beginning, Dr. Frank Conrad started broadcasting over his amateur radio station. People with wireless receiving sets listened to him."

Mary looked blank. "I never even heard of Dr. Conrad."

"He's an assistant chief engineer at Westinghouse. Most of the amateurs had to stop operating their sets, but Westinghouse got special licenses. They were allowed to continue their experiments in radiotelephone for the military during the War. There were two stations. One in East Pittsburgh near Westinghouse. The other one was at Dr. Conrad's home, a few miles away."

"My goodness, how weird to have a radio station in your house, Tom."

He leaned back in his chair, a contented look on his face. "After the war, Conrad went back on the air. He had a special land station and broadcast phonograph records. He got plenty of requests for records that ham radio operators wanted to hear. Then he began to air a program every Wednesday and Saturday night for the hams. His two young sons acted as announcers and played the piano. They were a big hit."

"How fascinating. Imagine having your sons do such a thing," remarked Mary, feeling bereft as soon as the words left her mouth.

"*I* can play the piano," squealed Lily, shaking her finger at Miss Cat.

Tom left the paper on the table and got up. "There's a show at the movie house in the Rocks. *Way Down East* with Lillian Gish. It's a silent melodrama about a young girl who has a rough life. Maybe we'll go this afternoon if you like. I'll put those groceries in the cellar now."

"Me, too," Lily rushed to the kitchen door and started down the steps. Tom grabbed the bags and followed.

Mary took the plush animals out of the chairs and began to heat vegetable soup and make cheese sandwiches for lunch. A lightness wafted. It wasn't often that Tom had the time to take her and Lily anywhere. He didn't even go to church with them on Sundays. His folks and a brother had passed away during the flu pandemic so he had no relatives to visit. When Tom wasn't at the railroad, he spent time at his workbench. Would it ever be possible for Tom to work regular days and be home in the evenings like Gertie's lawyer husband? That way they'd have a social life. The answer was no. Tom didn't have the education to snap up that kind of job . . . and educated people didn't want to mix with the uneducated.

When the food was ready, she opened the door to the cellar and called them to lunch. In a few minutes Tom and Lily came upstairs and took their places at the table. "By the way, Tom, I called Dr. Winter about the cod-liver oil. She said it would be a good idea to give Lily a physical and check her out."

"See about it then," he replied in a terse tone.

"I will. What time does the movie start today?"

He stared at her with controlled anger, his jaw square. "It doesn't matter. We're not going. I promised Lily I'd build shelves for her room. She wants to store her animals like Ben set cars on his shelves. I'll get started this afternoon."

Mary shriveled, the bite of sandwich in her mouth turning into a lump.

Chapter 6

As soon as he'd finished lunch, Tom rushed upstairs to measure the space for the new shelves, Lily trailing at his heels. Mary ran the hot water for washing dishes, her mind in a muddle. Was she taking second place in her own home? Why should what Lily wanted count more than what her mother wanted? Mary stewed, trying to fathom Tom's decision to cancel their movie date.

In a few minutes he returned to the kitchen with Lily and went to the cellar. Mary's wet hand darted out and grabbed her child by the shoulder. "You have piano practice to do now, honey. Get to it."

Lily pulled away. "I havta watch Daddy work."

"After you practice," said Mary, her eyes glittering. Lily scowled and headed for the parlor.

Mary hung over the sink, scrubbing the dishes with a vengeance. After a few minutes she stopped washing and stood still, wishing she had the wings of a bird . . . could fly to the highest treetop and find respite in its branches. Escape the frustration that was binding her up like a mummy. She was miffed about missing the movie. That would have meant several hours away from the house where she fluttered like a moth caught in a web.

The thought flashed that she might go to the movie alone. Step right up to the window and lay down her money to buy a ticket from the spectacled woman behind the counter. Slip into the dark movie house. Be ushered to a seat. In the gloominess, people would stare so hard it seemed their eyes were glued to her body. Wondering why a lone woman would come to view a show. It would take a basketful of nerve to do that, but the notion evaporated as quickly as it had sprouted. Tom would tell her she was a married lady and should never attend the theater by herself. If she did so despite his wishes, well, it was hard to even imagine the outcome.

She could hear Lily playing the scales. An idea sparked. Quickly Mary settled the last dish in the cupboard and went to the basement.

She made her way through the wet laundry she'd hung on the lines in the cellar that morning and approached Tom's workbench. He was hard at work sawing pine for Lily's shelves and was startled when he heard her made-up cough.

"Sorry to bother you," she said loudly. His hand stopped sawing in midair. She smiled. "Since you're busy making Lily's shelves, I'm going shopping this afternoon. I need material and patterns to make dresses for Lily to wear to school. I'll take her with me so she can pick out what she wants."

Irritation swept over him at being interrupted. The look faded. "That's fine," he said, laying down the saw. He wiped his brow with the back of his hand. "Be careful, Mary."

She nodded and took off.

Even though Lily had fussed when Mary told her that she couldn't stay home and watch her dad building the shelves, Mary knew that a trip to Pittsburgh would be like handing Lily a strawberry sucker. She always got something when they went shopping. "Something" was ice cream at Woolworth's lunch counter and a toy plucked from the table where everything cost under fifty cents.

Besides getting treats, Lily liked to drop the tokens in the box when boarding the trolley and grab a window seat. She pressed her face close to the glass as the orange streetcar stopped to pick up or let off riders, then whipped past houses in West Park, businesses in the Rocks and down Chartiers Avenue that hugged the river.

Lily turned to her mother as they crossed Point Bridge, standing high above the water, to reach Pittsburgh's shopping district. "I'd like to ride on that big boat down there."

Mary shivered, recalling the Titanic. After it struck an iceberg, the British steamer sank in 1912 on its first trip from England heading to New York City. She had no desire to ever set foot on a boat. "Maybe Daddy will take you for a boat ride, Lily."

They got off the trolley at Hornes. "Let's look at material first," commented Mary, stopping to gaze in the store windows at the fashions displayed on manikins. "Tell me when you see a dress you want, sweetie, and we'll find a pattern like that. Butterick has every kind of pattern under the sun. I'm sure we can copy any dress you pick."

Lily stared for a while before pointing to a short-haired model wearing a dress with bright buttons streaming down the front. "That one with the white stuff on the bottom," said Lily. "And I gotta have a pocket in my dress."

"That white stuff is lace on the slip peeping out, Lily. We'll try to find a pattern."

They hurried into the store and rode the elevator to the floor that held long tables stacked with yard goods. The melding of cotton, linen, silk and wool created an unpleasant aroma. Lily rubbed her nose. "It smells funny in here, Mother."

Mary chuckled. "It's all the materials mixed up together. We need to look for cotton, Lily. It will still be warm when school starts. That'll be the best fabric for September. We always have real hot spells then."

After fingering and smoothing bolt after bolt, they chose garden colors. Sky blue, green sprinkled with pink flowers, and a red polka dot remnant that was marked down. "Now we'll look for the patterns we need, Lily."

Mary led the way to the counter piled with books picturing women and children in different kinds of dresses. She lifted Lily onto a stool so she could leaf through the pages. It took an hour to find the right styles. Finally they left Hornes with a shopping bag, two patterns and enough material to make three dresses.

Lily brimmed with expectancy. "We're going to the dime store now, aren't we?"

Mary grinned, thinking her daughter was only satisfied when she was getting exactly what she wanted. "You know we are, honey. We'll have chocolate sodas or fudge sundaes with a cherry on top, whichever you want."

Lily sparkled. "I want both."

"I don't think so. You have to choose."

They headed to Woolworth's. A burst of energy swept through Mary. She was looking forward to sewing Lily's dresses on her Singer.

Lily's day was complete when they reached home. Tom had already finished the shelves and put them in her room. Lily rushed around, gathering up Miss Cat and Mr. Pup, two teddy bears, a monkey and three dolls. After setting them in their places, she announced that they had a new home.

"I'll stain your shelves in the morning before I go to work," promised Tom. "You'll have to move everything again and wait until the stain dries." He turned to Mary. "There's a letter for you on the kitchen table from Hannah."

"Good." Mary rushed downstairs. There'd been no word from her married sister in El Paso, Texas since Ben's funeral. They'd talked on the phone and received flowers but no letter. Hannah McGuffy Taylor wasn't a letter writer like Andy McGuffy.

Mary sat at her dressing table, unfastening the pins in her hair, letting it circle her shoulders. Tom was already in his pajamas, sitting on the edge of the bed, taking in her every move. "Did you get what you need in town today?"

She nodded. "I'll start sewing tomorrow. I'm anxious to do something. I like making dresses." She paused. "Wish we could have gone to that show today. I was really looking forward to it."

He sighed, crows' feet digging at the corners of his eyes. "Lily told me you got real mad when she went in Ben's room. It made her cry hard. I felt sorry for her. That's why I decided to build those shelves she wanted."

Mary swiveled around and faced him. "I told her never to go in there, Tom. She shouldn't be playing with Ben's toys. It's not right. She has her own things to play with."

"Do you want me to give her a whipping?" asked Tom, his face flushed.

"No! Don't ever whip her. It's terrible enough that you whipped Ben. You shouldn't have done that."

Tom drooped. "Kids have to be whipped when they do bad things. Yes siree. They have to learn. That's the way I was brought up."

"Whipping's wrong," spouted Mary. "And after I reprimanded Lily for disobeying me, you've rewarded her by making those shelves."

Tom grunted. "Lily wants Ben's cars. I don't see any harm in letting her have them. They're sitting on the shelf gathering dust."

Mary clasped her hands and sat rigidly. "Ben never wanted Lily or anyone else to play with his cars. It was as though they were his private property." She gave Tom a pointed look. "I'd say like the way you feel about your workbench. You don't want anybody else to touch it. His cars were the things Ben prized the most. Same as the gold ring he only wore on special occasions."

Tom groaned, wrinkles creasing his forehead. "We should change his room, Mary. Paint it a different color, get some new furniture. We can store his belongings in the coal cellar. Then Lily can go in Ben's room."

Mary squeezed her hands together harder. "No, Tom. I can't do that."

He ran his hand through his wavy hair. "We'll get somebody else to take care of it then. You won't have to do a thing. It will simply turn into a brand new room."

She sat there, her hands limp in her lap. "Gertie offered to help, but I want the room to stay exactly like it is."

Tom fingered the stubble on his chin. "The room will only keep reminding you of Ben."

"Everything in this house reminds me of Ben." The words echoed through the room. She closed her eyes and caught a fleeting glimpse of her child.

"Come to bed, sweetie. You'll feel better after a good night's rest."

Slowly she got up and moved to the bed.

"You didn't say anything about Hannah's letter. How is she?"

Mary stretched out and pulled the cover over her. "She's expecting. Her due date's in December. She didn't have any other news. She and Matt are fine."

"Good. She's been wanting a baby for a long time," replied Tom.

Mary's tears crept to the pillow. He snuggled his arm around her and held her close. She was cold as ice.

Chapter 7

Mary's Singer was in the dining room by the window where the brightest light filtered in through the sheer curtains she'd made. From where she sat, she could see the maples and the poplars leafing out in the backyard. Summer was wending its way to West Park. She worked at her sewing machine, relishing the hum of the motor as she made Lily's green dress with pink rosebuds scattered hither and yon. The pale blue dress was already finished and spread out on the buffet. Every time she passed by and gazed at it, her spirits lifted. Lily would love to wear the full skirt with a lacy slip peeping out below.

She finished the last seam on the green dress and laid it aside for hemming to be done by hand. Lily was playing the piano. *Fairies in the Moonlight* waltzed from the parlor through the archway into the dining room. Enlivened by the sensation that her child might be musically gifted, Mary took a deep breath. For a fleeting moment she pictured herself dancing in a bouffant gown and satin slippers, the gaze of bystanders following as she twirled across the floor.

Leaning back in her straight chair, she smoothed her apron and stretched until her body slackened like the elastic she sewed in the waist of Lily's pajamas. A smile caught her lips. Knowing that Lily's piano lessons had not been in vain was like having a pillow beneath her head. There had been days when she almost gave up the challenge . . . Lily was obstinate . . . refused to pay attention . . . banged on the keyboard whenever she hit a wrong note. Tom said Lily should practice after he left for work and didn't have to listen. He never cared for any kind of music, soft or loud, good or bad. But Mary remained stalwart, and now her daughter was playing the delightful melodies in *Piano Book One*.

Mary heard a knock at the front door, interrupting her reverie. "It's Gertie," she murmured, scrambling up to greet her best friend. Lily left the piano as Gertie came in and bestowed generous hugs on both of them.

She handed Lily a package. "I brought you something special, sweetie."

"You shouldn't have," said Mary, helping Lily tear open the box. "You're spoiling her rotten." Mary stopped short when she saw what was inside and drew back, her mouth agape. Reluctantly she lifted the gift out of the carton.

"A doll," cried Lily. She grabbed it from her mother, running her hand over the blue eyes with dark lashes, the pale lips, the well-built body. "It's a boy! It's a boy!" She held the doll up in the air. "See his shirt . . . his pants. They have pockets."

Mary shuddered, unbelieving. She turned to Gertie with questioning eyes, a sadness tugging at her mouth. "Why . . . why on earth?"

"I thought she'd like it," replied Gertie, her elation spinning into confusion. "Something new . . . something different." An afterthought. "She can put the doll in her playhouse."

"She rarely touches her dolls." Mary's words a whisper.

Gertie stiffened. She stepped back, befuddled. "I thought Lily was wild about dolls. I'll return it if you want."

"No!" cried Lily, grasping the doll. "No. He's mine. All mine."

Mary's face was red, her breath coming fast. She forced out her words. "The doll's yours, Lily. Thank Gertie for the present."

Lily's scowl turned into a smile. "Thank you, Gertie. Thanks."

Gertie patted Lily on the shoulder. "You're welcome, sweetie."

"I have to give him a name." Lily scratched her head, tilting the yellow bow that held back her straight hair. "I know," she chirped. "I'll call him Benny."

Gleefully she turned and ran up the steps, clutching the doll to her chest.

They sat in the kitchen, both of them shaken, teary eyed. "I'm awfully sorry, Mary. I never dreamed this would happen. Never entered my mind. Dumb me."

Mary wiped her face with her apron. "I can't believe . . . can't stand it." The words caught in her throat.

"I never meant to upset you, Mary. That's the last thing I'd ever do. I saw the doll in Kauffman's, and it beckoned to me. I've always been nutty about dolls. Knew I was coming here . . . wanted to bring something nice for Lily. I thought she'd love the doll so I bought it."

Mary was breathless. She opened her mouth and gulped some air. "I don't know, Gertie. Since Ben died, nothing's right for me in this house."

"I'm so sorry." She paused. "Have you gotten rid of his things?"

"No. I can't."

"I told you I'd be glad to help . . . or I could do it by myself if you want. Then I'm sure you'd feel a whole lot better."

"I don't think so. I'd like to live someplace else. I see Ben in all these rooms every day. Every night. He was so lively. Into everything. Always laughing or cutting up. Giving me hugs all the time. So much fun to have around."

Gertie's eyes narrowed. "Have you told Tom how you feel?"

"Not really, but he understands that I'm not myself anymore. I want to get away from the memories, but I can't. They're all right here, holding me tight."

"You should go places. You're cooped up all the time. Now that I'm almost done teaching until next fall, we can do things together. I've signed up for an afternoon class in June at St. Mary's in the Rocks. I'm going to make artificial flowers out of crepe paper. You won't believe how real they look, how pretty they are. I want to make some for my house . . . my friends. You ought to come with me."

"I'm not a Catholic. I'm a Baptist, Gertie."

"You know I'm a Baptist, too. No matter. Everybody's welcome no matter what church they go to."

"What about Lily?"

"They're having a program for kids. Storytelling and all kinds of games. Even puppet shows and movies. Lily would have a ball."

"I don't know." Mary was glum. She got up and began to make a pot of tea.

"You should talk to Tom about how you're feeling. I've never seen you so droopy, so miserable."

Mary rubbed the back of her neck. "I've been sewing for Lily. Making her dresses for school. I enjoy doing that, and I need to make dresses for myself. Staying busy keeps me from thinking about how it used to be."

"That's good, but I'd like to see you do something somewhere else besides this house, especially if you don't like it. Lily starts school in September. You'll be all alone when Tom goes to work. Alone most of the day and the evening, too."

"I never thought about that."

"Talk to Tom, Mary. You've got to talk to Tom. Tell him how you feel."

Mary sighed.

"Promise me you'll talk to Tom."

"I promise, Gertie."

A hard rain was beating on the roof and running in rivulets down the kitchen windows. Tom had finished his supper and was getting ready to head upstairs for bed. "I'm glad I beat the rain walking home. I'd have gotten a real good soaking for sure."

Mary began to clear the table and carry dishes to the sink. "We need the rain. The evergreens and rhododendrons are dry now since the snow's gone. The rain'll turn them fresh and shiny again so they're pretty."

"How was your day?" he asked, giving her a penetrating look when she moved closer to the table.

"Gertie came to visit. She brought Lily a doll."

"That was nice of her. She's a good egg."

"It was a boy doll."

Tom jerked. "Why'd she do that?"

"She happened to see the doll when she was shopping. She has always brought Lily and Ben a present when she visits."

"What did you say?"

"I was rattled no end, but I know Gertie didn't mean to fluster me. She offered to return the doll, but Lily wanted to keep it."

Tom's expression was serious, his eyes searching her. "I guess you'll have to get used to seeing that doll then. Maybe it won't bother you after a while."

"Lily named the doll Benny."

"Dang." Tom's fist hit the table. "What was Gertie thinking?"

Mary shook her head, anxiety hovering. "This whole house bothers me, Tom. I guess that sounds weird. A wonderful new home anybody would like, but I see and think about Ben all the time, regardless of what room I'm in. No matter how hard I try to block that out, it happens."

Tom got up and swept her into his arms. "Maybe we'll have to think about moving."

"We have a new house to pay for. How on earth can we move?"

He squeezed her tight, his tall frame towering over her. "We'll have to figure it out some way." He kissed her. "Let's sleep on it."

Tom was already in the land of Nod by the time Mary donned her flannel nightgown. She walked barefooted to the hall and peeped in Lily's room. Sound asleep, her arm wrapped around Benny. Lily had never really loved dolls. Mary glanced at the new shelves. Miss Cat and Mr. Pup rested on the top row. The bottom shelves harbored the rest of Lily's stuffed animals and her dolls.

Mary turned away and stood in the hall, mesmerized by the closed door to Ben's room. She stared. Ben had been like a flower in full bloom that was suddenly cut down. Misty eyed, she headed to bed.

Chapter 8

Mary woke before the sun had risen. The bedroom was still midnight dark. She tucked the cover around her neck, her ears tuned to Tom's breathing, steady, interrupted by an occasional snort. Being beside him made her feel safe. When she had been in bed without a husband at her side, she felt protected because her father was in the house. He died before she took off for Pittsburgh to find a job, leaving her mother in care of the house.

It was Mother's Day, the second Sunday in May. People were beginning to take notice of the date. They wore red carnations to show their mothers were alive . . . white carnations for deceased mothers. Mary wondered if Tom had paid any attention when he read the paper the night before. In a mood of impetuosity before he'd come home from work, she'd taken a red pencil and outlined the story on the front page. The article described how Julia Ward Howe suggested in 1872 that the United States have a Mother's Day. For several years, Julia held an annual Mother's Day meeting in Boston. Others followed her lead.

In 1907, Anna Jarvis of Philadelphia pressed for a nationwide observance. One year later, churches in Grafton, West Virginia and Philadelphia, Pennsylvania held Mother's Day celebrations. The service at Andrews Methodist Episcopal Church in Grafton honored the memory of Anna Jarvis's mother, Mrs. Anna Reeves Jarvis.

At the General Conference of the Methodist Episcopal Church in Minneapolis, Minnesota in 1912, a delegate from Andrews Church introduced a resolution, naming Anna Jarvis as the founder of Mother's Day. It received national recognition on May 8, 1914 when President Woodrow Wilson signed a joint resolution of Congress and recommended that Mother's Day be observed by Congress and the executive departments of the government. The following year, the President proclaimed Mother's Day as an annual national observance.

Lying there in bed with eyes shut tight, Mary mulled about what it meant to be a mother. Having a child was a gift, the most blessed thing in the world, but when the child died life was turned upside down. Mary dug her nails into the pillow, her mind woven into the past, wishing Ben had lived and that she'd be going to his room to kiss him good morning. She pictured his door shut tight, offering no welcome. Was she wrong in keeping Lily out of the room? Wrong in forbidding Lily to play with Ben's toys?

Tom turned over and grunted, reminding Mary that he wanted Ben's things stored in the cellar and his room redecorated. Made all new again from top to bottom as though Ben had never existed in that place. She cringed. The thought wasn't palatable. She slipped out of bed and hurried downstairs to brew a pot of tea. In the hour during daybreak she needed strength to face the morning.

The newspaper still lay on the kitchen table, the Mother's Day story highlighted in red. Tom's mother and father were deceased. It was unlikely that he had overlooked the article. Not her Tom with those keen blue eyes that could stare straight through flesh and bones.

She made her tea and sipped slowly, savoring as though it was nectar. She reread the story quickly, then found herself reminiscing about her own widowed mother still living in Cleveland. Mary had sent her a box of linen hankies, cookies and a newsy letter for Mother's Day. Sarah McGuffy had endured a pinch-penny life, abiding in a well-worn house that lacked every convenience except for a new icebox Andy bought after he enlisted in the Army. Sarah bore and reared six children who grew up fast like weeds in a flower bed. All the children managed to eke out a sufficient living despite little learning, except for Andy. He was the shining light of the family. Serving in the War and attending First Officers' Training Camp to prepare for an Army career that would set him apart from his brothers and sisters.

Her tea finished, Mary leaned back in her chair and surveyed the kitchen, becoming bright from the daylight creeping through the sheer curtains. She peered at the cupboards filled with food that had to be prepared and dishes to be washed and dried, the table that was set over and over again, the towels and linens that required washing and ironing, the linoleum that needed swept and scrubbed weekly. Pride swelled. With a hard swallow, she realized that she was in command of that kitchen. A duty she earned through the gold ring on her finger that affirmed wedlock to Tom Dunmore.

Tom was still in bed when Mary and Lily arrived at West Park Baptist, a quaint, yellow-brick church perched on a corner across the street from Stowe High School. The churchyard was covered with rye grass and edged by yews that boasted greenery all year long. When winter storms raged, the birds sought shelter inside the bushes that were quickly adorned with snow.

As she climbed the steps to the sanctuary, Mary was reminded of the day she had joined the little church after moving to Pittsburgh. She married Tom in the same setting and expected that he'd be beside her on Sundays, soaking up the sermon that flowed from the minister's heart and soul. Then they'd greet friends after church and hurry home to an extra-special meal prepared on Saturday. Instead, Mary found that Tom's railroad job turned their lifestyle upside down. He used it as an excuse for not going to church.

Mary felt relief as Lily scampered up the steps. Dr. Winter had examined her and stated that she was in excellent health. The doctor was emphatic. "Your child doesn't need a tonic." Lily wore her blue dress for the first time and was in an unusually receptive mood. One person after another stopped to remark about how pretty she looked. The lace on the petticoat bounced around Lily's slim legs as she walked and brought forth a giggle.

Lily hurried to the class for five-year olds. She usually told Mary about the Bible story the teacher related. Mary hurried to Fellowship, a session for young married couples. She always suffered an unease, sitting alone without Tom at her side when everyone else had a partner. One time Mary made an effort to explain that his job forced him to sleep late on Sundays and miss church. Afterwards, she regretted offering such a reason. Doubt flowed from the staring faces. Tom's failure to accompany her when he didn't have to work burned in Mary's mind.

On Mother's Day, the Fellowship's Sunday School lesson centered on Esther, a beautiful Jewish girl of long ago who became a Queen and saved the Jewish race from annihilation. While the teacher talked, Mary pondered long and hard, wondering if Esther had much education and how a woman could accomplish such a daunting feat. She wanted to ask if Esther ever became a mother but kept quiet, afraid of sounding stupid.

When the bell rang for dismissal, Lily came running with a nosegay of pansies. "Happy Mother's Day," she cried, propelling her arms around her mother's long skirt.

"It's lovely," replied Mary, pleasure taking over. She bent down and kissed Lily on the cheek.

"Miss Holly gave all of us one for our mother." Lily's voice turned somber. "She said we should be eternally grateful for our mothers."

Mary smiled. "I'm eternally grateful for you, Lily."

Back home after church, Mary was stunned to find Tom waiting in the parlor, standing man-tall and handsome in his pinstriped suit. "Thought I'd take you and Lily out to dinner in Pittsburgh. Happy Mother's Day, sweetheart." He handed her a small velvet box.

She gasped when she opened it and saw the gold chain. He put the necklace around her neck. "I'll wear it always," she said, her words smooth as silk. "It's awfully sweet you remembered."

"Couldn't help it," he said. "An angel reminded me."

Chapter 9

The sun was breaking through the clouds, and the birds were singing their "good mornings" with relish. She sat on the back porch, brushing Lily's hair 'til it glistened, finishing the task by fastening a bow on the top of her head. Mary took a deep breath. Somehow she was going to squeeze a memorable day out of the June sunshine. Learning to make crepe paper flowers would be something new, something challenging, something tantalizing. Help her escape the depression that was dragging her to the depths.

"Let's get ready." Mary got up. "Gertie's driving us to St. Mary's in the Rocks this afternoon. You'll have a great time, Lily. There'll be other kids your age and new games for you to learn."

"What will you be doing, Mother?" Lily's question hung in midair as they entered the kitchen.

"I'm going to find out how to make flowers out of paper. Gertie says they're pretty, almost like real ones."

Lily squinted. "Maybe I'll do that, too, then."

"The flower lessons are for the grown-ups, honey. They have games and movies for the children."

Tom returned from the yard where he'd been planting four-o'clock seeds, soaked the night before so they'd be sure to grow. His face was lined with fatigue, but he seemed to be in high spirits. "My Van Fleet roses are gonna bloom. Yes sir-ee, they're making it. I'd like to build a trellis for them to climb on this summer."

"You're always making extra work for yourself, Tom." Mary smiled at him. "But I believe a trellis covered with roses would be awfully nice."

"Since I'm off work today, I think I'll get started on that," countered Tom, setting the glass that had held the flower seeds in the sink.

Lily ran over to him and grabbed his hand. "I wanna stay home with you, Daddy. Can I? Can I?"

"Ask Mother. It's up to her," said Tom, running his damp hand through his hair.

"The classes start today, Lily. If you don't go, you'll miss out on getting to meet everybody and finding out about the exciting things they're planning for you. It's not good to miss any of the classes." Mary stood with hands on her hips, waiting for Lily's answer.

"Better do as Mother says." Tom pulled out a chair, sat down at the table and began to roll a cigarette.

Lily frowned, her gaze flitting back and forth at Mary and Tom.

"Go practice your piano, honey, while I fix lunch. Gertie will pick us up. The class starts at 1:30. We have to be ready to go when she gets here."

"I'd rather stay here with Daddy," grumbled Lily. She turned and glared at her mother, hesitated for a moment, then headed to the parlor.

When Lily was out of earshot, Tom said quietly, "Maybe you ought to let her stay home. I never get to spend much time with her. She'd like to watch me work on the trellis. Maybe she could even help a little."

Mary nibbled at her lip as music began to flow from the piano. She recalled her elation when learning she was going to become a mother for the very first time. How she thrilled to the stirring of new life in her own body, never dreaming that a child could ever cause trouble between its parents. Agitation nudged. Mary struggled to stay calm and began to pull food out of the icebox. She set the things on the counter and turned to Tom who was lighting his cigarette while he waited.

Determined to have a great day no matter what, Mary relented. "Go ahead and keep Lily while I go to class, Tom. She'll have to catch up next week."

Mary and Gertie entered the church hall where women had gathered for the flower class. The room was alive with chatter. Everyone stood near tables on one side of the room, oohing and aahing over the vases and baskets of crepe paper flowers on display.

"I've never see so many artificial flowers," declared Mary as they moved into the group. "I can't believe my eyes. They're absolutely fascinating."

Gertie edged closer to the display. "They're gorgeous. So many kinds. Roses, daylilies, columbines, hollyhocks. Everything under the sun is here. Look at those pansies over there and those white peonies. They're like honest-to-gosh real ones that have grown in the dirt . . . and you never have to water them."

Mary snickered. "I can't believe that I'm going to be able to make these. They look awfully complicated. I'll be happy if I figure out how to create one kind."

"I've seen some of these flowers before," explained Gertie. "They had an exhibit in the Homemaking Department at school. That's when I decided I had to learn how to make them."

They moved on to where supplies for making paper flowers were displayed. Green florist wire, green florist tape, Dennison crepe paper in rainbow shades, cloth or paper leaf material, and craft paint. Another table held an assortment of tools. Wire snips, glue, tweezers, darning needles, punches, and styluses.

A tall stylish woman with inky black hair and gray eyes approached the podium and introduced herself as Sally Kindle. She asked everyone to find a place at one of the tables set up for the students. "There are four big tables, ladies. You'll be able to spread out your materials and practice. We have 16 students. Four to each table plus a teacher. She will introduce you to flower making and get you started. You'll each have a Beginner's Kit and concentrate on making petals and a rosebud. Have fun everyone."

Mary and Gertie found their places and introduced themselves to Jean Karawan, the teacher, and to Anastasia Kustra and Lois Miscevich. Gingerly they opened their packets and began their practice under Miss Karawan's direction. The chatter in the hall died down to a hum, interspersed with an occasional titter as the women tried to shape petals out of paper.

Later that afternoon, Gertie drove Mary home. "I'm going to Woolworth's this week and buy some supplies, Gertie. I've fallen in love with crepe paper flowers. I'm going to practice making flowers. Just like I did the piano, but I can't play like Lily."

Gertie reached over and patted Mary on the back. "I'm glad you're feeling better. I knew that getting out and meeting people, doing something interesting would be good medicine for you."

Mary squeezed Gertie's hand when she got out of the car at home. "I don't know how I'd manage without a friend like you, Gertie."

Mary took a deep breath as she opened the door to the house. Being away for a few hours had steeped her in a sense of renewal, as though she'd been spirited to a carefree world where there was nothing to fret about or get upset. She rushed to the kitchen and called to Tom in the cellar. "I'm home, Tom."

She put the kettle on to fix a cup of tea and heard his footfall on the steps. He reached the kitchen, his face glowing with tension.

"What's wrong, Tom?"

"Lily . . . it's Lily," he sputtered. "I had to whip her."

"You what?"

"I had to whip her, Mary. She was real bad."

Mary glowered. "What happened?"

"She stayed with me in the cellar for a while. Then she wanted to go play in her room. When I went upstairs later to check on her, she'd moved Ben's cars to her shelves and set her dolls and animals on Ben's shelves. I made her put everything back the way it's supposed to be. Then I whipped her and made her stay in her room."

"I don't believe this," stormed Mary, turning off the kettle and rushing upstairs.

Ben's door was closed. Lily sat in her room on the floor, her face blotchy from crying, her arms clutching Benny. At the sight of her mother, Lily burst into tears and dropped the doll.

Mary gathered Lily in her arms. "You're all right . . . perfectly all right now. Don't cry."

Lily kept right on sniveling.

"Don't cry . . . please don't cry." She rocked Lily back and forth as the clock in the hall chimed the hour.

Mary glanced at the new shelves that had brought on the trouble. Miss Cat, sporting stiff whiskers and Mr Pup, showing off his toothless grin, were perched on top. The other animals and dolls rested on the lower levels.

Lily sniffled. "Daddy whipped me . . . with his strap."

"I'm sorry. Real sorry, honey." Mary hugged Lily tighter and began to ponder about how to manage the problem.

After a few minutes, she gave Lily a squeeze. "You should never have gone in Ben's room and moved his cars to your room. That was wrong. You've been told that several times, but you disobeyed."

Lily gazed up at Mary. "They're my cars, Mother. All mine now. Ben's gone so they have to be mine."

Mary flinched. She studied the child in her arms, wondering how she could turn life upside down like a stack of blocks tumbling to the floor. Words piled up in Mary's throat. "You must promise me . . . promise me right this very minute, Lily, that you'll never go in Ben's room again."

Lily dabbed at her face with her hand. "I should be allowed to go in Ben's room, but I promise, Mother."

"Let's go downstairs now, honey. I have some cookies and milk. They'll make you feel better."

Lily got out of Mary's lap. "Can Daddy have some, too, Mother?"

Mary nodded.

They met Tom coming up the stairs as they started down. "I'm having cookies and milk now. You can have some, too, Daddy."

While Lily was snacking on the back porch, Mary put on her apron and began to spread the materials in her Beginner's Kit on the dining room table. An urge to stay busy took hold, but she wasn't dwelling on making flowers, only preoccupied with what was happening. After telling Tom not to whip Lily, it was hard to believe he'd still do it. At the same time, the bond between mother and daughter was lagging while the one between father and daughter seemed to be growing stronger.

Tom came downstairs, a troubled look on his face. "I wanted to be sure she'd put everything back like it's supposed to be, Mary."

He glanced at the piles of crepe paper and ran his hand over one of the small tools on the table. "I see you had quite an afternoon of it. Seems like you had a mighty fine time at the flower class."

"The lesson was invigorating, Tom. I enjoyed it a whole lot, but I hate what happened here. You know my feelings about whipping."

"I'm sorry, sweetheart, but it had to be done. Lily has to mind us no matter what."

"How hard did you hit her, Tom?"

"I gave her a few swipes with the razor strap so she'd remember she did wrong. On her behind . . . not real hard."

Mary glared. She stood rigidly, her eyes glued to him. "If you ever whip her again, I'll leave you, Tom Dunmore. Honest to God I will."

He paled, his brows arching over his eyes. "I fixed the door on Ben's room. You won't have to worry about Lily ever going in there again."

"What on earth do you mean?"

"I locked the door. She can't get in."

He reached in his pocket and handed Mary the key.

Mary fingered it for a moment, then slipped the key in her apron pocket.

Chapter 10

In the beginning, Mary and Tom had experienced few disagreements in their marriage. Their conflicts centered on the house while it was being built. The kind of linoleum for the kitchen, which color to paint a room, what parlor furniture was suitable, and whether or not they could skimp enough to make payments on a piano. Mary wanted to learn how to play. She loved music.

But the arrival of two babies heralded a new host of problems. She and Tom had never talked about rearing children, only about wanting a boy and a girl. Years later, a page was turned in their marriage when Mary told Tom that she'd leave if he whipped Lily again. The distance between the couple gradually expanded to the point where they didn't talk as much to each other. Sometimes Tom failed to kiss Mary before going to work and held her close to his heart less often.

Acutely conscious that the space between them was getting wider, Mary worried about how to narrow it. She doubted if Tom would ever relinquish his stand about whipping a child. He'd been taught that corporal punishment always followed misbehavior and his father whipped him with a razor strap. In the aftermath, Tom whipped Ben several times and also took the strap to Lily.

On the other hand, Mary's determination held fast that her daughter would never feel that razor strap again. Every time she recalled the red stripes on her child's backside, Mary wondered why Lily gravitated toward Tom. It seemed as though he and Lily were in a loop, and she was left out.

Creating artificial flowers helped to fill the void creeping into Mary's life. Along with the Singer in the corner by the dining room window, the table became her workplace. She loaded it with rainbow shades of crepe paper, small tools, and pictures of flowers to be used as patterns. While Lily practiced the piano in the parlor, Mary fashioned paper blossoms in the dining room. Soon her skill developed to the point where she began to carry samples to show the class. Her pride flourished when Sally Kindle took her aside and said discreetly, "I'll put you on the list of paid teachers for the next flower-making class in September."

"I'd love to be a teacher," replied Mary. Her exhilaration rose even higher when friends offered to pay if she'd make them a bouquet. By the time Mary had finished the class, she had begun taking orders for crepe paper flowers, her first venture into the career world.

Lily celebrated her sixth birthday by inviting her Sunday School class to a party on July 14. She invited the friends she'd made at St. Mary's, too. The games, exercises, stories, puppet shows, and movies turned out to be fun while her mother attended class. Lily's grumpiness laid low. She was enlivened by having playmates. Her horizon broadened, thanks to the association with other children and participation in new activities. Mary rejoiced about Lily's brighter outlook. The neighborhood where they lived was sparse and lacked children who were Lily's age.

Nine girls and three boys bearing gifts arrived for the party. Mary admired the girls' dresses and stored ideas for copying similar outfits. A Gibson dress in lavender with a pretty kerchief at the neck, a square yoke dress in pink dimity, and an over dress in red and white dotted Swiss that flaunted a flared skirt and high collar.

Gertie arrived and helped Mary manage *Pin the Tail on the Donkey* and *Musical Chairs*. For the first time, Lily performed at the piano. She played *Hopscotch* and *Going on a Picnic* while the children marched in a circle. Laughter lilted as chairs were removed and one child after another failed to find a seat when the music stopped. Mary stood with her back toward the wall where a handmade casket had been placed a few months ago. Her thoughts flowed back and forth from Ben to the birthday party, but she forced a pleasant look on her face.

After the games were over, Mary told Gertie, "I'll let Lily open her presents before they eat ice cream and cake in the dining room. That way they won't gobble up the refreshments in a hurry so they can watch Lily unwrapping her presents."

"Smart idea." Gertie headed to the dining room. "I'll set the table while you help open the gifts. I know you want to keep track of who gave what."

"Swell, Gertie. The plates and spoons are on the table, and the ice cream cups are in the icebox. The cake's ready to put by Lily's seat. I did my best to make it pretty. After she blows out the candles and makes a wish, I'll serve the cake."

"I brought my camera. I can take pictures," offered Gertie. "Just think, by this time next year Lily will have finished first grade. She's growing up."

Mary sighed. "If only Tom didn't have to work and could be here to see everything."

"He misses all the good times," said Gertie.

Mary thought about Ben's not growing up. She smiled, but tears were flowing inside.

Chapter 11

West Park School was within considerable walking distance from Twelfth Street. Mary planned to accompany Lily on the first day of school but worried about her child's chancing the trip by herself after that. She and Tom finally decided that Lily wasn't old enough to go alone. More and more people were driving autos that made crossing the streets unsafe.

"I'm scared," said Lily as they left the house and began the trek to school. "Daddy oughta take me, Mother."

"He has to sleep," explained Mary with a twitch of her head. "You know he doesn't get home from work until real late. He has to stay in bed in the morning."

"You should'a let me bring Benny." Lily smoothed the skirt of her blue dress with her hand as they walked. "The kids would like him. Betcha nobody else has a boy doll."

Mary winced and walked faster, wondering if Lily missed Ben. She seldom mentioned him. It was almost like he hadn't ever existed for her. "You won't be playing with dolls at school, Lily. You'll have books to read and paper to write on. The teacher will help you learn how to do those things."

Lily began to skip, kicking up the dust with her patent leather shoes that she wore to church.

"Don't do that, honey. You'll ruin your Buster Browns, sure as the world. They're your Sunday best. You're only wearing them today because it's a special time."

Lily clutched her mother's hand. "I wanna go back home."

"You have to go to school. Everybody has to, Lily. You'll like it a whole lot. You can make new friends and learn how to read and write. It'll be exciting, believe me. I wish I could have gone to a modern school like you're going to. I didn't even have a desk to write on. We sat on hard benches and wrote in our laps."

Mary continued a steady stream of conversation, making mention of every house and auto they passed. One way to stop Lily from saying she wanted to go home, intent upon escaping the first day at school. Nothing was more important in life than an education, and Mary felt deprived by having a skimpy one.

They reached the brick school, hemmed in by a forbidding wrought iron fence. Children were running around the playground, used for recess when the weather permitted. "See how nice it is, Lily. You'll have good times here." Mary pointed. "There are swings and slides over there in the corner. See."

Lily tightened her clutch on her mother's hand. "I wanna go home."

They passed through the gate. "Come on honey. We're almost there." Mary headed to the entrance and started up the steps. Lily began to pull her backwards.

Mary grasped Lily's arm. "We'll be late. Come on. You can't be late to school, sweetie."

"I wanna go home, Mother." Lily screwed up her face as she struggled to escape her mother's grip.

Other parents with children gawked and hurried by. Mary pretended not to notice and kept her gaze on Lily, still struggling to get loose. At the door, Lily plunked herself down in the entrance. People began to take great care in walking around her, trying not to step on the little fingers spread over the mat like a fan or on the lace-edged petticoat peeping below her dress.

Mary bent down and leaned close to Lily. "Daddy won't like it when he hears that you acted like a baby at school."

Lily stared up at her mother, disbelief sprouting. She got up and went through the door.

A clerk stood inside, checking the names of new students against a list. "Lily Dunmore," said Mary. "She's had her vaccination."

The woman marked her paper, nodded agreement and motioned to the room on her right. "First grade. Miss Opal Griffith's class."

Lily grabbed her mother's hand and squeezed it hard as they entered the room, filled with boys and girls giving a once-over to the newcomer. A tall, wiry teacher approached. Mary introduced herself and Lily.

Miss Griffith smiled, her dark hair bristling around her pale face, eyes aimed toward the new student. "Lily will need a nickel every day if you want her to have milk at recess, Mrs. Dunmore. And when the weather turns cold, there's a cloakroom where she can hang her coat and store her boots."

"Of course," replied Mary, trying to act as though she knew everything that was expected in an up-to-date school. She glanced at the teacher's desk, topped by a worn Bible, a row of well-used books, and a box overflowing with sharpened pencils. In the corner of the room stood the American flag, its 48 stars catching the sunshine that drifted through the window. A stout wooden paddle was propped against the wall near the flag.

Miss Griffith led Lily to the first seat in the second row and told her to sit down. Lily settled at the desk that had a flip-up top, offering safekeeping for books, paper, pencils, and hoarded treasures. She turned around and glimpsed at her neighbors, then sank in her seat and stared at the blackboard.

"I'll be waiting for you when school lets out, Lily." Mary patted her shoulder and handed her a nickel for milk. "Put it in your pocket so you don't lose it, honey." After a quick goodbye Mary hurried away, loneliness shrouding her as the school bell tolled in the tower.

Tom was in the backyard when she got home, hard at work in his lush flower beds. Pulling out the weeds, trimming plants here and there, hoeing the ground until it was friable. His favorite pastime when he wasn't building something at his workbench. Mary glanced at the dining room table, brimming with supplies, tiny tools, and paper flowers in the making. A sense of well-being swept over her. At least she had something to do that she loved, something besides housework, an unending, repetitive task that required more muscle than brains.

She put on her apron and picked up a notepad on the dining room table. She'd started a list, showing how many orders had been filled for flowers and the price paid. Her money was still hidden in a pickle jar, stashed on the top shelf of the cupboard. She hadn't told Tom that she was selling bouquets either. The flower-making materials had been bought with her household allowance. She slipped the pad in her apron pocket that held the key to Ben's room and patted it lovingly. Knowing that she could accomplish something for money made her feel as smart as a man.

She packed Tom's lunchbox, then went to the door and called him. "I'll fix your meal a little early. I have to pick up Lily at school. There's only a half day because it's the first day. Tomorrow I'll walk her home for lunch, then take her back."

He left the garden, wiping his laced-up boots on the porch mat and heading to the kitchen sink to wash his dirty hands. "It'll take a lot of your time to get Lily to and from school."

"I'll manage, Tom. Don't worry your head about it."

He settled down at the table and rolled a cigarette. "I'm thinking about getting a pipe. I might like that. I looked at some nice ones down at Millard's drug store the other day."

"I wonder if smoking's good for you. You ought to ask the doctor."

"It relaxes me, Mary. Yes sir-ee. I only smoke at work on my break."

He picked up the newspaper while she began to fry bacon for his lunch. "Did you know women can vote now? It's in the paper. A bunch of tomfoolery I'd say."

She turned from the stove and stared at him. "Are you sure that's right? Can I really vote?"

He held up the front page for her to see the headline. WOMEN GET VOTE IN SEPTEMBER 1920. He laid down the paper. "Read it, Mary. The story tells how Negro men got the right to vote in 1867, but women weren't allowed to vote, no matter whether they were black, white, or any other color."

"I can't believe it, Tom. Gertie told me this would happen, but it doesn't seem for real." She reflected. "I guess I can go with you when you vote, and you'll show me how it works."

He guffawed. "Leave the politics to the men, Mary. That's our place. Women don't have any business interfering in politics."

She banged the side of the iron skillet with the butcher knife she'd used to slice the bacon. "Women ought to be full citizens, just like men. Equal players, Tom. No reason they shouldn't be, is there?"

He held up his hand in mock surrender. "You have enough to do with the house and looking after Lily. And you're into making those paper flowers. I don't see why you think you should vote or why you'd even want to vote."

"Because I want to have the same rights as men, that's why." She flipped the sizzling bacon over in the pan, letting the grease spatter. Quickly she went to the sink and held her singed arm under the cold water. "Women pay taxes, but they can't vote. Gertie teaches school, gets a paycheck, pays taxes, but she can't vote. No way that's fair, Tom."

He took a long drag on his cigarette. "We'll see," he grumbled.

Lily wasn't effervescent about her first day at school. "It was dopey," she replied after changing into play clothes and eating a jelly sandwich.

Mary kept probing. "What did you learn today, honey?"

"Rules." Lily sniffed and jerked her head from one side to the other. "Don't be late. Don't talk 'cept when you have to answer the teacher."

Mary eyed Lily. "I'm sure she wants you to learn good manners."

"She said we had to keep our hands to ourselves. Pay attention." Lily's voice took on a vibrato. "She uses the big paddle by the flag for whipping if we make any trouble."

Mary gasped. "Don't get into trouble, sweetie."

Lily was mum.

"What else did you do?" asked Mary.

Lily rubbed her nose. "She called the roll. Told us to say 'here' when we answer. That's silly. She can see we're here. Then she read the Bible, and we sorta said a prayer. After that we had to stand up and salute the flag. We practiced the Pledge. That took forever."

"Sounds as though you're off to a fine start and learned a lot your first day. I'm proud of you. Tomorrow you'll come home for lunch and then go back for afternoon class."

"Yeah," lamented Lily.

"It's time for your piano lesson now," said Mary, heading for the parlor. "The next lesson in your book has a duet. You and I can learn how to play together."

"I can play fine all by myself," twitted Lily, sliding onto the bench.

"I know, sweetie, but duets are for two people. In a duet, I play one part and you play the other. The music is written for two people. Maybe . . . just maybe if we learn to do it well, we can play a duet for Gertie or somebody. We could be in a recital some day."

Lily wilted.

"Play your lesson first," directed Mary. "Then we'll try the duet."

Half an hour later, Mary pronounced Lily's lesson a success. "You're doing fine. I'm proud of how well you can play. Now we'll try the duet called *Comin' Round the Mountain*. I have the secondo part in the bass. You have the treble. That's called the primo part."

Mary had spent half an hour learning her part. "Practice for a while, honey. Then we'll see how we do together."

Lily began, sight-reading the notes in a much quicker time than Mary had ever imagined. Mary joined Lily on the bench. "That's great, sweetie. Really great. You're doing beautifully. Now let's play together."

Mary had the easier part but soon found that she was no match for Lily who was playing in correct tempo and making few mistakes. After half a dozen starts and stops, Lily turned and faced her mother. "You have to practice," she said triumphantly. "You need it lots more than I do."

Mary flushed. Even though she was the teacher, she realized that her six-year old was right. Lily had more musical talent than her mother.

Chapter 12

The phone rang just after she'd gotten home from walking Lily back to school at lunchtime. It was Sally Kindle, offering Mary a teaching position in the flower-making class at the church.

She was surprised. "I'd love to teach, but I have to walk my daughter back and forth to school every day."

"Think about it and let me know right away," said Sally. "This class starts in October. Meets on Tuesdays 1:30 to 3:30. The teacher's pay is based on the number of students in each group. If you decide to teach, tell your friends about the course and invite them to join. Show them all the flowers you've made. They'll be interested."

Mary pondered. "I might manage one afternoon a week, but I'll have to ask my husband first and see what he says."

"Let me know by next week," said Sally. "We're offering a bridge class in October, too. That class is scheduled for Monday afternoons, 1:30 to 3:30. The fee will be the same as the one for making flowers."

"Let me get back to you after I talk to Tom," said Mary, a fire kindled that her life was taking on new turns.

Gertie dropped by after supper to see how Lily was doing in school. "Pete's gone back to the office to work this evening. Thought I'd find out how my favorite first-grader's doing."

Lily grinned. "We're learning to sing *Lucy Locket Lost Her Pocket*, Gertie."

"What's your teacher's name?"

"Miss Opal Griffith."

"I've heard that she's good. I bet you'll do very well in her class."

"I dunno." Lily wiggled her head. "Wanna see my books? They're up in my room on the shelves Daddy made me."

Mary headed to the kitchen. "Take Gertie for a look-see while I fix us some dessert, honey."

When they returned, Lily was clutching Benny. The bowls of vanilla ice cream sprinkled with chocolate jimmies were ready to carry to the back porch. Mary took a deep breath of the balmy air, relief overtaking her as they sat down to enjoy their sweets. Gertie gazed at the colorful flower beds and the pale buds aiming toward the trellis that Tom had fashioned beside the porch. "Those roses will be like an awning next summer. You're lucky to have a man who cares about plants and how the yard looks. Pete doesn't give a hoot. His mind's always on whatever case he's working. I have to see that someone mows the grass and prunes the shrubs. I don't have any yen or energy for planting flowers or tending to them." She fingered the purple beads around her neck. "I'm afraid I wasn't even good at making the paper ones."

"Don't run yourself down, Gertie. We can't be good at everything, can we?"

"No, of course not."

"Say, I haven't told you that Sally Kindle asked me to teach the next class."

Gertie grinned. "That's super, Mary. What a splendid opportunity for you."

"I'll have to ask Tom if I can. Since I walk Lily to school, it'd be rough on the day I teach."

"Tom shouldn't mind. I'm sure he wants you to be happy, Mary."

"To tell the truth, I don't know what he'll think."

Gertie straightened up. "You've got to do it, Mary. It'll be the same as taking a tonic. Getting out of the house, doing something you like, socializing with other people—I know that'll put more gusto in your veins."

Mary pointed to her chest. "But imagine *me* being a teacher."

"That's not hard to imagine. You're smart. You can do what you want to do."

Lily finished her ice cream, laid Benny in the baby buggy and wheeled it down the steps into the yard. Gertie's gaze followed as Lily pushed the carriage around the lawn. "She seems to be doing okay at school. Everything's neat as a pin in her room, too. That's unusual for a six-year-old, believe me." Gertie cast an inquisitive look at Mary. "I noticed that Ben's door is still shut."

Mary nodded. "Tom locked it to keep Lily from going in there. He gave me the key."

"How do you feel about that?"

Mary ran her hands over her lap. "I don't want her to go in there. Ever."

"How does Lily feel?"

"We haven't talked about it. She seems happy and never mentions Ben. If and when she wants to talk about him, I figure she will."

Gertie was reluctant. "I suppose so."

"Lily's doing great at the piano. We tried playing a duet." Mary tittered. "She even said that she can play better than I can. Guess what? She's right."

"I want to hear her play before I leave."

"Good, but we're not playing the duet yet," said Mary with a snicker. She became solemn. "I'd like to get Lily a piano teacher who has credentials."

Gertie leaned closer. "The music teacher at Stowe High gives lessons. You should talk to him. His name is Sean Foster. I don't think he'd charge a lot."

"Maybe I'll call him. I'm saving what I make from selling flowers. I want Lily to study with a professional so she can make the most of her talent."

"You need to think about yourself, too. You and Tom never go anywhere together. Pete and I belong to a bridge club. It's one of the few times I can drag him away from his office. We meet on the last Saturday night of the month and take turns at each others' houses."

"That sounds like having a good time. Sally Kindle said they're starting a bridge class at church. Maybe I can take lessons and teach Tom how to play."

"A swell idea. Then we could get together for a hand of bridge."

Mary doubted if a lawyer would want to socialize with a railroad fireman.

Gertie perked up. "Did you know that women can vote now? I can hardly wait."

"Tom mentioned it. He doesn't think I should vote." Mary began to stack the dirty dishes to carry to the kitchen.

Gertie eyeballed Mary. "You have to vote whether Tom likes it or not. Decide what party you're in and who to vote for."

Confusion captured Mary. She threw up her hands. "I don't know anybody who's running for office. Guess I'll have to start learning, won't I?"

"You can bet your life that *I'm* voting. Every woman should vote. Women have worked their heinies off to get the right to vote. Amendment Nineteen to the Constitution finally became law. Seems as though it's taken forever for that to happen. I intend to urge all my pupils to vote as soon as they're old enough."

Mary tapped her foot. "Tom won't ever be sold on women voting. He doesn't think that they should do the things men do. He believes men ought to take care of politics and run the country."

Gertie snuffled and swept a strand of hair back from her forehead "Women need to do their share and shoulder some responsibility. Believe me, we can do a lot more than run a house, have babies, and rear children. We proved that during World War I, didn't we?"

"I guess so," murmured Mary.

The next day Mary packed Tom's lunchbox while figuring how to tell him that she wanted to teach a class at St. Mary's. She'd already walked Lily to school and returned home to hang the laundry on the line where it was flapping in the wind. It was almost time to bring Lily back home for lunch. Mary decided to ask

Tom what he thought about his wife's teaching a class. Never in her harebrained dreams had she thought about actually becoming a teacher. She hadn't even set foot in high school, let alone a college.

Tom was relaxing at the kitchen table, breaking in his Wellington pipe while he scanned the paper. She gathered up nerve and faced him. Her words tumbled out. "I wanted to ask you something, hon. I've been invited to teach a class at St. Mary's."

He looked up, a furrow sprouting between his eyes. "What class?"

"Flower-making. The class I took when I learned how to make paper flowers. Sally Kindle, the leader, phoned and offered me the chance to teach. I'd get paid for every pupil I had in the class."

Awestruck, Tom cleared his throat huskily. "You don't have time to do that."

She plunked down in a chair. "It would only be one day a week, Tom. On Tuesdays, 1:30 to 3:30."

"What about getting Lily at school?"

"School lets out at four. I'd manage. If I was a little late, Lily could wait a few minutes in the school yard." She paused. "But that's not likely to happen."

He frowned. "You have enough to do, Mary. You don't need to work outside the home. That's *my* job. I'm the breadwinner here. A married woman's place is in the home."

She put her hand in her apron pocket, seeking courage from the key to Ben's room. "I'd like to do it, Tom. At least try. It helps me to get away from this house, especially now. I'd enjoy trying to teach. That's an important job. Teachers prepare everyone for their life's work . . . doctors, nurses, ministers, clerks, railroaders . . . even mothers."

Tom was rattled. He tapped his pipe on the table. "Teaching is a fine job for women who aren't married. They can devote all their energy to it."

"Gertie is an excellent teacher, Tom. She's married. I've heard nothing but good about her."

He laid his new pipe on the table and gazed at her long and hard. "I bet this all came about since you found out you can vote. It's not womanly to vote, Mary."

She stood up. Her face turned red. "Baloney, Tom. Voting had nothing to do with it. When I was in the class, Sally told me that she was putting me on her list as a possible teacher."

He glared. "What about voting? Are you gonna vote, too?"

"Sure. I'm hoping you'll help me. I don't know who to vote for."

"You'll have to figure that out all by yourself." His voice took on a gruffness. "And you can't go in the voting booth with me either. That's private. Like I've been thinking lately, women are never going to be satisfied. The more they get, the more they'll want. Next thing you know, some woman will be running for president."

Her eyes flashed. "That's the silliest thing I ever heard. A woman would never think of doing that, Tom."

He got up and slid the newspaper across the table towards her. "You'd better start reading to get educated if you're gonna be a teacher."

Mary swallowed hard. She'd have to do her darndest not to fail.

Chapter 13

Election Day 1920 arrived on the first Tuesday after the first Monday in November. Mary had to figure out who should get her vote. Tom was a dyed-in-the-wool Democrat. He said President Wilson's chance of getting what he wanted in the Versailles Treaty and the League of Nations was wrecked because too many Republicans elected to Congress voted against his ideas. In the aftermath, President Wilson collapsed and became bedridden.

Mary felt sorry for the President, but she didn't want that to be her reason for becoming a Democrat. Tom was no help. He remained mum about the candidates. "Make up your own mind. I'm not telling you how to vote. No sir-ee. No sir-ee."

After reading the newspapers, talking to Gertie and scanning the posters stuck round and about, Mary decided she was going to be a Republican. When her class met, she asked who was going to vote. Two hands popped up.

"It's your right now, ladies," she said staunchly. "Many women have spent years making this happen. Be sure you vote and keep on voting every time we have an election." Some of the women wore puzzled looks. Several said they'd vote.

Lucy Glocker spoke up aggressively. "My Ralph won't let me vote. Ever. He says women have no place doing that sort of thing. It's a man's place."

The remark jump-started an exchange of opinions. The women forgot about fashioning paper flowers. Sally Kindle approached to see what the buzz was all about, and Mary realized that she'd created a predicament.

"Vote every time you have a chance, ladies. Now open your kits," Mary said hastily.

Mary stayed busier than she'd ever been in her whole life. When the results of the election stormed the front page of the paper, she was pleased to find that one of her picks was a winner. She didn't know the candidate or how satisfactory he'd be as a councilman, but she'd accomplished as much as Tom. She had voted. It didn't matter how many winners he'd picked either. She and her husband walked to the poll set up in the school and made their choices separately and privately. Neither one ever asked the other how many winners they had chosen.

Her flower class appeared to be flourishing, and she was gaining competence in getting ideas across to the women. She tried to answer each question carefully, demonstrated the steps in making a flower, and helped those who were having trouble. Sally Kindle, armed with needle-sharp vision, came by occasionally to oversee the activities and ask if things were satisfactory. Mary smiled and shook her head in the affirmative. The money made from teaching and selling bouquets was filling up her Heinz pickle jar.

She had also joined the Monday bridge class and found that playing cards was even more fun than creating blossoms. One Saturday when Tom didn't have to work, she got out the cards and explained bridge to him. He latched onto her interest. They bent over the card table, studying the rules, dealing the cards, and making bids. Before long Mary gleaned enough courage to invite Gertie and Pete Schumaker over for an evening of bridge. Later on, thanks to Gertie, the Dunmores were asked to fill-in at the bridge club that met the last Saturday evening of the month. Mary was surprised to find that social or professional standings didn't seem to matter . . . only how well a person played bridge. She and Tom fit right in.

Mary had hoped that Lily would be an eager pupil, ready to soak up all the learning possible. Her daughter often complained about going to school. It wasn't her cup of tea. Lily's mood had been better when she accompanied her mother to flower class in the summer. Now, she wore a gloomy expression more often than a smile. The friends that Lily made at St. Mary's attended the Catholic school in the Rocks. None of them turned up in her first-grade class at West Park School.

Heeding Gertie's suggestion, Mary talked to Sean Foster about piano lessons. He agreed to teach Lily if she came to the school on Wednesdays after classes let out for the day. Lily took a liking to him right on and practiced the piano more than she studied any of her books. Mary paid for the lessons with the money she made. She was elated about Lily's studying with Foster, a friendly, easygoing teacher with a sparkle in his brown eyes.

The piano at Stowe High was hidden from prying hands behind the maroon curtain on the auditorium stage. While Lily was having her lesson, Mary hunkered down in a classroom and pored over books that she borrowed from the teacher's shelf. Her interest in Edith Wharton's *Age of Innocence* was so keen that she used a bookmark to save her place 'til the next week. Surrounded by a blackboard and a big, honey-colored desk piled with papers awaiting grades, Mary believed that she was getting a true taste of education for the first time in her life.

When Tom asked how Mary intended to pay for piano lessons, she braced herself and finally told him how she had been saving her money from selling flowers and teaching a class at St. Mary's. He sat in silence for a while, gazing toward the elm trees that were beginning to drop their leaves outside the kitchen window.

A shadow crossed his face as he reflected. "I never thought you'd be making money after we got married," he muttered.

"I'm glad I can do that, Tom. Never gave such a thing a thought until it happened. After I left clerking at the A&P in Pittsburgh and married you, making money flew out the window. It's good to know that I can still earn some." She moved back to the stove where she was boiling potatoes and frying steak.

Slowly he stirred cream in his coffee. "Better start keeping track of what you make. They'll be wanting you to pay taxes next."

She squinted at him. "Never gave that a thought either. I've been overloaded now that Lily's in school. Walking back and forth every day and keeping up with my flower and bridge classes, I hardly have time to clean house."

"Have you ever cleaned out Ben's room?" he asked flatly.

Startled, she stopped turning the steak in the pan. "No."

"That's a room going to waste. We're paying for something we don't use."

"No matter, Tom."

He stiffened and gritted his teeth. "We ought to move. Closer to the school. Then you wouldn't have to walk Lily all the time."

"I can keep walking, Tom." Her voice took on a shrillness. "Besides, it'll take us forever to pay for this house. Years and years. How on earth could we move?"

"I've been thinking. We might build a house near the school. Lily'd go by herself then. Save you time to do whatever you fancy. We could look at lots. If we built again, we'd rent this one until it sold. Ought to be easier to build the second time around."

Eagle-eyeing Tom, she tried to digest what he was saying. Moving? No way to fathom that. It had taken so much money and work to build their house that living elsewhere was incomprehensible. And if somebody took over the house, they'd change everything in it. Ben's room with its locked door and toy autos drifted in her mind.

She stood in a fog while the potatoes boiled dry and the steak turned crispy, imagining what it would be like to leave 1200 Twelfth Street.

Chapter 14

It was Wednesday, a chilly November day with dusky clouds nudging each other, threatening rainfall. Mary had a 1:30 appointment at Dr. Josephine Winter's on Broadway. A continual tiredness finally convinced her that she was overdoing. Teaching a class, taking a bridge lesson, walking Lily back and forth to school, and managing the housekeeping devoured her energy. She figured that Dr. Winter could prescribe a tonic that would bring back her feel-good days. The ladies in the flower class often chatted about the remedies they were taking to improve their health. Lydia Pinkham's Herbal Supplement was a favorite. Mary was in the mood to try anything for some relief.

She climbed the steps to the doctor's office, situated on the corner of Broadway across from where she and Lily caught the trolley to Pittsburgh. She admired the first and only woman doctor in West Park. Dr. Winter had graduated with high honors from medical school and practiced for ten years. She was married to Paul Bergman, who managed a bank in Pittsburgh. All of Dr. Winter's patients were women. No man had ever whipped up the courage to cross her threshold and ask for help.

The doctor propped her horn-rimmed glasses higher on her nose and greeted Mary with a handshake and a touch on the shoulder. "Why are you here?" she wanted to know, listening intently while Mary explained.

"I was hoping you'd prescribe something to give me more pep, Dr. Winter. I'm through teaching my flower-making class, but I'm doing a lot of walking and keeping busy at the house." The doctor nodded and told the nurse to put Mary on the table.

After her exam, Mary dressed and waited for the doctor's diagnosis. She expected to be handed a prescription that would put her on the road to well-being. Momentarily her spirits rose.

"I understand why you're so tired," said Dr. Winter, gazing at Mary across the desk. "You're pregnant, my dear. The baby is due around the middle of July."

Mary went blank. The doctor must have made a mistake. The message dug deeper in her mind and Mary blurted out, "Are you sure?"

Dr. Winter chuckled. "Right as rain."

"I never thought . . . never imagined . . . it can't be." Mary floundered, remembering how hard she'd tried to keep from getting pregnant.

Dr. Winter leaned closer, looking squarely at Mary. "You need to get more rest. Eat a healthy diet. Drink plenty of milk. Take care not to do anything too strenuous." The doctor eased back to a restful position in her chair. "But you already know all that. You've had two babies."

Mary fumbled for words, but her brain was speechless. Tom was searching for a lot where they could build a second house when they hadn't paid for the first one. If that wasn't bad enough, she was going to have another baby.

The rain had turned to snow when Mary and Lily left Stowe High. Lily clutched her book satchel under her arm. "Mr. Foster said I had a very good lesson today. He pasted a gold star in my book. Now I have a new piece to learn."

"That's splendid, honey. I'm glad you're doing so well."

The wind was blowing hard, sending chills down Mary's neck. She pulled the collar of her jacket shut and wished she'd worn a scarf. She'd never expected snow when she went to see the doctor in the afternoon. Nor being told that she was pregnant.

"We're gonna celebrate Thanksgiving at school," said Lily. "In our room. Miss Griffith said we'll act out how the colonists thanked God for the crops."

Mary's mind was blurred . . . hard to think of anything except that she was with child and had to tell Tom. She struggled to make conversation. "That'll be nice, honey. You'll learn a whole lot that way."

"We'll have a pretend stove where we cook the food," spouted Lily. "Miss Griffith said the Plymouth colonists let the children turn meat on spits in front of the fires they built outside."

Mary lowered her head against the wind fanning her face. "Do you have a part to play in the celebration?"

Lily shook her head emphatically. "Miss Griffith said everyone would have a job to do. We're gonna set a table. A great big one that you can fold up and put away. We'll have food like the colonists ate. She said our parents could bring some if they wanted."

Mary began walking faster, seeking warmth and wishing they were riding in one of the autos rumbling by. "I'm glad you have a fine teacher, sweetie."

Lily twittered and grabbed at the snowflakes fluttering down. "I hope it keeps on snowing. Then I can ride my sled."

"We need our coats," said Mary. "I'm getting out our winter clothes." In the back of her mind, Mary was trying to remember if she'd stored her maternity dresses in the chifforobe or given them to the Salvation Army.

She was enjoying a cup of cocoa when Tom got home from work. Two inches of snow covered the ground. Even though he'd shed his jacket and cap when he came inside, he appeared ghost-like upon entering the kitchen. His whiskers and eyebrows were glazed with new-fallen snow. He moved with weariness, a blue cast on his lips.

"My gracious, you're half-frozen," said Mary, rushing to the stove to pour him a cup of steaming coffee.

"It's mighty cold out there for sure," replied Tom. "What's left of my garden will be stiff as a board. I need to dig out my union suit in the morning."

He went to the sink to wash up, then sank in his chair and sipped coffee while Mary dished up dinner and set the plate before him. "What have you been up to today?" he wanted to know.

"The usual," she said, thinking it would be better to wait until he'd eaten before telling him about the baby. He'd be shocked but pleased . . . she knew he wanted another child. "Today was Lily's piano lesson. Mr. Foster says she's doing very well. He gave her a gold star."

"That's great, sweetheart. Too bad *we* don't get gold stars for what we do."

Mary was tickled. "What would you do with those gold stars when you got them?"

"Put them in the bank if they were real gold," quipped Tom.

She was relieved that he seemed to be in a good mood, in spite of being chilled to the bone after the trek from the railroad yard. If she had to walk those miles in freezing weather . . . well, it would be impossible for a woman. Then she remembered that she was doing footwork every day when she walked with Lily.

He picked up the paper and scanned it while he ate. "Wish I had those big-time stocks the rich are loading up on these days. We could pay for this house quicker."

"We'll get it paid off eventually," murmured Mary.

He looked up, his alert eyes taking her in. "Say, I've found the perfect lot for us. It's only a scant block from the school. You wouldn't have to walk Lily anymore. Maybe watch her cross Ninth Street where there's some traffic, that's all. The high school's close, too. I want you to take a good look at the lot right away. It's the size of this one. We could use the same house plan and make any changes you want."

She was flustered, her eyes pinned on him. "My heavens, you're moving way too fast for me, Tom. I can't even imagine building another house."

"It's for you, Mary," he said fervently. "I don't want you doing all that going back and forth every day. You have other things you like to do but can't on account of Lily."

"She'll soon grow bigger and be able to cross the street by herself, Tom. She's a smart girl. I'll teach her to look both ways and watch out for the autos."

Mary reached for the coffee pot and refilled his cup. Then she sat down at the table and tried to compose herself. "There's something I have to tell you, Tom."

He perked up. "What's that?"

"I went to see Dr. Winter today. I've been feeling run down lately." She paused while he studied her with questioning eyes. "The doctor says I'm pregnant . . . due around the middle of July."

Tom brightened and reached toward her, giving her hand a tender squeeze. "Land sakes, hon. Why on earth didn't you tell me?"

"I had no idea, Tom. I was as surprised as you are." A slyness crept over her. "Don't even know how it happened."

Tom laughed so hard he began to cough.

"Guess I'll have to send Hannah a card. She'll be pleased as punch."

He wiped his mouth. "Bet it's a boy, Mary. He'll have a room in our new house."

She felt a twist in her stomach. "We don't know whether or not it's a boy, Tom. And we already have a house. We don't need another one."

Tom became stern. "You're not carrying a baby and walking Lily to school and back every day. We've got to move closer for your sake."

"We'll see," she mumbled, knowing that she owned no property rights in Pennsylvania and he could do whatever he pleased.

Tom had already bedded down for the night and was sound asleep. Mary peeped in Lily's room to be sure she had enough cover. Benny was snuggled up to Lily under the blankets pulled high around her neck. Mary shut the door and stood stiffly, her gaze fixed on Ben's door. For an instant she thought about unlocking the door, then backed away. The key was in her apron pocket, hanging in the kitchen.

She closed her eyes. To save her life, she tried as hard as she could to picture another baby in Ben's bed . . . her own newborn . . . or leaving Ben's room behind for a total stranger to use. Finally she opened her eyes and padded reluctantly down the hall.

Chapter 15

Mary made cornbread with pecans, and Lily carried it to school in a basket for the Thanksgiving celebration. A dozen mothers attended the first grade's special day. Miss Griffith wore a long dress and apron, similar to a colonist's garb, and had her hair tucked in a crisp white bonnet. Standing by the table set up at the side of the room, she described how the custom of Thanksgiving Day spread from the Plymouth settlement in 1621 to the other New England colonies before becoming a national holiday.

"On November 26, 1789, President George Washington issued a general proclamation for a day of thanks," declared Miss Griffith. "For many years no regular national Thanksgiving Day was celebrated in the United States. Some of the states held the holiday, but others failed to recognize it."

She held up a large picture of an attractive lady with dark hair, fervent eyes, and a pleasant face. "This is Mrs. Sarah Josepha Hale, a famous editor of women's magazines and the author of the children's poem, *Mary Had a Little Lamb*. During the 1800s, she helped shape the outlook of thousands of women. She also persuaded President Abraham Lincoln to make Thanksgiving a national holiday."

After her introduction, Miss Griffith turned to the children and declared, "Now it's time for you to show how the early colonists prepared their food for Thanksgiving." The students came forward and played their parts in the front of the room where Miss Griffith had created a fireplace with cardboard boxes, paints, logs, and an iron arm for supporting kettles. Two girls hung a rubber turkey over the fire to roast, a black kettle placed beneath it to catch the drippings. Several boys took turns beating make-believe batter in a big bowl and poured the mixture in a Dutch oven sitting near the fire. The children set the table with a homespun cloth, napkins and plates that resembled wood but were made of paper. Cider filled the little bottles at each place. A fat pumpkin, grinning from ear to ear, graced the center of the table. Lastly, the children filled bowls with slivered turkey, carrots, peas, grapes, blackberries, honey and cornpone.

The mothers clapped when Miss Griffith pronounced the meal ready. The colonists sat down and bowed their heads in prayer, then ate the feast with their fingers. Miss Griffith passed cookies and fruit to the bystanders.

"That was fun," said Lily when they were on their way home. "Miss Griffith made us practice a lot. I was afraid I'd make a mistake. Get paddled."

"You did fine," replied Mary, patting Lily on the head. "Perfectly fine."

"I wish Daddy could have been there to see me. When I grow up, I'm gonna have a family and cook Thanksgiving dinner."

"That will be wonderful," replied Mary.

With Christmas peeping 'round the corner, Mary was relieved when Sally Kindle said another flower class wouldn't be scheduled until spring. It was gratifying to be paid for teaching, but half a dozen orders for red poinsettias lay on the dining room table, waiting to be filled. Then there were presents to buy, a tree to find and trim, extra cooking and baking as well as Yuletide cards and notes to write. She was already feeling very pregnant. Her breasts were fuller and her waist thickset. Favorite dresses didn't fit. It ruffled her to think about all the work piled on her plate. Worst of all, Tom was dead set on moving, in spite of a baby being on the way. Still, she reminded herself, the void between her and Tom was shrinking. She sensed it when he touched her, kissed her, and looked at her with nothing but love radiating from his blue eyes.

He'd taken Mary and Lily to view the lot he hankered after. He lit up when he mentioned that the stores and the schools would be within easy reach. His walk from work would get shorter, too, a godsend when the weather acted up. Mary's mind scattered like a handful of rice tossed at a bride and groom. She couldn't settle down about moving and hadn't said yes to Tom. Her sleep was threatened by dreams of being lost in rooms that were bare and led endlessly from one to another.

As they were having breakfast in the kitchen Saturday morning, Lily seemed agitated and asked grumpily, "Do we have to have two houses, Daddy?"

He laid his pipe down on the ashtray and focused on Lily. "We'll live in the new house, honey. We'll either rent or sell this house."

Lily frowned and began to rub her nose vigorously. "Why do we have to move?"

"To be near the school. Then you and Mother won't have so far to walk."

"Will the new house be like this one?" chirped Lily.

"The same . . . except for things your mother wants to change." Tom slapped his knee and horse-laughed. "Yes sir-ee, that could change if she changes her mind."

Mary was miffed. "You're the one who said that Beaver Board would make the living room look nice. Gertie has it in her house. So did the Langstons where we played bridge last week. It adds elegance when it's on a ceiling in a room."

His gaze was quizzical. "What about that bigger fireplace and mantel you said you'd like? And the flower window in the dining room?"

"The house ought to be as nice as we can make it," retorted Mary.

Lily squinted at them, shaking her head so hard the yellow bow on top wiggled. "I'm not moving. I'm staying here forever."

There was an eerie stillness while Mary and Tom digested Lily's declaration. After a few moments, Tom said, "You'll get lonesome all by yourself, honey."

"Hungry, too," chimed Mary. She rose from the table and gave Tom a stiff look. "I'm staying here with Lily."

Tom jerked, a flush coloring his cheeks. "No sir-ee, Mary. No sir-ee. You'll be in the new house with me."

"You know I'd never leave Lily," snapped Mary. She reached for the coffee pot on the stove.

Lily shot her father a receptive stare. "I'll move with you, Daddy. I don't want you to be by yourself in that new house."

As she refilled Tom's cup, Mary chewed at her lip until it bled. Lily had a habit of throwing a clinker in everything.

Chapter 16

Christmas arrived with a light snow casting a bridal veil over 1200 Twelfth Street. Lily squealed when she opened her eyes, peeped out the window and ran down the stairs to see what Santa had delivered. She had been firm about what she didn't want.

"No dolls," she ordered Santa. "Benny's my last doll." She stood by Santa's knee and refused to climb on his lap at Hornes.

Santa obliged. Lily scrambled through her gifts under the tree in the living room—pick-up sticks, puzzles, playing cards, checkers, colored pencils, writing tablets and story books. A red stocking, brimming with cookies and candy, dangled from the mantel. Mother's package held a blue poplin dress with long sleeves, sewn on the Singer after Lily was sound asleep in bed. Dad gave her a string of pearls with a bracelet to match.

They hovered in the background, watching Lily tear open her gifts from Santa. Tom presented Mary with a box camera to take pictures of the baby to come. She gave her husband a wool scarf, gloves and socks to keep him warm on those long treks from the railroad yard.

The fir tree, laced with popcorn and cranberries, the evergreen wreaths on the wall, and the stuffed turkey roasting in the oven wrapped the house in the smell of Christmas. After opening the presents, Tom moved to the kitchen to relax with his pipe, a cup of coffee and the newspaper. Lily was getting acquainted with her gifts spread out under the tree.

Mary gazed at the greeting cards lined up on the dining room buffet, along with a letter from Andy. He was doing well at First Officers' Training Camp. She was thankful that the World War had ended in November 1918, and she no longer worried about whether or not her brother would come back alive.

"He's downright handsome," said Mary, admiring the 8 x 10 picture he'd sent with his letter. She tingled with pride. Her brother was serving his country. It had to be inspirational for men to wear uniforms and perform the duties that protected their nation. A frown flitted. She hated that men were wounded and killed while defending their homeland. Still, men had to wage war to create peace, didn't they? She sighed, wishing that she could do something important like Andy . . . be someone who counted.

Mary began to set the dining room table, placing candles in brass holders on each side of a bowl of fresh greenery in the center. She wished her mother and sisters and brothers could join them for Christmas dinner, but the Dunmores were scattered miles apart. Her yearnings were interrupted by the telephone in the living room. When she hurried to answer it, Tom followed from the kitchen.

Matt Taylor in El Paso, Texas joyfully announced that Hannah had delivered that very day in the hospital and was doing well. The best Christmas gift possible. They'd named the baby Faith Hannah Taylor.

"Give Hannah our love and best wishes," said Mary before hanging up. She smiled at Tom and Lily. "Hannah had a baby girl today. They named her Faith."

"That's great news, especially on Christmas," cried Tom. "What a present."

Lily frowned. "Did Santa bring the baby?"

Mary glanced at Tom, then focused on Lily. "No, honey. A stork brought it."

Lily was puzzled. "When will I get to see the baby?"

"I hope Hannah and Matt will be able to visit us sometime," replied Mary. "They live a long way off, honey."

Lily scrambled to her feet and hurried toward the piano. "I'm gonna play the Christmas song Mr. Foster taught me. It's perfect for the baby." Lily plopped down on the bench and played *Away in a Manger*.

"That's very pretty," commented Mary. "One day you can play it for Faith and tell her you welcomed her into the world that way."

Lily eyed her mother. "I hope Mr. Foster likes that tie I gave him for Christmas."

Mary smiled. "He's probably wearing it right now."

She headed to the kitchen to check the turkey roasting in the oven, pleased that Lily liked taking lessons from Sean Foster. She was playing well and didn't even have to be told to practice anymore.

Mary opened the cupboard and stared at her pickle jar on the top shelf. The money filled the Heinz jar almost to the top. A tremor of happiness went through her. Making and selling paper flowers brought a sense of accomplishment that she'd never experienced when she was a grocery store clerk. On that job which paid her less than the male clerk made for doing the same work, Mary had to watch her p's and q's and do exactly as she was told, even if it seemed to be wrong. Now she was her own boss. Nobody could tell her what to do about her flowers.

Tired after a memorable holiday, Mary prepared for bed. After being on her feet a long time, an air of frailty surrounded her. She watched Tom as he undressed in a hurry, punched the pillows with both fists to fluff them up, then settled down in bed.

"Just think," he exclaimed. "Our baby will be six months old next Christmas, and we'll be in our new house. That'll be a great day, won't it?"

"Maybe I'll arrange for the stork to bring our baby and save me the effort," she wisecracked.

His laughter rolled across the room. "You'll have to figure out when you're gonna tell Lily about the baby. She'll see that you're getting bulky around the middle."

Mary drooped. Tom was not only looking forward to the birth of their baby. He was stirred up about building a new house as well. An uneasiness gripped her. She was still trying to come to terms with moving.

After slipping into her gown, she crawled in beside him. He reached for her, pressed her close and kissed her softly. At that moment the distance between them melted, and she knew the time had come to yield.

"You might as well go to the bank and get that loan for the lot," she whispered.

He kissed her again and again. "Swell . . . it's been the merriest Christmas ever, sweetheart. We'll begin building soon as the weather's right."

She felt him relax and listened to his breathing grow deeper. Before the Seth Thomas clock in the hall chimed five minutes later, Tom was sound asleep. She lay wide awake, thinking about Ben and how things used to be. She smoothed her hand over her stomach and was comforted by its fullness. When the clock chimed again she was asleep, dreaming that she had a baby boy on Christmas.

Chapter 17

Good fortune blessed West Park with a mild winter in 1921. It stopped snowing in February. The construction crew went to work, forming the footings and foundation and building the frame until a looming skeleton stood on the muddy lot. Mary and Tom used their plan for the Twelfth Street house but made each room several feet bigger.

"After all," noted Tom good naturedly, "we're moving up. Our second home needs to be bigger than the first one, doesn't it?"

Window seats on each side of the red brick fireplace in the living room offered storage as well as a place to rest one's bones and gaze out the window at the world passing by. The dark Beaver Board was placed on the white ceiling to form large squares that added a luxurious touch to the room. Tom even admitted that he liked the look.

A spacious porch graced the front of the house. Mary figured that he was thinking about making a wide swing for the whole family to enjoy. Every day she spent time leafing through nursery catalogs, deciding what plants would spruce up the yard and the flower boxes on the front porch.

After making peace with the decision to move, Mary's spirits surged. Shimmering hair, a flawless complexion and hazel eyes with glints of gold made her even prettier during pregnancy. She still walked Lily to school, stitched dresses on the Singer, and filled orders for paper flowers. When Sally Kindle offered a teaching stint in the spring, Mary turned it down, realizing that she would be taking on too big a load. One afternoon a week she played bridge at St. Mary's and enjoyed good scores. When Tom was off work on Saturdays, they filled in at Gertie's bridge club or honed their card-playing skills at home.

If they visited friends for bridge, Lily went along and had the company of other children. She stayed on the sidelines, refusing to take part in the games that were played. Lily made a habit of tucking Benny under her arm when they left the house and amused herself at the party by embroidering a sampler, coloring pictures or stringing beads that became pretty necklaces. Occasionally she hung around the tables, peering at Mother and Dad's hands and the cards being played as though she actually understood their bids. Whenever the family visited someone who had a piano, Lily was invited to play but pursed her lips and backed off.

"I don't know anything from memory," she'd say hastily, moving away from the keyboard. Mary knew that Lily could have played several pieces. Sometimes people coaxed, but it never helped. Lily was determined not to perform.

It was May before the new house was pronounced finished, and the crew let out an earsplitting hurrah of approval. Moving day turned out to be sunlit with birds flying high, fashioning nests in trees alive with fresh green leaves. The movers were on hand, ready to make the undertaking as effortless as possible. Clothing, linens, kitchenware and the like had already been stuffed into cardboard boxes, thanks to Mary. Tom had packed the food in the kitchen and the basement cupboards as well as every tool in his workshop. The doll furniture was carefully stowed in the truck, along with the house furnishings.

Ben's room had never been opened since the day it was locked. Tom put his arm around Mary and gave her a hearty squeeze. "I'm leaving it to you, love. Do whatever you wish." He walked away to assist the movers.

Mary wore the apron with the key still tucked in the pocket. She picked up her box camera and slowly climbed the stairs, Lily trailing at her heels. A glance in Lily's room showed that it was already empty, except for Benny. He was propped up in a corner. Mary braced herself before entering Ben's room. When two men appeared to clear out the furniture, she stood guard at the door.

"I have things to take care of in here," she explained. "Give me a little more time and come back please." They nodded and took off downstairs.

Mary dug the key out of her apron pocket and unlocked the door. Lily cradled Benny in her arms and hung back, unsure about whether or not to go in Ben's room.

Her mother motioned her inside. After sinking down on the bed Mary looked 'round, drinking up everything in sight while her daughter watched every move. Finally Mary rose, took down the curtains and blinds and flung open the windows, letting the sun fill the space with brightness.

"I'm going to take pictures of everything in this room, Lily. I hope they'll turn out." Mary moved about, operating the camera until the film was used up. Then she brought boxes from the hall and began packing everything stored in the drawers.

"Can I help?" Lily asked, her eyes begging to do something.

"Of course. Why don't you do the books on the shelf?"

Lily laid Benny down and began to work. Mary moved to the toy cars on the shelf. She glanced in the closet and picked up a basket. One by one she filled it with Ben's autos.

Then she turned to Lily. "You can have these, honey. They belong to you."

Startled, Lily dropped a book as she reached for the basket. "All mine?"

"All yours, sweetie."

Lily hesitated, then set the basket on the floor. She reached for Benny and dug in his little pocket. Slowly she drew out Ben's ring and handed it to her mother. "This belongs to you now."

Mary stood stock-still in disbelief, fingering the ring. "How . . . where on earth did you get this, Lily?"

"I took it off Ben when he was in the casket. I wanted something I could remember him by."

Dismayed, Mary shook her head, her eyes filling with tears. "I can't believe this . . . I just can't."

Lily broke into a smile. "*I* have Ben's cars now, Mother. They're mine."

Mary took off her gold necklace and slipped the ring on it. "I understand. I truly understand. *I* have Ben's ring now, Lily. It's mine."

Chapter 18

Mary had used a midwife for her first two births at home. But even though 50 percent of the births in the United States were attended by midwives, the number was dwindling. Tales and rumors abounded about infections, damaged babies, and deaths due to treatments bungled by midwives. More women were beginning to prefer physicians. Hannah sent Mary several pictures of Faith and wrote that she had used a doctor, birthed in a hospital, and all went well.

After the newspaper printed a story about Grace Abbott, a social work pioneer and Chief of the U. S. Children's Bureau, Mary wrestled with whether or not she should have a midwife or a doctor for her third child. Abbott had been fighting throughout the world for the rights of women and children. As a result, Congress passed the Sheppard-Towner Act in 1921, providing funds for employing public health nurses to train and supervise "untrained" midwives.

"There's been a lot of hubbub about midwives," Mary told Tom at the kitchen table one morning. "I know that Agnes Yeager did a fine job for me when Lily and Ben were born, but I'm thinking about having Dr. Winter instead."

Tension caught Tom. He straightened up in his chair. "Some doctors do things to hurry up deliveries, sweetheart. They can harm the mother or the baby."

"I've heard those stories, too," replied Mary, "but I trust Dr. Winter. She's a fine doctor. I may go to the hospital this time instead of staying home. Hannah had a doctor and went to the hospital. Everything turned out well for my sister."

Tom crushed his cigarette in the ashtray. "You ought to use Agnes again. She's always been good, hasn't she?"

"Yes. I've never had any trouble with Agnes. She's the best midwife I know."

"No use taking chances then, Mary." His gaze darkened. "Something might go wrong."

Mary glanced at him. "Don't you like Dr. Winter?"

He leaned back in his chair, impatience nagging. "I know Agnes much better than I know Dr. Winter. I'm relieved that the railroad doctor gives me my physicals every year, and I don't have to see another doctor. I'm certain it'd be a whole lot cheaper to use Agnes instead of paying a doctor. You'd have to go to the hospital. Dr. Winter wouldn't be coming to our house."

Stillness filled the kitchen. Mary, deep in thought, looked blank. Then she spoke in a thin voice. "I guess I'll have to go talk to my doctor about it before I make up my mind."

Dr. Winter greeted Mary heartily. "It won't be long until your baby's due."

Mary felt embarrassed, but she was desperate for a physician's opinion. "That's why I had to see you, Dr. Winter. I have to decide whether I should go to the hospital. I've always used a midwife."

"I know," said the doctor, settling down behind her desk and motioning Mary to sit. "That's been the practice in this town for a long time. I hope midwives take advantage of the new legislation that provides training for them. Then giving birth will be safer for both the mother and the child."

Mary sighed. "Tom thinks I should use my midwife. She's capable, but I'd like to stay in a hospital this time and have you deliver my baby."

Dr. Winter eased her spectacles up on her nose and gazed at Mary. "I worked as a midwife before I was able to enroll in Woman's Medical College of Pennsylvania. Many people didn't think women had any business being doctors. I'm sorry to say that feeling still prevails."

Mary clicked her tongue. "Men feel that way, don't they?"

Dr. Winter nodded. "I'm afraid they do. For a long time, women were barred from the medical schools by men. In the late 1800s, women were gradually allowed to get their foot in the door and study and practice medicine. Over 7,000 female physicians were practicing in America by 1900."

"That's a lot of women doctors," noted Mary.

"True. During the war, women became nurses. Some were trained. Others weren't, but they proved their abilities in the medical field. Unfortunately, the number of women doctors in private practice began to decrease after the war."

Mary frowned. "You're the only female doctor in town. Why is that?"

"Establishing a practice and making it thrive is a rough road for a woman to travel." Dr. Winter's eyes lit up. "During medical meetings, I've heard some female doctors say they were afraid the male doctors might choke them to death to get rid of them. I've been here since 1915 and wouldn't have survived without my husband's financial backing."

"He must be very proud of you. I'll bet he's your patient."

The doctor shook her head. "No. We don't treat members of our family. He goes to another doctor—a male physician down in the Rocks. No man has ever come to my office as a patient. I'm sorry to say, but most people think that I'm only a woman's doctor."

"What's your husband's name?"

"Paul Bergman." She noted Mary's quizzical look. "I kept my maiden name. Many women do that when they become doctors. I didn't marry until after I finished medical school."

Mary scratched her neck, a question jutting forth. "What's the advantage in using a doctor instead of a midwife?"

Dr. Winter leaned closer, her gaze squarely on Mary. "For one thing, you'd be in a fine hospital. Ohio Valley. Secondly, you'd have the best nursing care available. And finally, you'd have a doctor with considerable preparation and experience in delivering babies."

"That sounds perfect. Exactly what I want. Sign me up, Dr. Winter."

The doctor chuckled. "You'll have to make an appointment and come back for an exam, my dear. I want to check you out from head to toe before the blessed event."

Mary went home, uneasy about what Tom would say when she told him what she'd done.

She found Lily in the backyard, getting acquainted with a stray cat. Tom was in the basement, building a porch swing large enough for the family and a baby. On the spur of the moment, Mary decided to tell him the news and get it over with. No point staying on pins and needles until Lily was fast asleep.

Not wanting to chance the cellar steps in her condition, Mary called Tom to come upstairs. He reached the kitchen, sweat on his face, tiredness drifting over him. He'd found things in the house that needed tending to ever since they moved from Twelfth Street.

"You're working too hard, Tom. It's your day off from the railroad. You ought to take it easy," she said, hoping to entice him into a chipper mood.

"I want to hang the swing while the weather's warm. You can sit on the front porch with the baby." He cast a dubious look. "What did the doctor have to say?"

Mary took a deep breath. "I decided. Dr. Winter is going to deliver my baby."

"You what!" exclaimed Tom.

"I think it's safer," she said quickly. "It'll be much better than having the baby at home, especially on account of Lily. I wouldn't want her to be within earshot while I'm in labor."

"Why'd you do that?" he stormed. "Why didn't you talk it over with me first?"

"We did talk about it, honey. I told you I might have Dr. Winter."

He sank in his chair and reached for his pipe. "You should'a waited and asked me what I thought. Naturally she was gonna tell you to use a doctor."

His face was red. "I don't see why a woman wants to be a doctor anyway. That's a man's job."

Mary sank into a chair, aware that the baby was kicking. "It's close to the time. I had to decide, Tom. The doctor has to check me over first so I need to get on her list and go back for an exam. I didn't want to lose out. I'm sure Dr. Winter will be the best."

He lit his pipe and sat there brooding, dissatisfaction taking hold.

Lily appeared on the back porch, cuddling the orange kitten in her arms. She pressed her face against the screen door and stared at them. "Can I keep this cat?"

Mary sat in bewilderment.

Lily's eyes begged. "Please. She's so pretty. Please . . . please can I keep her?"

Mary swallowed hard. "No, Lily. We can't have a cat. Especially now. I'm going to have a baby. Pretty soon you'll have a baby to look after, sweetie."

Lily gaped. "We're gonna have a baby? A real baby? A baby girl like Faith?"

"I don't know whether it'll be a girl or a boy, honey, but it'll be one or the other."

Lily kept on pleading. "This cat needs a home. I already gave her a name. It's Kitty."

The cat mewed, and Lily put it down. "She's starving. Can't she have some milk? Please give her some milk, Mother."

Tom laid down his pipe and headed to the icebox. "I'll pour her a saucer, Lily."

Days passed into days. Rose Mary Dunmore was born on July 1, 1921 at Ohio Valley Hospital, not far from the new home on Broadway where Kitty basked in a pool of sunlight on Lily's bed.

Chapter 19

"She cries a lot," said Lily, watching Mary snuggle Rose on her shoulder in an effort to stop the baby's incessant weeping. "Why does she cry all the time?"

Mary stood at the nursery window, gazing at the flow of gold in the summer sky. "She has the colic, Lily. It's sort of like a stomachache."

"Do you mean she's sick, Mother?"

Mary turned away from the window. "No, she's just uncomfortable, honey. You've had a stomachache. Remember that time when you ate too much popcorn? I'm sure Rose will feel better straight away." Mary hoped that was true but an uneasiness haunted her. Something might be wrong, even though Dr. Winter had declared that Rose was perfectly fine. Still, the thought lurked that Ben had died suddenly, even though he was a rugged little boy one day and became breathless soon after. The same thing could happen to Rose, Mary reminded herself.

Lily eyeballed her mother. "Can I put Rose in the buggy and push it 'round?"

"Not until she's older, Lily. You'll have plenty of time to take care of Rose."

Lily flung her long hair back. "That'll be like I'm the mother 'stead of you." She scowled. "But I won't be able to nurse her like you do. I don't have any breasts."

"You'll have them when you grow up, Lily. No need to worry. I'm looking forward to you helping me, honey. Babies take a lot of attention and a lot of time. You can be a big help when you're not at school."

Lily scratched her head. "How soon does school start?"

"In September. You'll be in second grade, honey. We'll practice crossing Ninth Street. You can walk to school by yourself now that there's only one street to cross. You'll have to pay real close attention to those autos. When you come home at noon, I'll have your lunch ready."

"Why don't they fix it at school?"

"I don't know. I guess they don't have enough money to do that."

"My birthday's almost here. Can I have a party . . . get lots of presents?"

Mary squirmed. "I'm sorry, Lily, but we can't have a party with the baby so young. You'll still have ice cream and cake and presents from Daddy and me."

Lily thrust a mean look at the baby. "It's your fault I can't have a party, Rose."

"That's not a nice thing to say, Lily." Mary sauntered back and forth as she studied the nursery. With quiet deliberation, the furniture had been arranged so it was different from Ben's room. Still, she couldn't get him out of her mind, feeling his closeness whenever she entered the new nursery.

She recalled the look on Tom's face after Dr. Winter announced that the baby was a seven-pound girl. The twist of Tom's mouth, the bleak "Yes sir-ee" to Dr. Winter and the abrupt clearing of his throat left no doubt about his yearning. Men always wanted a boy who'd grow up and gift the family with a never-to-be-forgotten pride. The thought glistened. She'd hungered for a boy, too, but knew that she'd have whatever the good Lord intended.

She gazed at the blue-eyed baby and wondered if Rose would share Lily's incompatibility. Seemingly intent on opposition, no matter what the situation. Mary mused about what she'd read in the paper once. A child inherits half of his genes from his father and half from his mother. Hopefully, Rose Mary Dunmore would fix her eyes on the brightness in life instead of its darkness.

Lily learned to look both ways when crossing Ninth Street, but Mary and Tom decided that it wasn't safe for her to chance the streets to the high school for her piano lessons. On Wednesdays, Mary and Rose met Lily when school let out. They crossed the busy roads and walked with her to Stowe High.

Rose learned to love music when Lily took her lessons. With the baby in her arms, Mary danced up and down the hall at Stowe while Lily played rollicking tunes on the grand piano. Quite often Amos, the janitor, followed Mary, whirling 'round and 'round and 'round until he was dizzy, wielding his broom like it was his partner. Whimsy lit up his coal black face as he relished the dance.

In the beginning, Lily enjoyed tending the baby. While the weather was warm and Lily pushed Rose around the yard in the wicker buggy, Mary found time to fashion paper flowers and fill orders. The money stuffed in the jar paid not only for Lily's piano lessons but for cloches and plumed hats to show off at church on Sundays.

Mary was upbeat about her makeshift career. "I'm really accomplishing something worthwhile now," she'd confided in Gertie.

A wistfulness passed over Gertie. "You're doing really great, Mary. Remember that you have two wonderful girls to raise. That's the best accomplishment any woman can ever have."

Nevertheless, Mary missed playing bridge at St. Mary's in the afternoons. She decided to start an evening club of her own. With Tom working at the railroad and Rose sound asleep in her crib, there was no reason why she couldn't enjoy a delightful game of cards. In the fall, she invited her friends from St. Mary's to join the Evening Bridge Club that met every two weeks at her home. The women who joined pitched in for the cake and ice cream that was served after the game. Eventually, they voted to collect money for a high-score prize and a booby prize for the low-score.

Everything was tidied up and put away before Tom arrived home for his supper. It made for a bustling day, but Mary was enlivened by the renewal of her social life. Soon she found herself hunting in the paper and magazines for articles about how to play bridge. She was spurred to buy a small blackboard that was set up near the bridge tables. At each meeting she offered a brief lesson, focused on the requirements for an opening bid. It wasn't long before Mary became known as the contract bridge teacher in West Park.

Chapter 20

Lily's new teacher in second grade was Louise Musmanno. Miss Musmanno had bouffant, henna hair that she subdued in a snood at the back of her head. Her voice was high-pitched, echoing across the classroom like a blue jay's cry. She had a habit of bombarding the class with questions to make certain that everybody's mind was on the lesson. No child was left out when it came to question time.

The day arrived when it was Lily's turn to answer. She became rigid and her face went white.

"Speak up, Lily. Speak up. Three plus five is?" Miss Musmanno tapped her heel on the floor and waited for an answer. Impatience loomed on her face, the cheeks highlighted with orange rouge.

Lily's voice froze. She sat speechless, her eyes glazed over with fear.

Miss Musmanno held up her left hand and pointed three fingers at Lily. She raised her right hand and pointed five fingers. "How many are there, Lily?"

Lily felt her underpants getting wet. She pressed her thighs closer together and remained silent, thinking that she was going to die at any moment.

With a curl of her mouth, Miss Musmanno broke the silence and called on Walter Bennet, a Negro boy sitting behind Lily. His quick answer, "Eight," boomed over Lily's head.

From that day on, Lily knew that she could never warm up to Miss Musmanno. She'd have to squeeze through second grade as best she could.

When Lily's report card reached home and waited for Tom's handwritten approval, he was perturbed. He sat at the kitchen table where he'd finished his midnight supper, scowling as he examined the card. "I think Lily should get better grades than this, Mary. She reads well. I've listened to her many a time. She deserves more than a C-minus. Miss Musmanno also gave her a C-minus in arithmetic. That's not right either. Lily knows her numbers. I've given her problems and she gets them right."

"I'm disappointed, too, Tom, but Lily doesn't care for school. I thought she'd be an A student, but she isn't in love with reading, writing and arithmetic. Guess we all can't be at the top in that regard. I wish she'd take to school the way she takes to piano. She relishes her lessons with Sean Foster and plays very well. I'm pleased about that, and you should be, too."

Tom leaned back and gave his wife a searching look. "She doesn't get a grade for playing the piano, Mary."

Mary wrung her hands. "I know, but they learn to read notes and sing songs in class. The music teacher goes from school to school and comes by once a week."

Tom pursed his lips, wrinkles taking hold of his forehead. "I hear a lot of people complaining, mostly the ones who've crossed the ocean to work and make a home here. The Poles and Italians mix their language up with ours. The Slovaks don't understand what we're saying. When the Germans and Ukranians get together, it sounds like a bull fight, and the Jews and the Scotch-Irish squabble like roosters tussling over a hen."

Mary chuckled. "I'm glad our parents were Scotch-Irish. We're good and steady like the Scotch—warm hearted like the Irish. A lot of immigrants are in Lily's class. She says they're real smart, but they have a hard time with spelling and reading."

"Maybe they're taking up too much of the teacher's time," muttered Tom. "I've been thinking. I might run for the School Board. If I was elected, I'd make sure things got better in our schools."

Mary jerked, spilling her cup of tea in her lap. "I can't imagine why you'd ever expect to be on the board, Tom."

"I'd like to do it," he snorted, amused at watching her mop up the tea with a dish towel. "We need to move ahead in this world. If I was on the board, I'd tell them what needs improving. Some of the ways they're doing are wrong. Take this report card for instance. I'd find out how Miss Musmanno figured these grades. She can't be right. I know Lily deserves an A in reading."

Mary crooked her head and eyed him. "You've got to have a lot of education to be on the School Board, Tom. They want people with fine schooling."

He fumed. "Schooling isn't everything, Mary. You pick up from being around people. From your job. I had to learn the yard signals and operating rules . . . how to fire a locomotive with a scoop shovel . . . operate a stoker. I passed every one of those tests. I've learned plenty. I know enough to be on that board."

A gasp escaped Mary's lips. "I can't imagine you're thinking about getting involved with the schools."

Tom's eyes narrowed to slits. His face took on a flush. "No reason why I can't. You teach flower-making. Your education's no better than mine."

She flared up. "I teach women how to make flowers, but that's different from what schoolteachers teach. I think people on the board study and take classes so they can help the principals and teachers run the schools."

He stiffened. "I read the paper every day. Talk to all kinds of people in the know, especially those white-collar fellows I meet down street. I keep up on what's happening and what needs fixing. No reason why I can't help out on the School Board."

She sank back in her chair. "I still think you need more education for that kind of responsibility."

Tom picked up the pen on the table and signed Lily's report card with a flourish. "We'll see," he said defiantly.

Chapter 21

The house at 1200 Twelfth Street had been rented ever since Tom and Mary moved to Broadway in the spring. One morning after Tom spent several hours down street shopping and talking about the schools, he returned home to announce, "The Dingledines want to own our house instead of renting it."

Mary beamed. "Swell. Now we can relax and not have to clutch every penny."

Tom's eyebrows did a jig. "Well, I don't know about that, Mary."

She gave him a quizzical look. "What do you mean?"

He scratched his head. "I've been thinking about starting a business so we can make money. You know, something on the side while I'm working on the railroad."

"And how on earth would you manage that, Tom? You're finishing your stint at the P&LE when most folks are snuggled up in bed for the night. Have you figured out a way to add more hours to the day?"

"No, hon. I can hire somebody to look after the business while I'm working on the engine."

She dropped in the nearest chair. "Why can't we just ease up and have some time for ourselves instead of worrying about a business?"

"I'd really like to run a business, Mary. I know I can do it. Have a little faith in me, honey." His eyes had a pleading look that she'd never seen before.

She inhaled, trying to stop the off-beat of her heart. "Land sakes alive, Tom. Tell me what kind of business you're talking about."

He pointed. "See that icebox over there?"

"Of course I see it. So . . . ."

"We put 25 pounds of ice in there every week except in the winter when we use the window box to keep food cold. You know how much it costs to have that ice delivered by the truck that comes by."

"So?" Her gaze cut straight through him.

"If I built an icehouse out in the back beside the alley, people could buy ice here and get it much cheaper. Carry it home instead of having the truck deliver it to their door. They'd save money. This area is growing, and the schools and stores are nearby. There are bound to be plenty of people who need ice."

She gulped. "I'll have to admit that you come up with the most outlandish ideas I've ever heard of, Tom Dunmore. How long have you been concocting this notion?"

His laughter swirled through the kitchen. "It's been boiling in my head for a while." He gave her a penetrating look. "You didn't care much for renting our house and building another one, but we did it, didn't we? And you seem to be well pleased with the result. I haven't heard you complain any. Now I'd like to build something in our backyard that will bring in money to pay for this house."

She shook her head. "You don't have time to build an icehouse, Tom. You go to work in the afternoon and don't get home until midnight. Are you going to build the house in the dark instead of going to bed?"

He reached for his pipe on the smoke stand. "I'll hire a crew to do the work. I'm sure the fellows who built this house can put up an icehouse in no time flat."

"What do they know about building an icehouse?" Her words were tart.

"An icehouse has to have thick walls and a heavy door to keep the ice from melting. The ice will be delivered to us in 350-pound blocks that are scored. We can cut it in 25- and 50-pound chunks for the customers."

She swept a stray curl away from her face. "How did you figure that out, Tom?"

"I visited the icehouse in the Rocks where the trucks pick up their deliveries. There's nothing complicated about building an icehouse or cutting ice with a pick. We'll have a platform in the front. Sort of like a porch. The customer will order the size he wants. We'll cut the piece, bring it out and push it down the slide for him. That's all there is to it."

"You make it sound like child's play, Tom."

He grinned. "Yes sir-ee. Yes sir-ee. The girls will have fun out there for sure. Not every kid has an icehouse in their backyard. We'll close the business in the winter and open it the rest of the year when people buy ice. That'll be a first-rate way to make money. You won't have to spend time making flowers anymore."

"I love to make flowers," snapped Mary. "And I'm not going to quit either. My little business pays for Lily's piano lessons and a few other things I like."

He grunted. "I never said no about you getting into the flower business. I always let you do what you want whether it's right or wrong, don't I?"

Mary sat motionless, drowned in thought. She had to admit that Tom had given her the key to Ben's room. She'd sold paper flowers, started her own bridge club, and had Rose Mary Dunmore in the hospital when Tom thought they ought to use a midwife. On top of that, when election time rolled around next month, she was going to vote for Louise Krakowski, the first woman in West Park who dared to put her name in the pot for Commissioner.

Still, Tom did what he wanted, too, with only one exception. She'd threatened to leave him if he whipped their kids anymore. A thought nagged. How could she manage if her marriage somersaulted into a divorce? The husband in Pennsylvania wore the pants and had property rights. She didn't have any rights. Her ability to hold down a decent job was scanty, and there were two kids to tend and feed.

She watched Tom puff on his pipe while he skimmed the paper. He read everything he could get his hands on. If luck held, maybe he'd forget about running for the School Board now that he was set on starting a business. Besides that, she loved him and didn't want him embarrassed by coming up short when people found out he only had a grade-school education.

"I guess you'd better build that icehouse, Tom," she said after a while. "It sounds like a good idea to me. Maybe the work can be finished before the weather turns cold."

He grinned, laid down his pipe and came over to buss her on the cheek. "That's my girl." He gave her shoulder a soft squeeze. "The crew might be able to get it done by Christmas, honey."

I have to go see if Rose is awake," murmured Mary, deciding that marriage was turning out to be one change after another instead of the serene, simple life she'd always imagined.

Chapter 22

Christmas Day in 1921 was the best one ever for the Dunmores. Rose was almost six months old, and Lily was a healthy 7-year old. The family lived in a spanking new house. To add to that, some of Mary's kin arrived on Christmas Eve.

The icehouse had been finished lickety-split, exactly like Tom predicted. It stood at the rear of the house, beside the alley where customers could easily load the ice into their cars, trucks, or wagons. A fence lined the rest of their property in the backyard.

"I'll plant roses there in the spring," Tom told Mary as he stared out the kitchen window on Christmas afternoon. "They'll climb over the fence and make it real pretty. I wish it was spring now so I could start selling ice."

With tongue-in-cheek, Mary replied, "I can hardly wait for that icehouse to open, hon." She looked in the oven, eyed the big turkey and squirted it with melted butter. "Now, let's go join the folks. I don't want to miss anything."

Words were streaming when Mary and Tom entered the parlor. Andy McGuffy, on leave from First Officers' Training Camp, was delighting everyone with tales about his adventures. Mary felt pride every time she looked at her brother. She tried to imagine being in his shoes. He was tall and handsome in his olive-drab uniform with the U.S. insigne on the collar. A man dedicated to protecting his country from harm, even though it meant he might be injured or die while performing his duties. She shuddered, wondering how women could stand being Army nurses. Then relief swarmed. No doubt they'd always stay way behind the battle lines . . . be 100 percent safe for sure.

Andy had given Sarah McGuffy a ticket to ride the train for the first time in her life from Cleveland, Ohio to Pittsburgh, Pennsylvania. With hair grandma white and eyes star bright, she relished a visit with her family.

The Taylors had also arrived from El Paso, Texas to spend Christmas with the Dunmores. Hannah cuddled Faith, wearing a smile above the dimple on her chin. Matt and Hannah celebrated Faith's first Christmas birthday with a lace-trimmed dress, pink rattles, and a little rubber doll that cried Mama when it was squeezed.

Lily huddled by the Christmas tree, trimmed with handmade paper ornaments and strings of cranberries and popcorn. She stayed close to Rose who lay fast asleep in her wicker buggy. When Hannah urged Lily to play the piano, she shook her head and sidled over to lean against Andy's leg for comfort. He wrapped his arm around her.

"Guess I'll be spending more time in here now that I have a radio to listen to," said Tom, turning it on. "I'm sure glad Santa didn't forget me."

"Santa didn't bring it," retorted Lily. "Mother gave you that radio."

Everyone smiled when Tom put on his earphones and tuned into KDKA. He glowed when the announcer on Pittsburgh's first radio station talked about the weather. "Isn't that something! Yes sir-ee, we'll always be able to tell whether it's going to be sunshine, rain or snow."

"You'll have to move your smoke stand in here," commented Hannah. "I know this is where you'll be hanging onto that smelly pipe of yours."

"No." Tom wagged his head, his mouth twisting at her remark. "Soon as the weather warms up, I'll be at the icehouse, seeing that it's running right."

Matt seemed perplexed. "Who's going to manage the icehouse when you're at work on the railroad?"

"I'll find someone," replied Tom with confidence. "I've been scouting around for a dependable fellow who wants a part-time job. Plenty of men are looking for jobs that don't take much training or experience."

Lily spoke up. "Daddy says I can help at the icehouse."

Hannah grimaced. "For goodness sakes, what could you do, Lily? You're only a girl. Girls don't have any business around an icehouse."

Lily glared at her aunt. "I can do it. I know I can and Daddy said I could, so there."

Everyone roared except Mary who shot Lily a dark look.

Hannah, miffed about the comeback, placed Faith in Matt's arms and headed for the kitchen. "Come on, Mary. Let's get dinner on the table. I'm starved."

Tom adjusted his earphones. "I want to hear the news, folks. I'd like to know if more snow's on the way."

When the weather report ended and a band began to play Christmas carols, Tom took off his earphones. "Don't care a thing about that racket," he muttered.

After a day of talking over old times, opening presents, and feasting on a meal with all the trimmings, the activities turned to finding beds. The Taylors were given Mary and Tom's bedroom. Grandma McGuffy slept with Lily. Mary stayed in the nursery with Rose, and Tom and Andy made up their beds on the roomy window seats in the parlor.

Mary slipped out of her shoes and relaxed in the kitchen, sipping hot cocoa and thinking about the day's happenings. Andy joined her as soon as Tom began to snore.

She perked up when Andy came through the kitchen door. "Why aren't you asleep?"

He poured himself a cup of cocoa and sank into Tom's chair. "I'll have my sleep when I return to camp. I never get to spend time with my big sister anymore."

Mary chuckled. "You haven't called me that in a long time. I can't believe that you're ten years younger than I am. You were the baby in the family, and I helped take care of you. I even changed your diapers."

He grinned. "I miss those long talks we used to have. You kept me on the right track, telling me how important education was in making a decent living. Then you left home, got a job and married Tom after a while." He shook his head. "Believe me, Sis, it's easy to lose touch with your family."

Mary stretched out her legs and crisscrossed them. "We all live far apart now and nobody writes anymore. You're the only one who sends me a letter. Now and then I get a picture postcard from Hannah with a few words scribbled on it. Nobody else bothers."

He set his cup down and rubbed his chin. "Gotta shave in the morning and write in my journal. It keeps me up on what happens every day. Even if it's only a line or two, I try to put something down."

"When you were fighting, I'm sure you didn't keep a journal, Andy."

"You're right about that. I was thinking about staying alive, but sometimes when things were quiet at night, I hunkered down in a trench and scribbled a note or two."

"I bet you were scared out there with guns firing and grenades going off. I'm sure I'd be trying to run away."

Andy cringed. "Some of the fellows tried that, but they were always caught and brought back."

She was startled. "Did you ever run away?"

"No. I told myself I had to fight and stay alive. I did, thank God."

She removed the bobby pins from her hair at the back of her neck and let the tresses fall about her shoulders. "I wish you'd brought that nurse along that you date. I'd love to meet her."

He twitched. "Amanda and I broke up."

"For heaven's sake, why?"

"It didn't pan out, Sis. She was dead-set on a career. She wanted to settle in one place. Build a reputation as an outstanding nurse. Work her way up to a position in a hospital where she'd be in charge. Amanda didn't want to move around like I'll probably do as an officer. Darn it, I cared a lot for that girl. I miss her, that's for sure, but no way she'd give up her plans."

"I'm awfully sorry, Andy. I figured she'd marry you and have babies."

"Afraid she didn't have that notion. While we were going together, Amanda was taking a management course to help her move up the line."

"There'll be other fish in the sea, Andy. You wait and see."

He gave her a penetrating look. "I may never marry. Marriage and an Army career don't always mix. I've heard of wives as well as engaged gals taking up with someone else during the war."

Mary gasped and shook her head in dismay.

Chapter 23

Loneliness cloaked the house after the Christmas visitors left. The decorations and gifts disappeared. The Dunmores settled into their routine. Lily returned to school, came home for lunch and hurried back. She had no taste for classes but tried to do what was expected of her. Making friends was a task for Lily. Shy and self-conscious, she tended to distrust people. The highlight of her time at school . . . her piano lesson.

"I'm gonna be on the stage some day playing the piano," she told her mother. "Just you wait and see."

Mary looked forward to her Evening Bridge Club when friends gathered 'round. She yearned for afternoon bridge at St. Mary's but knew that attending would mean placing Rose in the church nursery. Plagued by the fear that Rose might catch something from a sick child, Mary played it safe and stayed home. She spent her time studying and teaching bridge and filling orders for make-believe flowers.

Rose was a bundle of company. She lit up the day with smiles and didn't fuss when put down for her naps. She reminded Mary of Ben. Sometimes Mary looked at the pictures taken on the day that Ben's room was unlocked. Memories flooded back . . . the basket heaped with tiny cars . . . Ben's gold ring. She recalled Tom's gasp when she told him how Lily had gotten the ring and given it back. He was astonished.

As time passed, Rose became an explorer, climbing everywhere she could on her chubby legs and poking her fingers into any nook that offered an invitation. She found out what was movable and what was stationary. Naturally, anything that could be clutched in her hand would fit in her mouth. Mary took care that every cupboard was shut tight.

For a while she appreciated Lily's taking charge of Rose. Lily copied Louise Musmanno, pointing or snapping fingers whenever she wanted the baby to do something. But as Lily's caretaking increased, the glamour of playing mother and teacher became smudged. Lily complained. She never had to change diapers but was supposed to tell Mary whenever the baby needed a fresh one. Lily also tended Rose at mealtimes, cleared the table and dried the dishes that Mary washed. The Golden Rule prevailed . . . family members helped each other. Nevertheless, the seed of resentment was planted in Lily.

When compliments from family and friends flourished regarding Rose's easygoing nature, jealousy also sprouted. Lily watched and listened with indignation clouding her sky. "Everybody likes the baby more than me," she complained.

Lily's report cards continued to bear average grades except for one subject. She had an A in music. Tom sputtered the day he read her report. Mary hung over him as he signed his name in black ink. She sensed the rage boiling in him.

He thrust a shrewd look at Lily. "Would you like to be a teacher some day?"

A frown took hold of Lily. She spoke up. "No. I'm gonna play the piano, Daddy."

Tom gritted his teeth. He peered hard at her. "What good would that do, Lily?"

"I'd like to play for people who like music. I want to be somebody important up there on the stage."

"I see," Tom muttered although he didn't.

He scratched his head and pondered. "A teacher is mighty important, Lily. She's up in front of the room like it's a stage, writing on the board, talking to the pupils, showing them how to do something useful. Something worthwhile."

Lily squinted at him. "That's different than playing a concert, Daddy."

He swallowed hard and cleared his throat noisily. "I've been thinking, honey. You never play with that doll furniture in the cellar. Rose likes dolls a whole lot. She'll have fun with the furniture I made. I'll build you a nice desk to put down there, exactly like your teacher's. You can pretend you're teaching a class while Rose plays house."

Lily folded her arms across her chest and faced her father. "I don't wanna desk, Daddy. I'd rather have a big piano like Mr. Foster's that's on the stage. Chills run all over me whenever I play on it."

He scowled. "I can't build a piano, Lily. And I can't afford a grand piano either. You'll have to be content with our upright in the parlor. In fact, it's not even paid for."

Lily leveled a sharp gaze on him. "Don't make me a teacher's desk, Daddy. I'll never use it. It'll just go to waste." She hurried away.

"She doesn't want to be a teacher," cautioned Mary when Lily was out of earshot. "Let her be herself, Tom."

He sniffed. "I want her to be a good pupil, Mary. Having a teacher's desk might spur her to do something besides playing the piano."

Mary clutched her hands in desperation. "Lily simply is Lily. She loves music and thinks school is a drag. That's not likely to change, Tom."

In the days that followed, Tom not only built a teacher's desk with drawers lined up on both sides. He made a chair with a straight back to be its neighbor and set up a brand-new blackboard that he ordered from a catalog. He called Mary to come down to the cellar to see what he'd accomplished before Lily arrived for lunch.

"She can do her school work and watch Rose at the same time. And you can do whatever you want upstairs, honey."

Mary swallowed her anger. "The desk is awfully nice, Tom. I hope Lily uses it." She gave him a crisp look. "Keep in mind that Lily has musical talent and wants to play the piano. Mr. Foster says she'll be able to perform in the orchestra when she reaches high school."

"Playing the piano will never get her a job," argued Tom, his eyes flashing.

"She can *teach* piano and get paid for it," fired back Mary.

He grunted and walked away to tidy up his workbench.

Tom was smiling when Lily came home at noon. "I've got a surprise for you," he said the moment she walked in. "Let's go look in the cellar."

For a second Lily seemed perplexed, then resignation dawned.

Mary glared. "She has to eat and get back to school, Tom."

"I know. This'll only take a minute. Come on, Lily." She followed him down the steps.

Tom pointed to the desk he'd made. "See what I built for you. You can teach any kind of lesson you please."

Lily glowered. "I don't wanna teach a lesson," she declared, turning away and rushing up the steps.

Tom thought about all that he and Mary had endured to give Lily piano lessons. Making her practice and listening to her bang the keys when she hit a wrong note. To top it all, Lily refused to perform, even when she was coaxed to play at school.

During his morning jaunts down street, he began to drop in at the high school. Before long, Jack Thompson, principal, and Nick Pecori, assistant principal, knew exactly who Tom Dunmore was. He told them that dissatisfaction was brewing regarding the state of the public schools and that changes needed to be made posthaste. His first complaint—parents needed a voice in what was happening in the schooling of their children. Secondly, parents should be able to watch any classes they chose and offer suggestions about making them better.

Thompson and Pecori shifted glances at each other whenever Tom explained his views about teachers, especially those in the lower grades. They were shocked about some of his ideas, especially when he said the main thing his daughter learned at school was to hate it. Privately, the principals hashed over whether or not a railroad fireman had the smarts to sit on the board with men who had high school diplomas and had taken a college course or two.

When Tom described the classroom he had produced in his cellar, aimed at turning Lily onto learning, Thompson was impressed. He told Pecori, "If he cares that much to do all that work, he'd be a good person for the board, even though he hasn't been to high school. He'd go the extra mile to fix whatever we're doing wrong."

Pecori thundered, "If Tom Dunmore can fire up an engine on a locomotive, maybe he can fire up our school system. Certainly he can do no harm. Let's figure out how to get him elected."

Chapter 24

When the weather turned warm and the snow melted, Tom hired David Carson to run the icehouse. Most people called him Dave. He had a slim face with smooth skin and hair streaked by gray that gave him a distinguished appearance. His body was lean and well muscled. Known as a handyman, he was always on call to help out with any problem that popped up around the house. A sluggish sink, a light on the blink, a roof that leaked . . . Dave was the person to call.

All of the Dunmores were on hand when the icehouse opened. Tom had spread the news regarding his homemade business by word of mouth and placing signs in the store windows where he traded. Mary stood on the icehouse platform, looking forlorn with Rose in her buggy, tended by Lily.

Mary had to admit to herself that she'd never seen Tom so elated. He tapped his foot while Dave cut 25-pounders from the first block of ice. Without a second to waste, Tom picked them up with tongs, carried them out on the platform and sent them down the chute for the customers. The air was ripe with cheers from onlookers in the alley.

When Tom asked for Mary's reaction, she made it very clear. "I'll never work out here, Tom. Never. It's not befitting for a lady."

Lily was beside herself with glee. "Daddy told me he's gonna fix a stand where I can make ice balls to sell, Mother. Soon as school's out for the summer."

Mary's eyebrows edged up a notch. "You're not hanging around out here either. Girls don't do that. I won't have it, Lily. It's not ladylike."

June arrived and the sun blistered down, turning pale complexions ruddy. In spite of Mary's protests, Lily stood by the counter Tom had built, scraping ice into flakes and forming ice balls. After setting a ball in a pleated paper cup, she squirted it with whatever syrup the customer preferred . . . orange, lemon, lime, or cherry. Mary even helped make the sweet stuff and admitted she had fun. It cost a nickel or five pennies to cool one's throat. When word got around, kids lined up in the alley to buy ice balls.

Before long, Tom was struck with another idea and decided to try his hand at making root beer. He bought a Hires Root Beer Kit and mixed the dry root beer extract with water, sugar and yeast at a cost of five cents a gallon. After washing the bottles with boiling water and Octagon soap, he poured the brew into bottles and sealed the caps to ensure good carbonation. Then the samples were set in a cool cabinet downstairs. After two weeks, Tom opened the bottles, tasted the root beer and declared the test a success. His homemade root beer went on sale at the icehouse.

Mary cringed when she saw her washtubs being used in such a fashion, but she was powerless to do anything about it. "I won't make root beer on the day you wash clothes," promised Tom.

One thing Tom wasn't telling Mary. Even though Dave was hired to do the work, Tom spent every minute he could spare at the icehouse, talking to customers about the need for improving the schools. It came as no surprise that many people didn't like the way teachers were treating their kids and wanted that to change.

Tom contrived his own secret campaign and began hinting that he might run for the vacancy on the board, even though he had a full-time job plus the icehouse to run. "Changes need to be made and that can only happen one way, Mary. Yes sir-ee, somebody who has a beef about the schools has to have a hand in fixing them."

As his ice business prospered, so did Tom's determination to win a seat on the board. Mary had an inkling that her husband was moving in that direction, but she had no idea about his success until the ladies in her Evening Bridge Club mentioned that their husbands believed Tom could improve the schools if he was elected. Mary was rankled . . . his lack of education would be detrimental to the board and open the public's eyes to the fact that he didn't have much schooling.

Her breath was coming hard and fast when she confronted him in the kitchen. "You have a good job on the railroad and the icehouse to worry about. Why do you want to have anything to do with the School Board?"

"We'll soon have two girls instead of one who hates school," he responded. "Things have to improve. Lily would like learning if her teachers were better at what they do. I want Rose to be a fine pupil . . . not copy the awful attitude that Lily has. She's never even sat down at the desk I made. All she cares about is the piano."

"Lily warned you, Tom. She told you she didn't want that desk. All your sawing and hammering for nothing."

"I oughta give her a good whipping. Make her use it whether she wants to or not." He flushed as he saw Mary recoil. He threw up his hands. "I know . . . I know. Don't worry. I won't use the strap on her again."

Mary gripped her hands together. "You'd better not, Tom Dunmore."

"You know they paddle kids at school," he countered. "What are you gonna do when the teacher paddles Lily?"

Mary glared. "She'd better not or she'll have to answer to me."

A slyness twinkled in Tom's eyes. "If I was on the board, I'd stack up all those paddles in the schools and put a match to them. We'd pass a rule that no teacher and no principal could give even one lick with a paddle."

Mary sucked in her breath. "That'd be wonderful, Tom." For the first time a streak of lightning zipped through her. Tom might do some good on the board after all.

Sally Kindle phoned to see if Mary was interested in teaching an afternoon bridge class in the fall. "So many women have signed up we plan to hold two classes instead of one."

"I'd love to, Sally, but I can't. I have to keep Rose while Lily's in school. I'm afraid to leave Rose in the nursery. You understand, don't you?"

"Of course I do, but we'd really like to have you. I've heard that you know a whole lot about the game and would be a fine teacher."

"Keep me in mind for later when Rose starts school. Maybe I can do it then, Sally."

After she hung up, Mary was disgruntled. Tom worked on the railroad, ran the icehouse, and was aiming for a seat on the board. He could do anything he wanted.

Even though she loved Lily and Rose with all her heart, they tied her down at home. She was itching to try something new, something exciting, something invigorating, but it would be a long time before the girls were old enough to stay by themselves.

Gertie dropped by in the afternoon. They settled in the kitchen and pasted photos in an album while Lily played *Kitten on the Keys* for Rose in the parlor.

"I want you and Tom to come for bridge on Saturday night," urged Gertie.

"Of course we'd love to, Gertie. Tom's off work this Saturday, but I don't have anyone to keep the kids."

"Bring them along. You can lay Rose down on the bed, and she'll go right to sleep. Lily can bring her books or anything she wants to pass the time."

Mary gazed out the window at a sparrow settling on the clothesline. "That might work. I don't know what I'll do if I don't get out of this house once in a while."

"Sounds like you have cabin fever, honey."

Mary dabbed paste on the last picture and shut the book. "You're lucky. School starts pretty soon. You can leave the house. I had to turn down Sally Kindle's invitation to teach a bridge class. I'd have a ball doing that, but I can't because of the kids."

Gertie cocked her head. "You could have an afternoon class here at home. How about that?"

"Sounds super, but it won't work while Rose is little and into everything. I can't manage her and teach bridge at the same time."

Gertie finished her cookie and folded her hands in her lap. "I heard that Tom might run for the School Board this fall."

Mary was wide-eyed. She groaned. "I'm afraid he's going to do it."

"Why be afraid, hon? I think he has a good chance of being elected."

"It worries me, Gertie. You know that Tom doesn't have much schooling."

"From what I've heard, Tom has some mighty good ideas, Mary. A friend of mine said Tom thought parents should hold regular meetings at the schools. Talk about the problems and how to solve them. That would be one way to improve our system. The federal government has developed a few programs to aid education. Goodness knows, women in private organizations and some of the churches have been trying to better the schools, too, but much more needs to happen."

Mary was perplexed. "I'd like to learn about what they're doing at Lily's school. Maybe the women in our town could form a group and get permission to visit the classes."

Gertie perked up. "I know the National Congress of Mothers was formed a while ago with the intent to streamline the schools, but we need local cooperation. I'd like to see an organization in West Park that involves teachers, parents, and pupils—the whole community in making the schools succeed."

Mary rose and carried the teacups to the sink. "That's exactly what my Tom wants."

Gertie nodded. "You ought to encourage him to get elected. He could open the door to jacking up our schools."

A smile brightened Mary. "You've made my day, Gertie. For the first time I feel sure that Tom might do something worthwhile by being on the board."

Chapter 25

Mary stood at the back door window in the kitchen, watching the autumn leaves blow off the trees and dance across the lawn. She peered at Dave, chatting to a customer at the icehouse, and knew that he was savoring being top dog for a while. Rose sat in the playpen, building a two-story house out of the red and blue blocks that Tom had made for her.

Now, before going to work, Tom spent the mornings telling townsmen how he'd improve the schools if elected. Right after a breakfast of eggs, bacon, and fried cornmeal mush with butter and syrup, he hurried down street to win votes. Mary had finally conceded that it was possible for him to win a seat on the board. With a smirk, she'd announced that he might even get her vote.

His signs were printed with bold letters and set in the stores where he traded on Broadway. VOTE FOR TOM DUNMORE, WEST PARK SCHOOL BOARD. Mary worried that he was eating too fast, inviting indigestion or something worse, but she was glad that he'd finally cut down on his smoking. He had no time anymore to relax with a cigarette or a pipe of Prince Albert and read the paper in the morning. The radio wasn't turned on to hear the news and the weather report. Still, Mary thought they were more devoted since she'd approved of his venture into politics. However, the idea hovered that instead of loving her, he might fall in love with a seat on the board. What would life be like if he won? Times change and we have to change with them, she told herself.

She moved to the stove and grabbed her gingham potholders to lift the roast pork out of the oven. Its outer skin was baked to a crispness. Reaching for the ladle, she dipped juice from the pan and basted the meat. No doubt Tom would relish a slice of pork after he finished work at the yard and hurried home.

Lily arrived from school and complained when she found that he wasn't home. "Daddy's never here anymore when I eat lunch. I hate that, Mother."

"He's terribly busy, honey. Maybe he'll get back before you have to leave."

Mary lifted Rose from the playpen and set her in the high chair that Tom had fashioned. With a brimming smile, Rose stretched her arms toward her sister.

Lily held her hands up in the air and headed to the sink. "Gotta wash my paws, Sis."

Rose began to make music, banging her spoon merrily to and fro on her plate while Lily washed her hands. On the way to the table, Lily reached for the spoon. Rose dropped it on the floor and giggled.

Lily made a monkey face at her sister. "I won't let you play with Benny if you're bad." Rose stuck out her tongue and offered an impish grin.

Lily turned to her mother who was shaking her head at the girls. "I wanted to tell Daddy that Miss Morton asked me to play a prelude. It's for the Thanksgiving skit the sixth graders are giving."

"How splendid, honey. I'm very proud of you." Mary gave Lily a squeeze on the shoulder as she sat down at the table.

"I'm not gonna play for Miss Morton, Mother."

Mary focused on Lily, "For goodness sakes, why not?"

"I don't wanna." Lily gulped her glass of milk and picked up her peanut butter sandwich.

"Use your napkin, Lily. You've got a white moustache."

Lily wiped her mouth with the back of her hand.

"Why don't you want to play the piano like Miss Morton asked?"

"I might make a mistake, Mother. I'd be shaking like a leaf up there in front of all those people."

"You said when you grew up you were going to play the piano on the stage . . . become a concert artist. Doing what Miss Morton asked would be a good experience. You'd be on the stage, playing the piano before a lot of people."

Lily shuddered. "Not good. No way. I'm not doin' it, Mother."

"You should if you're going to play the piano for a living."

Skepticism swam over Lily. Her brow wrinkled. "I'll live right here with you and Daddy. I'll play on the stage whenever I feel like it."

"Land sakes, where did you ever get that idea? The world doesn't work that way." Mary stood with hands on hips, facing Lily. "When you grow up you'll get married and move to a place you call home, just like your father and I did."

Lily sniffed. "I'll do exactly as I want. You'll see, Mother."

Mary took a deep breath, trying to rein in her temper. Bringing up children was hard. It might be easier if she'd gone to high school, she told herself, but there was no way for that to happen at this stage of life. All she could do was read everything she could get her hands on and hope for the best. A speck of sunshine . . . Tom might be able to borrow books from the school if he was elected. Maybe she could get some learning that way. Become smarter and be able to handle kids better.

Lily finished her sandwich and sat still while Mary combed her hair and fastened the bow on top of her head. "Wish I had her hair," muttered Lily, ogling Rose's curls. "Then I wouldn't need a dumb bow."

Tom walked in and Lily jumped up. She eyed him with belligerence while she explained Miss Morton's request. "I wanted you to know that she asked me to play for her skit, but I'm not doin' it, Daddy."

He gave Lily an unyielding look. "You ought to do what the teacher wants. Maybe that'd bring up your grades."

"Miss Morton teaches sixth grade. She doesn't have anything to do with my grades. Miss Nora Duse gives me my grades, Daddy."

Lily gave Rose a poke on the arm as she walked past her high chair. Rose retaliated with a swift kick that missed Lily's backside.

A grimness hung over Tom. He settled down at the table. "Think about making a good impression. It helps when people have some reason to like you."

"I don't care," retorted Lily. "I'm not gonna take a chance hittin' wrong notes and spoilin' the piece. Gotta go now or I'll be late. The first bell's rung." She slipped out the door and stopped long enough to pet Kitty, sunning on the porch rail.

Tom reached for a cigarette while Mary fed Rose macaroni and cheese. "I wish Lily would cooperate at school. "If I get on the board, I'd sure hate to have a daughter who's barely making it at school."

Mary winced. "Maybe she'll change when she gets a little older. They say a daughter is like her mother, but Lily and I don't have much in common right now."

Tom shoved his cup across the table to Mary. "She was the firstborn," he lamented. "I never thought a girl would be hard to raise."

Mary poured Tom's coffee and finished feeding Rose. "I worry about Lily. She's ill-humored a lot. Ben was always good-natured and easy to get along with. Rose is the same way. I hope she doesn't change."

Tom leaned back, stared at the ceiling and pondered a moment. "Maybe they were born too far apart."

Mary chuckled. "Nothing we can do about that now, is there, Tom?"

"Don't worry. It'll work out, sweetheart." He sniffed the air. "That roast sure smells mighty fine. You're a better cook than my mother was, Mary."

She glowed. "You'll have pork and sweet potatoes when you get home tonight, hon. Sometimes I wonder how your stomach stands being fed supper at midnight."

Tom stroked his chin. "I've been thinking, Mary. When Lily gets home, have her take Rose downstairs to play with the doll furniture. See if Lily shows any interest in that desk I built. I'm still hoping it won't go to waste."

"I'll do it, Tom, but I can't make Lily play schoolteacher."

He ground his cigarette in the ashtray and grunted. "Guess I'll go listen to KDKA while you pack my lunch. I'd like to get a radio for the kitchen."

After getting up, he paused. "I forgot to mention that I ran into Paul Bergman on the street corner. I was talking to him about the schools . . . how they needed improved. He said he'd like to play cards with us sometime. I told him you'd be phoning Dr. Winter about getting together for a game. This Saturday might be a good time."

"I'd love that." Mary smiled. Playing bridge with Dr. Winter and her husband would be something she could look forward to.

Chapter 26

Mary phoned Dr. Winter on Friday. She was delighted when the doctor accepted her invitation to play bridge Saturday evening. There was the possibility that she might be called to the hospital unexpectedly, but that didn't happen often.

When Lily arrived from school, Mary told her that she wanted Rose to play in the cellar. "She's getting old enough to enjoy your doll furniture now, sweetie."

Lily screwed up her face. "I was gonna practice."

"You can do that later, Lily."

"I'm taking Kitty downstairs then. *She* can play house with Rose."

Lily went outside to fetch the cat while Mary took Rose to the cellar. The September day was sunny, sending rays of light through the windows. Rose headed to the dolls seated around the table in the playhouse. Lily had moved them from her bedroom shelves, now taken up by samplers, scrapbooks, and Ben's toy cars. Benny stayed on Lily's bed, along with Kitty who snoozed on the chenille spread. Miss Cat and Mr. Pup still held the top shelf in the bedroom but were no longer first choice.

Rose was exploring the playhouse when Lily came down the steps with Kitty at her heels. The cat hightailed it to the desk and began to wash herself with an instant vigor.

"She'll scratch the finish, Lily. Put her somewhere else please."

Grudgingly, Lily snuggled Kitty and set her on the doll bed that showed off a crocheted spread.

Mary stood back and surveyed the desk, placed a few yards away from the playhouse. "It's very nice, Lily. Looks like it came from the furniture department in Hornes. Your father did his very best work when he built this desk for you. Believe me, you're a mighty lucky girl."

"It looks like Miss Musmanno's," mumbled Lily.

Mary pulled out a drawer. "You'll have room to store everything you need in here." She sat down and tried out the straight-backed chair. "This goes perfectly with the desk. You can do your lessons and not be bothered by a single soul."

Mary got up and moved to the blackboard Tom had bought. She ran her hand over the slate. "You have this to write on, too. It's like your teacher's." Mary picked up the chalk in the tray and printed Lily's name in big capitals.

"I'm doing lessons in my room, Mother. I like it up there. I'm never coming down here to study."

It dawned on Mary that she was wasting time, trying to persuade Lily to appreciate the desk. Tom should have listened when Lily said she didn't want it. He'd simply have to live with his disappointment.

On Saturday morning, Mary was making a devil's food cake for the bridge party when the phone rang. She'd just cracked the third egg and begun to blend it with the sugar and butter when Tom answered the call. She could hear him talking amiably in the parlor. In a few minutes he stood in the doorway, a broad grin on his face. "Guess what?"

She stopped stirring. "What?"

"That was Jack Thompson, the principal at Stowe High. He wants to see the desk I made for Lily."

"Who told him you'd made a desk?"

A sheepishness wafted over Tom. "I mentioned it some time ago."

"Whatever for?"

Tom rocked back and forth on his heels. "I wanted him to get the drift of what it takes to help kids succeed in school. Thompson said my idea of having a special place to study at home was a novel idea. He asked if he could come by this afternoon to see what I've done."

Mary beat the batter harder. "I can't ruin this cake," she murmured to herself. "It's for the company tonight."

She stopped beating and turned her attention to Tom. "I don't understand why he wants to look at the desk you've built. Being a principal, I'm sure he's seen plenty of desks."

Tom stood still. "I'd better go be sure that everything's shipshape downstairs. Maybe I need to do a little sweeping or dusting." He disappeared.

When she'd finished adding sifted cocoa and flour to the bowl, Mary poured the batter in the pan and set it in the oven. She wiped her brow with a tea towel. Why in heaven's name did Jack Thompson have to drop by when she was getting ready to entertain Dr. Winter and her husband? Then an idea hit hard.

She rushed down the steps. Tom was in a lather, rubbing the desktop with a rag soaked in furniture polish that filled the air with a pungent odor. She glanced around. He'd lined up a row of metal chairs they used for picnics in the backyard. A wastebasket, bookcase and lamp had been moved beside the desk. The things that had been on Tom's workbench were awaiting their place on the polished wood—a mug filled with pens and pencils, a yellow tablet, and a tray filled with paper.

"Why on earth are you going to all this trouble, Tom?"

"Can't hurt anything, can it? Maybe it'll get me a vote."

"What are you going to do if the principal wants to talk to Lily?"

Tom stopped rubbing. He stood stiffly, sweat beading on his forehead. "Never figured on that."

"Lily might not pay your desk any compliments, Tom."

He cleared his throat huskily. "Thompson said he'd be here around two. Why can't Lily be in the backyard, pushing Rose around in her buggy or making ice balls at the icehouse?"

"We'll see," replied Mary, almost running up the stairs to find out if she'd ruined her devil's food cake.

Jack Thompson arrived at two o'clock sharp. Tom opened the door and welcomed him inside. Nick Pecori followed. "We both came. Hope you don't mind," said Thompson. "I thought we ought to have some photos of what you've done. Nick is the photographer at Stowe High."

Tom gulped. He'd never thought about anyone taking pictures of his work.

After Mary was introduced, the men went downstairs. Lily had been forewarned that someone from the high school was coming to visit. She'd been told to tend Rose in the backyard and not come inside 'til the company left. Mary pinned one eye on the backdoor window and one ear on what was happening in the cellar. Thompson had a package tucked under his arm when he entered the kitchen. She was real curious about that bundle.

She eyed the cake that was cooling on the counter after being taken out of the oven. She wished it could be frosted but that job had to wait until the men left. Icing was something you beat without stopping until it was ready to be put on the cake. The talking, specks of laughter, and the clicking of the camera drifted up the stairway. Mary itched to be down there with the men, but she was afraid to take her gaze off Lily who was wheeling Rose at a fast pace around the yard.

Then Mary heard Tom coming up the steps. "Mr. Thompson wants to meet Lily and ask her questions."

Mary turned queasy. "Did you tell him she's busy tending to her baby sister?"

Tom nodded. "He wants to take Lily's picture, too."

"I'll go get her then." Mary hastened outside and gave Lily a spur-of-the-moment lecture. "Be on your best behavior. Answer Mr. Thompson's questions politely. He's going to take your picture. Smile."

Mary picked up Rose and followed Lily downstairs. She hovered in the playhouse, trying to keep Rose amused.

Thompson moved forward to shake Lily's hand. "Hello there, Lily. I'm Mr. Thompson, the principal at Stowe High School. I'd like to take your picture at this fine desk your dad made for you."

Wary, Lily drew back her hand as soon as Thompson let go.

Tom pulled the chair out from the desk and motioned Lily to sit down. She moved slowly. Thompson stared at her when she was seated. "She looks awfully small in that big chair. Let's try something." He opened the package he'd brought and laid half a dozen spanking new books on the desk. "Why don't we let Lily sit on some of these? That way she'll look taller in the picture."

Tom propped Lily up on *English for Business*, *American History*, and *Science Education*. With a twinge of embarrassment, he turned to Thompson. "I didn't want to make the desk a size that would fit her perfectly right now. She'll grow . . . be able to use it clear through school to graduation."

"Right," said Thompson, motioning Pecori to take the picture.

Pecori focused the camera on Lily. "Give me your very best smile."

She grinned, elated that the principal wanted her picture.

"What do you think of the desk, Lily?" asked Thompson when Pecori finished posing her in several ways.

"It's exactly like Miss Musmanno's."

"That was her teacher in second grade," explained Tom.

Thompson smiled at Lily. "I'm sure you're a good pupil. What do you like about school?"

"It takes up my time," declared Lily.

Thompson chuckled. "I guess that's exactly right. I'm looking forward to having you at Stowe High some day. You'll like it. You're lucky to have a dad who wants you to do well in school, Lily."

When Thompson was ready to leave, he thanked Tom for letting him see his homemade study. "Every parent should have something like this at home to help their children succeed in school. I'm leaving these books here. Lily can use them later on."

Mary was ecstatic after the men left. She could hardly wait to examine the books but that would have to wait. The cake needed frosting and the house put in apple pie order for the bridge game with Dr. Winter and Paul Bergman. "Don't you think it's funny for a married couple to have different last names, Tom?"

"Yes sir-ee. Yes sir-ee. Dr. Winter should have changed her name to Bergman when she got married." There was a sparkle in his eye as he gave Mary a quick hug.

He turned to Lily. "How did you like having your picture taken?"

"Okay I guess, Daddy. Wish I could see my picture."

Lily's wish came true on Tuesday morning when Tom showed her the Gazette. Her picture brightened the front page. She sat sedately at the desk, her nose in a book titled *Algebra 1*. The story described how Tom Dunmore had fashioned a study in his cellar that would entice his children to become good pupils. The final paragraph noted that Tom Dunmore was running for the Stowe School Board in the November election.

Chapter 27

The air was brisk on Election Day 1922. There wasn't a cloud in the sky. Mary had been afraid it might rain and people wouldn't turn out, but the weather cooperated. Before heading to the poll, she waited until Tom had voted and returned home to tend Lily and Rose. Mary tittered as she grabbed her pocketbook. The last time Tom baby-sat was when he had to mother Lily while Rose was being born at Ohio Valley Hospital. He'd enjoyed being with Lily but was relieved when Mary returned home and he could go back to a man's job.

Feeling high-spirited, Mary headed to the polling place in the school and stood in line, awaiting her turn to enter a curtained cubicle. She counted the number of men and women voting . . . three dozen men, only five women. But it was early morning, and most people voted later in the day. The women were probably washing breakfast dishes or making up slept-in beds. Mary caught the eye of every woman in line and gave them an admiring smile. Why didn't more women vote? Were their husbands standing in their way? Why did some ladies think that men were the only ones who deserved the privilege of voting?

Louise Krakowski ran for Commissioner in 1921. "It's the law now," Mary had declared. "Women are full citizens and equal players. We're not taking any power away from the men."

The first female to run for office in West Park was soundly defeated. Not only were many men overjoyed about Louise's downfall. A considerable number of women clapped their hands and spouted, "Leave politics to the men, ladies. A woman's place is in the home."

Louise had more than her helping of nerve to think she was fit for public office, according to the critics. She got her comeuppance when she was soundly beaten by a man. Mary feared that no woman in town would ever step onto the political stage again. It might require some clever conniving for a female to take her rightful place in the community.

The thought crossed Mary's mind that she'd voted Republican during the last election. Today she was becoming a Democrat. Arthur Anderson, the

Republican opponent, managed a hardware store on Broadway six days a week, 8 a.m. 'til 8 p.m. Art was a heavy-set man with a dark moustache, a bulbous nose, and brows that hung like awnings over his eyes. His booming voice caught everyone's attention when he opened his mouth. Art was well liked in town for his congeniality and easygoing nature. If her husband wasn't running on the Democratic ticket, Mary knew she'd cast a vote for Art Anderson.

In case Tom was elected, Mary wondered how their lives would be affected. When they first started playing cards, she recalled thinking they'd be snubbed as bridge partners. She'd been flat wrong. The Schumakers had welcomed them into their circle of friends . . . so did Dr. Winter and her husband. Nobody ever asked if they'd graduated from high school or taken a college course. Mary hoped no one would inquire about Tom's educational background. Even though he'd only been to grade school, he handled a tough job at the railroad, built two houses for his family and ran an icehouse on the side. That had to take plenty of know-how.

The morning after the election, while waiting to hear whether or not he was victorious, Tom became antsy. He smoked one cigarette after another, emptied a pot of coffee and kept his earphones on, hoping to catch the election returns on the radio. Mary was thankful that Lily was at school. Otherwise, she'd be playing the piano and he'd be telling her to practice when he was at work.

"They oughta have the votes counted by now," growled Tom. "I want to know where I stand before I leave for the yard . . . not have to wonder all day and all night how the vote turned out."

She tried to pacify him. "There are bushels of paper to wade through, hon. It's hard work to count those votes. I'm sure the officials want everything to be absolutely correct."

"Suppose so," he muttered. "I'd like to see their system myself . . . know exactly how they count those votes."

Mary was rolling crust for the apples she'd peeled and sliced for a pie when the phone rang. She listened intently while Tom talked to Harold Kimble, the election official. As soon as Tom hung up, he let out a howl and headed to the kitchen. He stood tall in the doorway, a smile brimming. "Yes sir-ee. Yes sir-ee. I knew I could do it. I knew it, Mary. I got 378 more votes than Art did!"

Mary wiped her hands on the dish towel and wrapped her arms around him. "I'm glad you won, hon. Now you can make things better in our schools."

"I'll have to find out what day they meet. I need to get together with Thompson right away and figure things out. Then talk to my boss so he'll know when I have to be off work."

Mary let go of Tom, her face in a pucker. "Won't that be a problem? It's not like you're asking off because of sickness or a birth taking place in the family."

Tom wagged his head. "Nah. Don't forget, I belong to the Brotherhood of Locomotive Firemen. My boss and I are on friendly terms. He knew I was running for the School Board and thought that was okay. Even said he'd vote for me, and if I won it'd be a feather in my cap . . . a railroader sitting on the board."

"He sure was nice about letting you off when I went to the hospital to have Rose."

"Yes sir-ee. And thanks to President Wilson, I got more pay when Congress passed the Adamson Bill. It gave all the freight train and yard service men an 8-hour day with time and a half for overtime."

Relief swam over Mary. "That's a step up. You get paid for every hour you work and extra pay when you work extra." She shook her finger at him. "Don't ever do anything to make your boss or your company mad at you, Tom."

He clicked his tongue. "There are always a few scabs who want to make trouble, but the Brotherhood doesn't go along with that. We're conservative and like to work things out in a peaceful way."

When it was time for Tom's first meeting with the board, Mary urged, "You have to wear your suit and a white shirt."

A groan escaped his lips. "Are you sure about that?"

"If you're going to play the part, you have to look the part," advised Mary. "You don't want to wear your overalls and blue work shirt, do you?"

"Course not."

"Wear that pretty tie with the American flag on it, Tom. That should strike the right note."

He remembered finding a shiny new penny on the street the day before. He stuck it in his suit pocket, hoping it would bring good fortune like a lucky piece.

It was dark by the time Tom left for the meeting. Lily pressed her face against the cold windowpane and watched him hurry down the walk. "Why does Daddy have to go to school at night?"

"Because he won the election, sweetie. The people in our town gave him the most votes because they knew he'd find ways to make the schools better."

Lily turned from the window and faced her mother. "The first thing Daddy needs to do is fire Miss Musmanno."

Chapter 28

The phone rang while it was still dusky outside the bedroom windows. Mary pulled herself from bed and made her way down the stairs, wondering who could be calling before daylight had broken.

It was Andy. "I'm sorry to wake you at this hour, but I'm afraid I have bad news."

Mary sensed that a rock had fallen in the pit of her stomach. "What is it?"

"Mother died late last evening at the hospital in Cleveland. I'm letting the family know."

After discussing the arrangements, Andy hung up and Mary went to the kitchen to make a pot of tea. While the water boiled, she sat in her flannel nightgown with her arms hugging her knees, seeking warmth in the chilly room. She reminisced about the last time she saw her mother. It was a year ago when Andy brought Sarah McGuffy to their new house on Broadway to spend Christmas with the family. Sarah loved hymns and hummed along when Lily played her favorites. Often Sarah rested in the spool rocker, reveling in contentment while she cuddled Rose or Faith in her lap.

Lily had stood by, her eyes vivid with interest. "I'm not a baby anymore, Grandma. I don't sit in laps. I've grown up now."

Gratitude flowed, along with Mary's tears. She was thankful that Sarah had spent her last Christmas with the family.

The Dunmores rode the train from Pittsburgh to Cleveland as deadhead passengers. "It's wonderful that we can travel on a pass, Tom. I remember buying a ticket when I left Cleveland and moved to Pittsburgh. Now I don't have to worry about how much it costs."

A Pullman Porter helped stow away their luggage, and they settled down for their first train trip. When the conductor came by, he showed the girls how he kept the passenger records tucked in his railroad cap. They were tickled. He let them hold his ticket punch and railroad pocket watch. Before moving on, he pulled out two small packs of peppermints and caught Mary's eye. She nodded assent, and he gave them to the girls.

"The conductor not only punches tickets. He calls out the stations," explained Tom. "He'll let us know when we get to Cleveland. If we were taking a longer trip, let's say to some far off place like California, we'd have our own room where we could relax and eat our meals . . . or we might go to the diner. When night came, the room could be turned into a double-decker bedroom. The Porter would make our beds and pull down the upper berths."

"That'd be better than a picnic," chimed Lily. "When can we go to California, Daddy?"

"Later," said Tom, winking at Mary.

Grandma's house was surrounded by rose bushes, petunias, daisies, lilies, and morning glories that furnished a rainbow all summer. Now in November, snow laid a white blanket over the yard, a rustic bench and well-worn lawn chairs. The Dunmores knocked at the front door and were met with hugs, kisses, and handshakes from the family they hadn't seen in a long time or had never even met.

Everyone gathered in the parlor. The children took to the carpet, amusing themselves with the pencils, tablets, crayons, coloring books, and blocks that Mary spread out.

"How about everyone telling us about themselves? That way we'll catch up with each other right away," suggested Andy as they settled down.

"Grand idea," said Hannah. "You're the youngest one here. How about you starting off, Andy?"

"Okay, Sis. Most of you know that I served in the World War. I was in the 82nd Infantry Division. The Army's my career, and I hope to advance some day. Now I'm in Officer's Training Camp at Fort Riley, Kansas." He grinned. "And I'm still single, believe it or not."

A smile flashed over Rebecca's pretty face. "Girls love men in uniform. Somebody will nab you real fast, Andy."

He shook his head. "That's not likely, Becky. Remember, I don't get to meet many women." Andy motioned to Patrick, a well-muscled, friendly looking fellow.

Pat turned to his wife. "This is Anne Marie. And that's my two-year old girl, Florence, playing with those blocks on the floor. The look-alike twins are Jack and Joseph. They're four now. We're expecting another baby in about a month. I'm a manager in Cleveland at Best Tires. I hope to keep rolling along until I own a tire company."

"You'd better keep rolling along in that tire business," remarked Raymond. "You'll have another mouth to feed pretty soon." The room was sprinkled with laughter.

"And what's your job, Ray?" asked Pat.

"I'm a bookkeeper at First National. I plan on being the bank president some day. I'm not married either, but you can bet I'm playing the field every chance I get."

Everyone guffawed.

Matt spoke up. "Hannah and I live in El Paso, Texas. We like it there a lot. Faith was born on Christmas Day two years ago. I'm a senior post-office clerk now. I'd like to stay with the post office, keep moving up the ladder and retire in style when the time is right."

Hannah gave him a nudge. "I can promise you that he's not going to retire any time soon. I want to travel and see the world when Matt gets his vacations. Until then, I'm staying at home looking after Faith and Matt."

Andy pointed to Becky. "It's your turn now, girl."

She grinned. "I work in May's Department Store downtown and enjoy clerking. You meet a lot of people and help them pick the right thing. I'm in the dress department. Of course, I love good clothes and get snazzy bargains whenever they have sales. So far, I haven't met the man of my dreams, but I'm keeping my eyes open."

Andy focused on Tom. "Guess you and Mary are last."

Mouths fell open when Tom told them he worked on the railroad and didn't get home 'til almost midnight, ran an ice business at home nine months of the year, and had been elected to the School Board recently.

"You're so tied up working that Mary must get terribly lonely," commented Ray.

"Don't believe it," sparked Mary. "I make and sell crepe paper flowers, teach a flower-making class, have an evening bridge club and take care of the kids and Tom."

For a moment the room was dead quiet. Then Lily broke the silence. "I'm hungry. When are we gonna eat, Mother?"

Andy glanced at his watch. "I made reservations at a nearby restaurant. After we finish eating, it'll be time for us to go to the funeral parlor. I've also arranged for someone to keep the kids."

On the train headed home to Pittsburgh, Mary settled into the plush seat, laid her head back and closed her eyes. She submitted to comfort, feeling Tom resting beside her and knowing that Lily and Rose were already asleep nearby. Thoughts turned to her mother and father, buried next to each other in the graveyard, hidden behind their country church with a bell in the steeple. James had passed away long ago, leaving Sarah to fend for herself and the children on a meager life insurance check. Now her parents were together again, as they should be. A feathery snow had drifted down and veiled the headstones, blurring their letters into namelessness. While the minister offered the closing prayer, Mary remembered opening her eyes and gazing at the family, holding hands in a circle around the graves. She pasted that picture in her mind, thinking it was the last time she'd ever see all the McGuffys together again.

Chapter 29

It was an icy cold evening. The gas fireplace was lit, giving the parlor a shred of furry warmth. For the first time, Lily was allowed to stay up to celebrate the New Year. School bells and church bells rang in McKees Rocks at midnight. The nearby West Park Firehouse whistled its welcome while fireworks blasted off all over town.

Lily stood at the parlor window, watching the colors explode in the starry sky. "Is the New Year here yet?"

Mary glanced at the clock on the mantel. "One minute past midnight. It's 1923."

Lily was breathless with excitement. "You should'a let Rose stay up to see the fireworks."

Mary shrugged. "She was too sleepy. I hope the noise doesn't wake her."

"When are *we* gonna get some fireworks to shoot off, Daddy?"

Tom had his ears pinned to KDKA. A frown crossed his face at being interrupted. "Maybe we'll have some sparklers on the Fourth of July. You'll like them."

Lily scowled. "I want to celebrate the New Year right now, but we don't have any fireworks."

Mary moved away from the window. "We'll have ice cream instead. Let's go to the kitchen, honey."

Still intent on listening to the radio, Tom kept on smoking while Lily trailed after her mother.

Mary settled down with Lily at the table. "Almost everybody makes resolutions for the New Year . . . something they'd like to do that's hard for them."

"What's *your* resolution?" asked Lily, diving into her bowl of chocolate ice cream.

"I'll read as much as I can. Those school books downstairs on your desk are going to waste. I'll try to learn all I can from them."

Lily groaned. "That's the same as being in school, Mother."

Mary nodded. "Your father's on the board now, sweetie. You ought to be pleased that your dad belongs to such an important group. He's already been to his first meeting. They called it an orientation. He got an inkling about what they wanted to accomplish this year."

"What's he supposed to do on that board?"

"He'll offer ideas about how to make the schools better. We'll have to wait and see what happens."

Lily sniffed. "Well, at least I got my picture in the paper 'cause he's so crazy about school."

"You're old enough now to make a New Year's resolution. Make one and find out if you can stick to it through thick and thin."

Lily threw up her hands. "Guess I can practice the piano more . . . get ready to give concerts."

Mary stared at her daughter. "I wish I had your musical gift. You play the piano beautifully and should perform when people ask. Why don't you start doing that when they want you to play? That'd be a mighty fine resolution to make."

Lily jabbed her spoon into the ice cream. "I'll play for people when I feel like it, Mother."

Mary was serious about making the most of her time. Her resolution—read as much as possible every day. The books that Jack Thompson had left on Lily's desk were pure delight. Mary planned to devote her energy to one book at a time instead of lumping them together. She started studying English and was amazed at how much there was to soak up. After thinking hard about what she'd learned in grade school, she recalled hearing something about a noun and a verb. But . . . she never knew there were predicates and adjectives and adverbs and prepositions. No wonder it took 12 years to become a high school graduate.

Sally Kindle had already invited Mary to teach another flower-making class, but she refused. She was still afraid of putting Rose in the nursery. Sally also mentioned that the Women's Club of Pittsburgh was seeking a contract bridge teacher. The thought of teaching a class uptown sent shivers through Mary. She tossed the idea back and forth and finally dredged up enough nerve to phone for the particulars. Teresa Pulaski, the director, filled her in on the details but said an interview was required before employment could be considered. Mary knew she'd have to hire someone to keep the girls if teaching in Pittsburgh was ever to become a reality. Besides that, Tom might not allow it. He was attending his second board meeting that evening. She decided to find out if he'd let her have a sitter.

As soon as Tom hung his coat on the hook by the cellar steps and laid his notebook on the kitchen table, Mary approached him. Her heart leapt up and down as though it was dancing. In an effort to calm herself, she smoothed her hand back and forth over her chest and took several deep breaths. Then she faced him head on. "I want to know how you feel about getting a baby-sitter for the girls."

He gave her an anxious look, wriggled his head and turned toward his chair. "Why on earth do you want to do that?"

She flinched. "Guess it's for the same reason you have for wanting to be on the School Board."

His gaze skimmed over her. "What do you mean exactly?"

While she started a pot of coffee, she told him about talking to Teresa Pulaski. "I'd really love to teach that class in Pittsburgh if I can get the job, Tom."

He sat there, seeming perplexed. "I'd think you'd rather be at home. Isn't that why you started your evening club . . . and threw in free lessons to boot?"

She joined him at the table while waiting for the water to boil. "I'm fond about my bridge club, hon, but that's not like teaching a class in Pittsburgh. Imagine me getting paid for giving bridge lessons to a roomful of women who want to learn."

He leaned back in his chair and slapped both knees. "Afraid my imagination won't stretch that far."

"Well, I'd adore it. But if I was lucky enough to land the job, I'd have to find somebody to keep Lily and Rose once a week. I don't know anyone who'd want to do that. The women I know are either tending their own kids or going places so they can get away from the house for a while."

He sat quietly, pondering about what she was telling him.

She filled a plate with chocolate cookies and set it on the table. "How was your meeting tonight, Tom?"

"Fine. Real fine. We talked about what we needed to get done this year. Everybody has different ideas about things we should tackle."

"What was your idea?"

A cough grabbed him, and he held his handkerchief over his mouth until the coughing stopped and he could talk. "I'd like to look in on all the classes. Get a better idea of what's happening between the teachers and the pupils."

She filled his coffee cup and sat down. "I'd think the school would have somebody who'd do that sort of thing."

"Jack Thompson said someone from the university comes by every year to visit some of the rooms. He talks to the teachers and makes suggestions and comments. That's fine I guess, but I'd like to sit in on the classes and see what's happening."

"Did they say you could do that?"

"Nah. Not the way things stand now. The board would have to vote on it. I'd like to get some town folks to form a group that's interested in helping the schools. We'd have to find a place to hold our meetings. Then see if we can figure out what's good and what's bad in those classes and set about making improvements."

The impact of what he was saying hit Mary. She leaned closer and spoke excitedly. "Once you have a group put together, you could invite them to our house and get things started, Tom."

He was stunned. "That's a neat idea, sweetheart. Yes sir-ee, that's a mighty neat idea. Everybody has more time now. It's cold weather, and they're shut-ins. Not out and about, running around doing things. I could set up a meeting for a Saturday when I'm off work."

She rocked her chair back and forth while she gave the matter some thought. Then her eyes glistened. "What a great plan. Now that you have that problem fixed, help me find a sitter so I can go for an interview about that job in Pittsburgh."

His fingers tapped the table. "How about Dave Carson? He's not running the icehouse right now."

She squinted at him. "I never heard of a man being hired as a sitter."

Tom took a sip of his coffee and set the cup down. "He's his own boss. He does odd jobs for everybody. He must have some free time on these winter days."

Mary leaned back and wriggled her head. "I don't know." She straightened up and gawked at him. "It seems awfully weird, hiring a man to look after Rose and Lily. Weird as all get out. What in the world would my friends think? They'd believe I was plum nutty to pay some man to take care of my child."

"Don't worry about that, sweetheart. Some people think I'm plum nutty because I believe I can make the schools work better." He picked up the cup and finished his coffee. "Guess what? I'm gonna do it anyway."

Mary leaned forward and clasped her hands. "I know Dave's trustworthy. I've watched how he works at the icehouse. He likes the girls and they like him."

"That's true, Mary."

She burst into a grin. "Great! First thing tomorrow, ask him if he'll baby-sit for me."

Tom gave her a shrewd look. "Ask him yourself, Mary."

Her lips twisted as she reflected. "I'll do it," she said after a moment.

One week later on a frosty Saturday afternoon, Tom and Mary sat in the parlor, exchanging ideas with three men and a dozen women who had expressed interest in improving the schools. Mary took notes during the meeting while Dave Carson played games with Lily and Rose in the cellar.

Mary had already been interviewed by Teresa Pulaski and was hired to teach an afternoon class for ten weeks. Every time Mary thought about teaching bridge at the Women's Club of Pittsburgh, delight streaked through her from head to toe. Nary a doubt in her mind now that she'd stepped into a career.

Chapter 30

Mary was exhilarated the day she began teaching Contract Bridge at the Women's Club of Pittsburgh. She had dressed carefully for the occasion, wearing a dark blue circular skirt in walking length and a white tucked blouse with a high neck and long sleeves. Her chestnut hair was caught in a knot at the back of her neck and held by combs edged with pearls. She wore the gold bracelet that Tom had given her before they were married.

The meeting room was quite large and well-heated by radiators to fend off the chill of the wintry day. Mary realized that she needed to speak as loud as possible to reach every table. A good-sized blackboard had been set up, offering writing space for illustrating a Point Count Table. Later on in the lesson, she intended to explain the requirements for an opening bid. Then the play would begin with the participants shuffling and dealing the cards.

Mary circulated, stopping at tables to observe, answer questions and provide help. In no time, she began to memorize the names of the women. It was easy to pinpoint those who already knew something about playing bridge. She decided to place those ladies at strategic tables the next week so they could help the stragglers catch onto the game.

As she rode the street car home in the late afternoon with the after-work crowd, Mary enjoyed a sense of comradeship and began to feel as though she belonged, even though she didn't know any of the passengers. A few of them were already nodding off for a nap as the trolley zipped along the rails on West Carson Street beside the Ohio River.

It was well past six o'clock when Mary walked in the house and shed her wool coat and broad-brimmed hat laced with sprigs of holly. She was surprised to find that Dave had already heated some leftovers he'd taken from the window box and fixed supper for the girls.

"I didn't expect to be this late, Dave. I hate that you went to so much trouble. It was mighty nice of you to feed the girls. I'll bet you're hungry."

"Millie will have supper ready for me as soon as I get home. I was glad to fix a bite for the kids. Didn't amount to a hill of beans. The kids were hungry, and I knew you'd be tired after a day in Pittsburgh, Mrs. Dunmore."

She ran her hand over her forehead. "Please call me Mary. I must admit that I'm bushed after being on my feet all afternoon."

"Bridge is a hard game. You're awfully smart to teach it."

The compliment spread a flush over Mary's cheeks. "Did the girls behave all right?"

Dave glanced at Lily and Rose. "Sure did. We had a great time, didn't we, girls?"

"He read us stories and we made up some." Lily's eyes widened. "I played the new piece I'm working on for him."

"Good. I like to hear that you're playing the piano for Dave, honey."

Lily let out a moan. "I wish he taught school and could be my teacher 'stead of that dull Miss Grigsby."

Mary winked at Dave. "That's an honest-to-goodness compliment. You can't do any better than that, believe me. I never heard of a man teaching grade school."

He chuckled while Mary got her pickle jar out of the cupboard to pay him. "I'll count on you being here next week. Same time, Dave. Okay?"

"Sure. Glad to do it," he said as he left.

She sat down to catch her breath, and Rose climbed into her lap. "Don't like it when you go 'way."

Mary gave Rose a fat squeeze. "I wasn't gone long, sweetie, and now I'm back home. We'll have dessert after I eat some supper." Guilt was already nagging because she'd let someone else look after her girls.

When Tom came home, he wanted to know how Mary's bridge class turned out. "I loved it, simply loved it. The women were nice and seemed very interested. Some of them already knew quite a bit about bridge. The others were afraid that they'd never be able to figure out how to play."

"It's befuddling at first, but they'll catch on, Mary. I did, especially with a good teacher like you." He put his arm around her and gave her a kiss.

"How was your day?" she wanted to know when he let her go.

"Okay except that it's getting awfully cold when I walk home. I'm already into my long underwear so I can't do any more to stay warm."

"Wish we had a car. Then you could drive and not have to freeze."

He washed his hands at the kitchen sink and took his place at the table. "We can't buy one of those four-wheel contraptions. No sir-ee. Maybe later. I don't have a need to drive right now. My mind's set on what I need to do to help the school system."

She dished up his dinner and set it on the table. "Saturday's your day off, and our group is supposed to meet. We need to find a bigger place where we can get together. Last time we met everyone said they knew somebody else who wanted to join."

"Right." Tom slathered butter on his warm rolls. "I talked to Thompson this morning before I left for work and asked him if we could use the gym for our meetings. I meant to tell you, but you were getting dolled up for your bridge class. Thompson said it would be okay as long as we moved the tables and chairs and put them back. Of course, we're not supposed to neb around the building either. He said he wanted to sit in on our first meeting so he'd know exactly what was taking place."

Mary nodded. "Wonderful. I'm glad the principal's interested. He should be."

"We can ask Dave to baby-sit for us so we don't have to worry about the kids acting up at the meeting," said Tom.

"That's a good idea. If we took the girls, no telling what Lily might say about her teachers."

"We need to think up a name for our group, Mary."

"I've been pondering on that lately. How about Parents for Better Schools?"

Tom laughed. "That's right to the point. Let's go with it."

Thirty people showed up at Stowe High for Saturday's meeting. Ten men and twenty women. The auditorium buzzed with excitement. People renewed acquaintances, got to know one another and shared gripes about the schools.

"I think having the meeting here in the gym instead of our house encouraged a lot more people to attend, Tom. They seem to feel freer about expressing their opinions."

"Yep. Seems like a real nice crowd. I'm pleased. Wish me luck, Mary."

She gave his hand a hearty squeeze before he walked to the table up front, called the meeting to order and began to explain what he wanted Parents for Better Schools to accomplish. "All of us know things about the schools that we'd like to change or improve. We need to get involved. Find out exactly what's going on and what we can do when something goes wrong and needs to be fixed. Most of us don't have much spare time. Our jobs and caring for a family take a big chunk out of our days. Still, if we work together on the problems we see in the schools, we're bound to help our kids do better."

Tom was surprised when the crowd clapped loudly. He glowed with the response and continued. "I figure that the first Saturday evening in the month is the best time for us to meet. Jack Thompson has been kind enough to let us use this gym. We thank him for that privilege."

Everyone smiled at the principal who had entered the room. "I'm pleased to do that," noted Thompson with a wave of his hand. "I'm looking forward to doing whatever I can to make the schools work better."

"Fine," noted Tom. "This evening, we'll divide into small groups. Five persons to each group. I brought notepads to pass out. Pick a leader in your group. The leader will make a list of the problems that you see in the schools. After half an hour, each leader will come up front and talk about the problems that were mentioned. Then we'll discuss what action might be taken to remedy the situation."

He glanced at Mary who was sitting in the front row. "Please stand, Mary."

She looked perplexed but did as Tom asked.

He spoke to the audience. "We need a secretary to keep notes about what happens in our meetings. I would like to recommend my wife, Mary Dunmore, as secretary. If you want her to be the secretary, please raise your hand."

All the hands in the room went up except Mary's.

Tom grinned. "Fine. Mary Dunmore has been selected by acclamation to be the secretary. I'm sure she'll do a fine job."

Everyone laughed and began to move into a group.

Chapter 31

The year following Tom's election to the board in 1922 was packed full for Mary. As secretary, she filled three yellow tablets with notes about the meetings of Parents for Better Schools. When the leaders listed their gripes, Tom asked the members for ideas that might resolve the problems. He wrote the suggestions on the blackboard for the audience to ponder. Mary recorded every word.

She was elated about what was happening in the schools, even though there were plenty of squabbles among principals, teachers, and PBS members. The school system certainly couldn't be turned around in one fell swoop, but she disliked the bickering and the lengthy note-taking. Yet, she realized that it was important to soak up various opinions and keep track of events for future reference. Tom was pleased with how she was digging in. Most of their conversations hinged on what was wrong in the classrooms and how to make them better. When it came to improving the schools, they clasped hands in togetherness.

Tom's trips down street in the mornings after breakfast took on a new life. Instead of hunting for groceries that were on sale, he spent his time urging folks to join PBS and jack up the schools. On the heels of the first meeting at Stowe High, he had met with the six group leaders. After considerable debate, they developed three by-laws, stating the organization's goals for grades 1 through 12. Mary asked Gertie to type them and run off copies on the mimeograph. They were passed around at the meetings and posted in the schools for everyone to read.

PARENTS FOR BETTER SCHOOLS
BY-LAWS

1. Parents are expected to provide a home atmosphere conducive to learning.
2. Students must be respectful of others, at home and at school.
3. Parents are free to visit a teacher and ask for help when problems arise.

It wasn't long before the Italians, Polish, Germans, Slovaks, Africans and Irish wanted to know more about PBS and began coming to the meetings. They learned how to talk and understand each other, regardless of their heritage. New friendships took root and flourished like wild flowers in a meadow.

Mary was overjoyed when asked to continue her bridge class in Pittsburgh. Other teaching offers arrived, but she shut the door because there weren't enough hours in the day. She still held her Evening Bridge Club at home. It gave her a chance to keep current with the happenings around town. How else would she know that Joyce Wolfe was trying to enroll in a Presbyterian seminary and become a minister, despite being warned that a woman was not allowed to preach from the pulpit . . . or that Anna Aral begged her husband to let her open a beauty shop after she'd finished a cosmetology course.

Leon Aral thundered, "Nyet, Anna, nyet!"

Mary felt blessed that orders for her bouquets began coming to her door again. Friends admired their brightness that cheered up rooms in the dead of winter. Once in a while a gentleman asked her to make a bunch of flowers for his wife's birthday, but nobody ever complained about Mary setting up a business in her home . . . perhaps because Tom managed an icehouse in his backyard.

Even though the work was painstaking, Mary blossomed when she made flowers. After her handiwork on an order was finished, contentment wrapped its arms around her. Housekeeping chores and cooking never brought such pleasure. If Mary found any spare time, she kept her New Year's resolution and studied a textbook.

Tom was overloaded, but he hankered to be busy. At the Island Avenue Yard he shoveled coal left-handed and coordinated the movement of the scoop shovel from the tender to the firebox by opening the fire door by a foot pedal. He helped the locomotive engineer, checking signals and engine performance and oiling engine parts. Railroading ran in his blood. When Tom read about the Diesel-Electric Locomotive being designed and built, he told Mary that he wanted to try his hand at that kind of engine. He declared, "For sure, it'll take a whole lot of learning, but I'll do it if the opportunity ever comes."

Dave Carson was available to tend the girls in cold weather, but Mary and Tom spent fewer Saturday evenings playing bridge. Tom listened to the radio in the parlor more than ever now that earphones weren't needed. He settled down in his spool rocker and relaxed with a cigarette or pipe, digesting the weather report and the programs that featured narrators and announcers. The French doors between the parlor and the dining room remained open so Mary could listen while she created flowers. Lily and Rose amused themselves with checkers or puzzles and pored over the Hearst comics in the paper. Orphan Annie, Andy Gump, Buck Rogers, and Blondie were their favorites. Thanks to the funnies, Rose began reading before she entered first grade.

As soon as the snow melted and warm weather turned the corner, Tom ordered ice from the company in the Rocks. The icehouse was unlocked, and Dave chipped the blocks into 25- and 50-pounders for the customers waiting in the alley. Tom took to the cellar to start a batch of Hires root beer.

When school let out in June, Lily scraped ice balls to sell while she kept an eye on Rose. During the afternoons that Mary taught in Pittsburgh, the girls tagged along and snuggled up in a corner to play games with their own deck of cards. Afterwards, Mary took them to Woolworth's and let them buy something from the bargain table as a reward for their good behavior.

The family enjoyed the porch swing on summer evenings. Mary laid a straw rug on the floor and filled Tom's homemade planters with geraniums, ferns, and violas. Kitty curled into a furry ball on the wicker end table, stacked with dog-eared magazines and old newspapers. The girls were ordered not to step foot off the porch. They watched the cars driving up and down Broadway. After fussing about which machine was best, the Hupmobile with an open-air rumble seat won out.

"Buy a car like that and take us for rides, Dad," they begged.

Tom shook his head and clicked his tongue. "No sir-ee. You don't need a machine. Your legs can take you wherever you need to go."

He walked them to the drug store where they were treated to ice cream cones filled with two scoops of their favorite flavor.

On the day in September that Miss Adeline Grigsby laid Lily over a desk and swatted her bloomers, Mary reminded her husband of his promise to burn every paddle in the schools if he was elected. Tom still believed that paddling deserved a respectable place in education, but he hankered to heal his breach with Mary. He began by telling Lily it was wicked to sass grown-ups.

Lily promised she'd never do it again but insisted that Miss Grigsby was a dumb teacher. "Why should I have to memorize three poems and recite them in front of the class? All those beady eyes and grins make you forget every single word you learned."

Tom escorted Lily to school the next day and stood by while she apologized to Miss Grigsby. Later, he enjoyed a private discussion with the teacher. When Tom held her at bay, Miss Grigsby's pink complexion turned whiter than Lily's bloomers. Before he left, the teacher stowed the paddle in the cloakroom out of sight. Tom planned to visit Principal Thompson straight away and discuss how paddling could close a student's eyes instead of opening them to the goodness of an education.

Santa arrived at the Dunmores on Christmas Eve and piled gifts under their fir tree, aglow with ornaments and garlands of popcorn. By happenchance, Santa left a box filled with sparklers and a note, saying they would only burn if a match was put to them on New Year's Eve. On that night, Mary and Tom sat in the living room, watching Lily play a polka while Rose whirled around the room until she was out of breath and flopped on the floor. She clamped her hands over her eyes, trying to recover from the dizziness.

Tom eyed the clock on the mantel. "It's time to light the sparklers now. The New Year's almost here."

They bundled up in their winter coats, hurried outside and stood on the sidewalk as whistles began to make themselves known all over West Park.

Tom showed the girls how to handle the sparklers safely. Then he lit them. "Be careful and don't get burned now. That's real fire you're playing with."

Lily and Rose were enchanted. They watched the brilliant sparks scatter in the crisp night air and disappear like they'd never existed.

Mary kept quiet, thinking how blessed her family had been in the memorable year gone by. She prayed that 1924 would be just as fruitful.

Chapter 32

New Year's resolutions for 1924 had been made and forgotten by the time winter set in with a vengeance. Lily complained about being frozen after walking to and from school, even though she wore a wool coat, scarf, hat, and gloves. Whether it was raining, snowing, or a clear day, she pulled on rubber boots. The floor of the school was always drafty. Overshoes kept her toes warm.

"The cloakroom's stacked full. It takes forever to get everything off and in its place," complained Lily to her mother. "Then you have to put it all back on when you go home."

Mary took a deep breath. "Be glad you have things to wear, honey. Some people don't have any clothes to keep them warm."

A sense of relief swept over Mary. Thank heaven her sewing skills kept the family well dressed. She'd even fashioned ear muffs for Tom to wear on his long walks from work. The elastic held them tight on his ears. He thought he looked kooky, but no matter. Who saw him walking through the tunnel and on the streets when it was almost midnight?

"I wanna go to school with Lily," crowed Rose. "Can I?"

"Not 'til you're older, sweetie."

"Will you make me dresses, Mother? Pretty ones like Lily's."

Mary laughed. "I promise that you'll wear everything she grows out of."

Lily faced Rose with a taunting gaze. "You get my hand-me-downs, 'stead of new stuff, Sis."

Mary scowled. "That's not a nice thing to say, Lily."

When Tom stepped in the door that night, Mary thought he didn't look well. "Are you sick?" she wanted to know.

"Nah. Just tired. The wind was in my face all the way home tonight. It started me coughing."

"I hope you're not coming down with something." She hurried to pour his coffee while he washed up at the sink.

"Don't worry. You know I never get sick, sweetheart."

Pleasure rippled. She loved when he called her sweetheart. Moving to the big pot on the stove, she ladled the homemade vegetable soup she'd made for him.

He took his place at the table and began crumbling soda crackers into the steaming bowl before he began to eat. "This is mighty good. You're the best cook in town." A cough caught hold. He covered his mouth with the blue work hanky he kept in his pocket.

Mary hovered. "I'm worried about you. That hacking sounds really awful."

"Don't worry. It's only a winter cold, that's all." Still, he had a hard time getting supper down in between his coughs.

The next morning, Mary had no doubt that Tom needed to see the doctor. He'd tossed in bed all night, kept her awake, and finally gone to the kitchen for coffee because he couldn't sleep.

"I sure hope you don't have the flu," worried Mary. She thought about Ben and how fast it had overtaken him.

"I'll be okay. It's only some darned bug making its rounds. Guess I'll have to call in sick. Don't let the girls come near me. They might catch something."

By 10 o'clock that morning, Mary phoned Dr. Winter for an appointment and arranged for Dave Carson to care for the girls. Tom called the dispatcher and said he couldn't work because of illness but he'd be back soon. To tell the truth, he was feeling so rotten he didn't fuss about being examined by Dr. Winter who was only supposed to treat women.

Mary stayed in the waiting room while the nurse took Tom's temperature. The doctor peered down his throat and took his blood pressure and pulse. After listening to what was going on in his chest, she asked Mary to come in.

"He has to go to the hospital."

The doctor poked her horn-rimmed glasses higher on her nose and focused on Tom. "You need a chest X-ray and some tests that can't be done here. Your fever's high, and I don't like the sound of that cough."

A scowl streaked over Tom. "It's only the crud, that's all. I'm used to getting the stuff. Railroaders catch the bug all the time in the winter. I'll be fine in a few days."

The doctor frowned, a furrow forming between her dark eyes. "After I view the X-ray, you might have to stay in the hospital for a while."

Tom began buttoning up his shirt. "No need for me to go to Ohio Valley, Doctor. I can rest cheaper at home. My wife knows how to play nurse, believe me."

Frenzy captured Mary. "You have to do exactly what the doctor tells you, Tom." She turned to Dr. Winter. "Can't you give him something to tide him over?"

"No, not until I have more information regarding his condition."

Tom stood up. "You mean you won't give me some pills? Just this once you could try some kind of medicine and see if it works. I don't need to go to the hospital."

Grimness pervaded. "Warm liquids, aspirin, and gargling will ease your throat some. That's all I can prescribe right now."

"I'll try that then. I've gotta get back to work. I have a family to support and a board meeting's coming up."

"You need to be in the hospital while we do some tests and find out what's wrong." Dr. Winter's voice was firm.

Tom eased toward the door.

"No more smoking," ordered Dr. Winter. "Not even one cigarette, Tom."

"I can't live without my tobacco, Doctor." He slipped his hand in his pocket to make sure his smokes hadn't been stolen. "Come on, Mary, we've gotta go."

Dr. Winter faced him. "If you go home, your girls might catch what *you've* got, Tom."

He stopped in his tracks.

"My nurse will call a cab that'll get you to Ohio Valley right away, Tom."

He was given a hospital gown to wear and put to bed after his tests at the hospital. Tom lay quietly except for his coughing which filled his mouth with a bloody mucus. The nurse left tissues and a waste can by his bed.

Mary sat quietly with hands clasped, thinking how life had changed overnight. It seemed like a bad dream. How could she be in the hospital, waiting for Dr. Winter to tell her what was wrong with Tom? He'd always been healthy. His physicals at the railroad pronounced him fit.

To gain a measure of respite, she phoned Dave and told him what was happening. He said not to worry, the girls were fed and in bed . . . he'd stay the night if needed. Mary decided to take a cab home after she talked to the doctor.

It was past 9:30 p.m. when Dr. Winter walked through the door, looking weary and drained. Mary sensed that the news wasn't good, even before the doctor opened her mouth.

Dr. Winter eyed Tom. "I'm sorry that you're feeling so wretched. You had an upper respiratory infection when I examined you this morning, but the tests show that you have pneumonia now. You'll have to stay in the hospital until your condition improves. After you're well, you can go home."

"What rotten luck," grumbled Tom.

"You'll be treated with sulfa. That's a mighty fine drug. It has helped many of my patients. Hopefully, you'll feel better real soon."

Tom groaned and wiped his mouth. "I've gotta get back to work."

"In good time," replied the doctor.

A nurse appeared with Tom's medication. Dr. Winter took Mary aside. "I'll drive you home. I know you've had a rough day and need to get some rest."

In the car, the doctor confided in Mary. "I didn't want to tell you this in front of Tom, but I have to get your opinion. His X-ray showed that he has a tumor in his right lung. He's been a heavy smoker for a long time. He'll have to give up tobacco. I think we should wait until he has recovered from pneumonia before telling him about the tumor. How do you feel about that, Mary?"

She gasped. "I don't believe this, Dr. Winter. It's unreal. A couple of days ago my husband seemed fine."

Dr. Winter shook her head. "I'm very sorry. I know this is terrible news, but I had to tell you."

"What can you do about the tumor?" asked Mary in a shaky voice.

"We won't make any decisions about that until he recuperates from the pneumonia. An operation might be possible, but a surgeon will have to study his case. Of course Tom must be told, but telling him now might cause him to backslide. I thought you'd want to wait until he has improved."

Mary nodded. "That makes good sense to me. We should wait a while. Frankly, I can't believe this is happening. It's like a nightmare."

"I know," said Dr. Winter. "It's even hard for me to believe."

On February 3, 1924, when snow was falling in West Park, Tom Dunmore died from double pneumonia at Ohio Valley Hospital. Mary was by his side. He never learned that he had a tumor in his right lung.

Chapter 33

Mary lived in a haze during the weeks following Tom's death. Friends from every corner of her world streamed in to offer condolences. Her far-away relatives sent flowers and phoned. Gertie came by in the evenings to plump up comfort and see if she could help in any way. Food was stashed in the kitchen as well-wishers expressed their sympathy, according to tradition. No matter what their nationality, they sensed that offering sustenance was appropriate and needed. Early on, Mary learned that it didn't matter what country people came from. They could be sympathetic and caring toward someone who had suffered loss. PBS members—an Italian, a Slovak and a Ukrainian—sent condolence notes that praised Tom's creating a group, tuned toward improving West Park schools.

Even though life seemed surreal and ravaged, Mary traveled through her normal routine except for canceling her Pittsburgh class, scheduled on the day after the funeral. Lily kept going to school and taking piano lessons. They attended church every Sunday. The evening bridge class met as usual at the house.

When it was time for PBS to meet, Mary took charge like Tom would have wanted. She presented *Reasons for Poor Classroom Performance,* the program that Tom had prepared before his illness. During the meeting, Mary became President of PBS by acclamation. At Mary's request, Gertie accepted the position of Secretary.

Dave Carson hovered at the Dunmores, keeping coal in the furnace and shopping from the lists that Mary made. He didn't want to accept any pay, but Mary insisted. A letter from the railroad arrived, stating that a life insurance check would be forthcoming. For the first time she worried about whether a woman with two children to raise could stretch the money far enough. Since she had no property rights and little control under Pennsylvania's common-law system, it never entered her mind to talk to Tom about how she would manage if he passed on. No way in the world she ever imagined that he'd be gone at age 39. Men usually lived until they were in their early 50s unless they met with an accident or foul play.

Frequently Mary reached for the Bible and searched for answers, hoping that she could fathom why her beloved son and husband were both snatched away so early. She lived a wholesome life according to The Ten Commandments. Nevertheless, the thought lingered that she had done something wrong and was being punished. After failing to find anything in the Bible that supported such a notion, she consoled herself by telling herself, "Surely the Lord will show me the way."

Rose often asked, "When is Daddy coming home?" Mary always told her that he was in Heaven, waiting for the time when the family would all be living together again.

Lily screwed up her face and declared, "I miss Daddy something awful, but I don't want to be in Heaven now. I'm gonna stay right here in this nice house he built."

Mary pondered about the years ahead. She yearned for a good-paying job like many men had. How glorious to have enough money to support her family and not have to worry. She pinpointed what she wanted for Lily and Rose. Aside from being healthy, they must graduate from high school. Go to college. A few females were trying to enroll nowadays, but the door often slammed shut in their faces. Then the "weaker sex" had to take jobs offering low pay and no future. She didn't want her girls to settle for being store clerks. They must take college courses and graduate. Instead of marrying soon after high school like most girls, her daughters needed to get more education and delay the wedding bells. There would be plenty of time to keep house and mother babies.

At nightfall, Mary lay down in the four-poster bed and sensed a lingering emptiness as her arm stretched over the bare space beside her. When remembering brought her no slumber, she rolled up Tom's worsted union suits and stuffed them by her side. Pressing herself against the comforting flannel finally brought forgetting and sleep.

The week before the School Board met, Jack Thompson came to visit. He commiserated with her for a while and talked about how much her husband had helped the school system. Mary was flabbergasted when he asked her point-blank if she would take Tom's seat on the board.

Dumbfounded, she replied, "I never thought . . . no. I can't do that. I wasn't elected by the people like my Tom was. It wouldn't be right, Mr. Thompson."

The principal faced her head-on. "Tom's ideas about helping the schools were well accepted. The board looked forward to his input. You know more than anyone else about the plans he had. You've been the secretary and done considerable work in that regard. It's all written down. There's no reason why you won't be a capable person on the board. The group has already accepted you if you'll agree."

She quivered and wondered if this was a dream. "I'll do it," she murmured.

When the news spread that the School Board had accepted a woman, heads nodded and shook, tongues wagged and eyes cast disbelieving looks. A number of Mary's friends congratulated her. Some said nothing at all. Several measured every word they spoke while a few made blatant comments.

Sally Lyone sputtered, "It's the same as stealing, Mary Dunmore. I hope you can't get away with it."

"Don't you know you're stepping on men's toes?" demanded Arlene Cowan.

Mary kept right on, trying to look pleasant and unconcerned.

In the months that followed, Mary read every library book she could find related to education. She focused on creating harmony instead of discord in the schools. As the President of PBS, she offered programs leading to vigorous discussions. The members talked about ways to encourage pupils to study, the danger in setting goals too high, and balancing school activities and outside activities. A dozen parents even agreed to serve as classroom aides when needed.

Mary kept the board members informed about what was happening in PBS. They were invited to the meetings and showed up occasionally. She tried to promote an amicable relationship between the community and the schools. All the while, she developed her own abilities, despite the criticism directed toward her by folks who felt that women had no business being leaders.

Chapter 34

Mary was getting ready to settle down in the dining room and work on her bridge lesson. She'd just been to the cellar, shoveling coal and dumping out ashes. It was an ice-cold day. She hoped the chill wouldn't keep the ladies in Pittsburgh from coming to class.

When she glanced out the window, snow was falling. She pictured the girls trying out the new sled Santa had brought at Christmas. Quickly she scribbled a note for Dave and left it on the kitchen counter.

Dave, If there's enough snow, let Lily and Rose sled ride in the backyard. Be sure they're bundled up real good and don't let them get wet or they might get sick.

Mary sat down at the dining room table, loaded with paper flower materials, and turned to her notebook. The French doors between the parlor and the dining room stood open. A smile glimmered. Rose was practicing the piano. Under Lily's tutelage, Rose had begun lessons and was learning lickety-split. Kitty settled on the bench, purring when the notes were sweet, crouching behind the couch when they became discords.

It crossed Mary's mind that in some ways she was lucky, even though she'd lost her son, husband, and mother in the past five years. Her blessings struck a responsive chord. She was paid for teaching bridge and serving on the School Board. The flower business brought in dollars, even though she only took a few orders because planning the PBS programs gobbled up her hours. The members would quit coming if the meetings weren't invigorating. Most of all, she wanted Tom's dream of improving the schools to stay alive.

An hour later, Mary finished preparing her bridge lesson. Rose and Kitty were in the cellar, playing house with the dolls Lily had discarded because "I don't give a hoot about any of them except Benny. He can stay on my bed with Kitty."

Mary went to the kitchen to fix lunch. She stopped short after a glance out the window. The trees were dressed in white and loomed like Halloween ghosts.

Snow showered down, dancing in whatever direction the wind was blowing. She figured the overloaded clouds were dumping their flakes to get relief.

Momentarily she eyed her feet and wondered if her boots would keep the wet stuff from ruining her Sunday shoes, always worn when she taught in Pittsburgh. Another glimpse out the window told her that it would be useless to hold class. The wind was whirling snow over everything in sight. Women probably wouldn't venture out in that kind of weather, even for a good card game. She went to the phone and called the Women's Club. The class had already been canceled by Teresa Pulaski.

Lily arrived home, shivering from head to toe. "School's closed," she shrieked delightfully, pulling off her coat and hat with one swoop. She tugged at her boots with both hands. "I'm sure glad I don't have to go back this afternoon."

Rose came upstairs and squealed when she saw Lily. "You look funny. Your hair's all white."

Lily shook her head hard, scattering flakes over the linoleum. "It's awful out there, Sis. I'm stayin' inside where it's nice and warm." She grabbed Kitty from Rose's arms and smoothed her face against the cat. "I love to hear her purr. She's humming a song just for me."

The phone rang, and Mary hurried to the parlor. When she returned to the kitchen, she told the girls, "Dave says all the schools are closing. Travel in Pittsburgh and the surrounding towns is impossible."

"That's scary, Mother," moaned Lily.

"We'll be fine," answered Mary. "Dave said he'd help us if we needed it." She shrugged. "I'll have to keep the furnace going, that's for sure."

The afternoon was spent with the girls fussing about what to do because it was too frigid to go outside. They couldn't sled ride. "You'll have to wait 'til the storm's over. You'd freeze out there right now," warned Mary.

They pulled out their board games and sat down by the gas fireplace in the parlor. Mary made cocoa and topped the mugs with marshmallows. "This is yummy," said Lily. "We ought to use this fireplace all the time. Then you wouldn't have to shovel that dirty old coal, Mother."

Mary shook her head. "The fireplace can't heat this big house. Besides, gas costs more."

She turned on the Crosley radio. The KDKA announcer described the difficulty people were having in getting home, even though they'd left work before quitting time. Trolleys stalled on various routes because their tracks were snowed under. The car barns were filling up with trolleys that couldn't move. Cabs, autos, and buses became snowbound on the streets.

The reporter said that not only schools would close. Stores, banks, and industries were shutting down. Church staffs called in to cancel their services for the rest of the week. The newsman warned against shoveling snow since it could bring on heart attacks. "It won't do any good because the storm is continuing."

Mary felt helpless, like she did when Tom died so unexpectedly. It seemed impossible that she was in a two-story house with snow piling up around it and two children and a furnace to tend. The idea flashed that big snows could cause roofs to collapse. She shut her eyes and murmured a prayer.

When supper time arrived, Mary opened cans of chicken soup and made cheese sandwiches. She worried about whether there'd be enough milk. Two quarts were delivered on the front porch every other day, but the storm would keep the milkman from making his regular route. She always put milk in her coffee but left it out. If the bottled milk was used up, she'd give the girls canned milk that was stored in the cellar cupboard.

They were eating in the kitchen when the lights went out. "What happened?" cried Lily.

Mary hurried to the window. She could see lights way off in the distance, but the nearby houses were dark. The street light wasn't burning either. "I guess the storm damaged the lines or a tree fell on a line. We'll have to be patient, girls, until they fix whatever's wrong."

She moved to the counter and began rummaging in the drawers. "Where's the flashlight? Where are the candles?" Finally she found a flashlight, then remembered that the candles were in the cellar. The only time they were used was during Christmas. She hadn't even gotten them out this year.

Fear nibbled. She pointed the meager light down the pitch-black cellar steps. "Guess we won't use any candles, girls. I'm sure they'll fix the electricity right away." She bit her lip, aware that she probably wasn't telling the truth. No telling how long it would be before the electricity came on . . . might even be days. Maybe she should call to report the outage. She picked up the phone. It wasn't working either.

By bedtime, the house was getting cold. The furnace blower that sent heated air through the registers had cut off when the electricity quit. Mary remembered that the water line could freeze when the temperature dropped. Tom always made sure that the spigot had a slight drip to keep that from happening. Hurriedly she tended to it.

"If you want, we can sleep in my bed tonight," said Mary. "That way maybe we'll all stay good and warm."

"Hurray!" shouted Lily. "Hurray!"

"Me, too. Me, too," sang Rose.

After climbing the steps, guided by the flashlight, they piled into bed without brushing their teeth or changing into nightgowns. Kitty nestled at the foot of the four-poster. With a girl tucked on each side, Mary was grateful that they'd stay warm. She thought about Ben and how he'd have relished the adventure of being snowbound. Finally, she fell sound asleep.

In the morning, the Dunmores awoke to a pristine world. Mary stood at the bedroom window, soaking up the stillness of the street. Nothing was moving—no people, no cars. The only thing stirring were the birds, searching for food that had vanished.

"It's beautiful," she sang. "The snow hid all the dirt in the world. Everything is pure white." Tom came to mind. He wouldn't have been able to walk to the railroad yard and back home in the deep snow. Maybe he'd have been trapped with no way to get home. She trembled at the thought.

The girls tumbled out of bed. They climbed on the loveseat and pressed their noses against the window panes. "We can see everything now. Not have to feel our way around in the dark," spouted Lily.

Rose rubbed her nose to warm it. "Look. The cars are covered up with snow. I'm freezing. It's awful cold, Mother."

"Put on an extra sweater and your wool socks," said Mary. "I'm going to make breakfast. Let's hope the gas stove and the water are still working."

The sun shone bright when afternoon came, making the snow dazzle even more. People were pulling snow off the roofs with rakes, brooms and ski poles and trying to rescue their cars. It was a herculean task. Workmen came by, throwing salt to encourage melting. Neighborhood men pitched in to clear the streets with shovels so cars could begin to move. Later in the day, a big machine pushed the white stuff up high against the curbs to clear the street, making it impossible for people to dig the snow out of their driveways.

In the evening, Mary and the girls cheered when the electricity and the phone were restored. The house began to warm up as the blower started working. A sense of relief surfaced while Mary stuffed coal in the furnace with all the might she could muster. "Wish I had a strong back like a man's," she griped.

They ate supper, gathered close to the fireplace while listening to the radio announcer who described what was happening in town. Who could believe that 26.2 inches of snow had fallen on downtown Pittsburgh and the surrounding burbs? People, stranded at work, sought refuge in hotels or wherever they could find shelter. Travelers were left in a lurch at the Pennsy Station until the railroad tracks could be cleared. The reporter said the National Guard had arrived to enforce a temporary law that forbade entering the Triangle in autos. Icicles hung from the sides of buildings. One man was killed when he was struck in the head by ice falling from a window. Crews used power shovels, coal loaders, and muscles to fill city trucks with snow that was dumped in the rivers.

"Most workers can't get to their jobs," Mary told her girls. "The steel mills will lose lots of money. Besides that, it will cost plenty to clean up this mess. Allegheny County will have to pay for all of it."

Sunday arrived and life was returning to normality in West Park. Snow started to melt and people were getting ready to return to work. The milk delivered on the porch froze and became snow cream, good enough to gobble down. Lily and Rose built a grinning snowman in the yard for all to admire. Dave pulled the girls around the block on their sled. School was reopening on Monday.

Late in the evening when the girls were fast asleep, Mary stood at the window, her gaze on the houses with their roofs frosted with snow and the lights shining brightly inside. She figured Tom was peering down on her and he would be proud. His family had weathered the storm.

Chapter 35

She sat in the dining room, making blue irises for Wilma Warchak to match her newly-painted blue bedroom. Mary was in a meditative mood. The winter had been unusually mild, reminding Mary how her life had been turned upside down two years ago by the 1925 storm that shut the family inside a snowbound house with no electricity or phone. The Dunmores discovered they could manage. They even toasted marshmallows in the fireplace.

With the coming of spring and the closing of school in the offing, Mary's thoughts focused on her girls. They were as different as night and day. Rose arrived home every day, bursting with enthusiasm about what she'd done in class. Her chums often came to the house. If the weather proved bad, they spent time in the cellar with the doll furniture or the classroom Tom had fashioned.

On the other side of the coin, Lily went to school only because she had no choice. She shied away from mixing with others and dreaded entering Stowe High as a freshman in the fall. That meant facing new teachers and new classmates. Her only comfort was in knowing that she'd be taking piano lessons every week from Sean Foster.

After finishing a flower, Mary laid it aside and moved to the window for a breather. The grass was becoming green in the back yard. Soon the days would turn warm and bushes would sprout, bringing buds into blossom. She gazed at the icehouse. Dave was sending a 25-pounder down the slide. He broke into a grin as the ice landed in a wagon. The customer handed Dave the money, and they chatted for several minutes.

Dave was a blessing. Along with the income from Mary's sidelines and Tom's life insurance, the money made at the icehouse kept the household running and paid Dave's wages to boot. On occasion he took charge of the girls. Mary considered herself an honest-to-goodness breadwinner now. Her friends still raised their eyebrows and babbled when the subject of paying a sitter came up. Some women declared it a crime for a man to tend children.

Mary left the dining room and headed to the front porch to pick up the paper, delivered like clockwork on the steps every morning. A screaming headline met her eyes. She rushed back inside and settled down to read the news.

LINDBERGH MAKES FIRST SOLO FLIGHT ACROSS THE ATLANTIC

On May 20, 1927 at 7:52 a.m., Charles Lindbergh headed the *Spirit of St. Louis* down the dirt runway of Roosevelt Field in New York. With four sandwiches, two canteens of water and 451 gallons of gas, Lindbergh took off while 500 people watched. On the evening of May 21, he crossed the coast of France, followed the Seine River to Paris and touched down at Le Bourget Field at l0:21 p.m., 33 1/2 hours and 3,600 miles later. The crowd of 100,000 swamped the plane the minute he came to a stop. In an instant he turned hero, named *Lone Eagle*. He was the first to fly the Atlantic alone.

A daredevil barnstormer and expert mechanic, Lindbergh worked as a United States Air Mail Service pilot in 1926 and pioneered the airmail routes between St. Louis and Chicago. He wanted to win the $25,000 prize offered for the first New York-to-Paris nonstop flight by Raymond Orteig, a Frenchman who owned hotels in New York City. Lindbergh visualized St. Louis as an aviation hub. He persuaded Harold Bixby, Head of the St. Louis Chamber of Commerce, to sponsor his flight with a $15,000 budget.

Many aviators placed faith in the increased power and safety of multi-engine planes. Lindbergh believed that multiple engines increased, rather than decreased, the odds of engine failure. He said that less weight—one engine and one pilot—meant increased fuel efficiency and allowed for a longer flying range.

Ryan Airlines Corporation in San Diego, California, built the plane for $6,000. Under Lindbergh's supervision, Donald Hall was Chief Engineer and Designer. Housed in a defunct fish cannery, the special plane was completed in only two months. Extra fuel tanks were added. The wingspan was increased to accommodate the additional weight. The main fuel tank was placed in front of the pilot's seat rather than behind it. Lindbergh didn't want to be caught between the tank and the engine in case the plane was forced to land. That meant that he could not see directly ahead. If necessary, he could watch the sky in front of him by making shallow banks and peering out the window on each side.

When completed, the plane weighed 2,150 pounds and had a 46-foot wingspan. It was powered by a *Wright Whirlwind Engine*, estimated to perform for over 9,000 hours and outfitted with a mechanism that kept it greased during the transatlantic flight. To lessen the weight, Lindbergh left behind a parachute, radio, gas gauges, and navigation lights. He wore lightweight boots and sat in a flimsy wicker chair instead of the usual leather pilot's seat. During the dangerous trip, he had to fight fog, icing, and sleep deprivation.

Lindbergh's gigantic feat electrifies the whole world. Undoubtedly, honors will be heaped on him as long as he lives. Surely many countries will present him with prestigious awards for his colossal achievement. He is the first person to make a solo-nonstop flight from New York to Paris.

Mary stared at the picture of Lindbergh on the front page . . . a handsome man to be sure. How would it feel, being a nobody one day and a hero the next? Must be like a dream. She tried to picture flying a plane with only its floor underfoot instead of solid ground. Mary cringed. Once in a while she'd dreamed about driving a car, but even that was scary. Flying a plane would be terrifying. No woman would ever want to be a pilot and chance losing her life.

She took a deep breath and turned to the rest of the paper. Another headline caught her eye. NEW EASTERN STAR CHAPTER FORMS. The Eastern Star was a fraternal organization of Master Masons and their wives, widows, mothers, daughters, and sisters. They promoted charity and goodwill through supporting social and charitable projects. She remembered that Tom was a Mason when they married, but he couldn't attend the meetings after beginning work on the railroad.

I'd like to join, but I already have too much to do, Mary reminded herself. Caring for the girls, teaching bridge, working on the board, chairing Parents for Better Schools, but . . . belonging to the Eastern Star sounded intriguing.

She carried the paper to the dining room table and cut out the information about how to petition for membership. No way she could ever fly a plane, but maybe she could become a star some day.

Chapter 36

It wasn't long before Mary had enticed Gertie to join her in applying for membership in the Order of the Eastern Star. Their petitions were carefully completed and submitted. During September, they attended a meeting where a ballot determined that they were accepted as members. Mary and Gertie received letters, advising that they were to be initiated into the Eastern Star, Ohio Valley Chapter, No. 438, McKees Rocks, Pennsylvania.

"Can we call you Star now, Mother?" asked Lily.

Mary flashed a smile. "No. I'm not a star."

"It'd be fun to call you Star," countered Lily.

"She's Mother, not Star," chirped Rose.

The Eastern Star Initiation was held on the first Monday in January, 1928. Mary was relieved. She'd been afraid that the School Board meeting would coincide.

"I'm worn to a frazzle," she complained after the program when Gertie was driving her home. "I'm sure glad we both got through it without flubbing up."

"Everything went just fine. Don't worry. We didn't make a mistake."

Mary heaved a sigh. "We can enjoy the activities now. They have plenty of social events as well as projects they do to help needy people."

"There aren't any Eastern Star meetings in July or August, Mary, but we'll have plenty of nights to relish. Maybe after a while you'll decide to become a Worthy Matron, get elected and buy a beautiful dress to wear for the initiation."

Mary snickered. "Bosh, I'm too young to be called a matron, Gertie. Don't forget, I'm livin' it up in the Jazz Age."

"You don't look your age, girl, so there. If you'd bob your hair real short like they're doing now, you could easily be taken for 28 instead of 38. You oughta try it and see." Gertie hesitated. "Have you ever thought about getting married again?"

Mary's eyes widened. "Heavens no. Such a thought never entered my head. I still love Tom."

"Life would be easier if you were married, hon. You could stop worrying about whether you'd be able to send your girls to college."

"I'd never find another husband like Tom." Mary puckered up her face. "Remember Al Jolson's song, *A Good Man Is Hard To Find*? Anyway, I'm doing okay money-wise as long as I watch my budget and don't overspend. I just have to be careful."

"Don't ever buy any stocks, Mary. You could lose money that way."

Mary tittered. "Land sakes, I never invest in stocks, Gertie. I don't have that kind of money. I know nothing—a goose egg—about stocks. Tom didn't buy any."

"Pete dabbles in stocks, but I don't pay any attention to what he's doing with the money he makes. He'll always take good care of me even though I teach school. The $980 I make every year goes right in the bank."

"Gosh, with two incomes you'll never have to worry about money, Gertie. If the icehouse fares well, I teach bridge and stay on the board, I'm sending my girls to college so they can have careers like men. I don't want my girls to come up short like me. Lily will be the first one in the family to go to college after she graduates from Stowe High. Seven years later, it'll be Rose's turn. I get fluttery all over thinking about it. Wish my turn would come."

"What college are you considering, Mary?"

"One in Pittsburgh. I want to keep an eye on my girls."

"How does Lily feel about college?"

Mary rolled her eyes. "I haven't mentioned college to her. She gripes all the time about school. Lily never cared about classes. Says she'll be a concert pianist some day. Reverend Dryer asked her to play hymns for Sunday School. She actually said she'd do it. I didn't think that would ever happen."

Gertie seemed puzzled. "You'd better find out how she feels about college. I don't want you to get your hopes up and make plans while she's kept in the dark. She might pitch a fit about going to college."

There was a pause before Mary said, "I'm afraid Lily won't like the idea."

"What grades does she make?" Gertie wanted to know.

"Average ones mostly, but she gets A's in music. Sean says he'll let her play with the orchestra next year. I'll just have to wait and see how that works out."

"Sounds as though she might like to major in Fine Arts, but Lily needs better grades. The powers that be at college don't welcome females with open arms unless they have good grades and want to be schoolteachers. If she was a daughter or a relative of a faculty member that would help. I think Lily's best chance of being admitted is an A average."

Mary dug her feet into the floorboard. "Somehow it'll work out, Gertie. It has to. If it were Rose, I wouldn't worry. She likes school and plays for the kids to march in from recess. She loves to do that. They get a big kick out of marching to the music."

"Super." Gertie stepped on the brake and eased the Model-T to a stop in front of Mary's house. She turned to Mary. "You realize that Rose and Lily have different personalities. Lily keeps to herself. Rose is friendly. That'll help her get wherever she wants to go."

Mary opened the car door. "Lily's standoffish, but she'll outgrow that. I'm sure she'll go to college and graduate. So will Rose."

"Don't count on it," murmured Gertie as she drove off.

Chapter 37

Mary's ideas about college plunged like the stocks did on Black Tuesday, October 29, 1929. U. S. common stocks lost 10 percent of their value in a flash. On one day, desperate speculators sold 16,400,000 shares. Thousands of players saw their investments vanish in the worst stock market crash in Wall Street history. The exact reasons were unknown. Most observers thought the cause to be widespread abuse of securities markets by insiders and the inadequate disclosure of financial data by companies.

Floored by the news, people huddled on the sub-treasury building steps across from the New York Stock Exchange. Nobody could believe or would ever forget the moment they learned that America's financial heart had been scarred. Devastated buyers flung themselves out of the windows, high above Wall Street.

Weeks later, radios and newspapers reported that Americans were acting in outlandish ways. They lavished their money on expensive automobiles, travel, and vacations. Jazz bands, dances, sports, and motion pictures took over the scene. New timesaving appliances eased housework and enticed wives to fritter their hours away from home. Young flappers went wild with skimpy skirts, silk stockings, bobbed hair, and flashy make-up. Drinkers, furious about Prohibition, sought relief in the illegal speakeasies. Gangsters became bootleggers.

"I don't think President Hoover's doing a good job," complained Mary to Dave as they chatted in the kitchen one morning. "By darn, I'm sure sorry I voted for him."

Dave reached for the pay Mary handed him. "I think Hoover's done as well as he could. The stock market crash wasn't his fault. People who borrowed money to buy stocks and turn rich overnight got slammed. To make things worse, Congress passed the Smoot-Hawley Tariff Act on the heels of the stock market crash. It raised tariffs sky high. Then foreign countries followed suit. Now trade's coming to a dead stop."

"I read that our farmers are going broke," responded Mary. "I'm worried. People in all kinds of companies are losing their jobs these days, no matter how long they've worked there. Everybody says we're headed for a terrible depression."

Dave scratched the stubble on his chin. "I'm afraid that's the truth."

Mary lowered the gas under the beef stew she was making. "I hope the icehouse keeps running. I'd sure as the world hate to lose that income. It's not a lot, but every little bit helps."

"It'll soon be time to shut the icehouse down. Winter's coming," muttered Dave. "My handyman jobs have slowed to a trickle 'cause people are out of work and don't have a dime to spare."

Clouded with uneasiness, Mary gritted her teeth. "My girls have to go to college, and I have to keep up the payments on this house. I'm wondering about my bridge class in Pittsburgh. I hope that doesn't fold. My contract's up at the end of the year. Maybe it won't be renewed."

Dave gave her a devilish grin. "I expect those fancy ladies you teach are plenty well off. Don't worry. They'll still have enough money for bridge lessons."

"Maybe you're right, Dave, but who knows? Their husbands probably lost plenty in the crash." She pondered. "If I had a decent education, I'd be able to get a real job now."

"Even if you'd graduated college, you wouldn't find a job. There aren't any." Dave moved toward the door and stared out the window. "I've gotta get back to the icehouse. I see a customer out there."

When Rose came home from school, Mary gave her a doughnut and milk. "What did you do today, honey?"

"We had more words to learn. Ten new ones. And Miss Grigsby gave us homework. We're working on multiplication tables." She scratched her forehead. "I like words a lot more than numbers, Mother."

Mary chuckled. "Guess you won't be an accountant then."

Rose's blue eyes gleamed beneath her thick lashes. "What's that?"

"Someone who works with numbers . . . who knows how to add, subtract, multiply, and divide real well. If he works in a bank, an accountant has to keep up with how much money comes in and how much goes out."

Rose took a big bite of her doughnut. "I like money, but I don't want to count it all day."

"The accountant doesn't count money that way, sweetie. He operates a machine that prints numbers on paper. That way they have a record of what's happening to the money."

"Oh, I see." Rose finished her milk and took her empty glass to the sink. "I'm gonna get Kitty and take her downstairs. I'll start on my homework."

"Fine. I'll look it over when you've finished, honey."

Rose was still in the cellar, spouting a multiplication table to Kitty when Lily arrived from school. Mary decided, no matter what, she was going to find out how Lily felt about college. "There's something we need to talk about, sweetie."

Lily plopped into a chair. "What's that?"

"I hope you've been thinking about what you're going to do after you graduate from high school."

Lily's eyebrows arched. "I'll take piano lessons . . . give concerts."

Mary spoke firmly. "First, you have to go to college."

Lily sat up straight. "I'm not going to college, Mother. Not ever. I hate classes. Mr. Foster says after I graduate I can take piano lessons at Pittsburgh Musical Institute."

A cough nagged at Mary. She cleared her throat and peered at Lily. "You'd be taking piano lessons in college and playing recitals so you could perform for the public. Piano would be your main course, but you'd also have other classes—English, Math, and Science."

Lily glared. "I don't care a hoot about those things, Mother. They don't help a pianist one bit."

Shrewdness swam over Mary. "I've been studying those books Principal Thompson left in the cellar for you. I learned scads of things from them and got a big lift."

"Whew." Lily jerked her head back and forth. "I'd rather play the piano and forget all that other stuff. It's bad enough doing homework now. Miss Torino assigned a theme for English class. It's due next Monday."

Mary inhaled, trying to stifle her anger. "What are you going to write about?"

Lily snapped her fingers. "Guess what? We don't get to pick a subject. Miss Torino gave us one. *Tips for Doing Homework*. She told us to describe every single step we should take to get the most good out of doing our assignments."

"I want to read your paper when you're finished, Lily. Better get started. Rose is doing her homework in the cellar. Maybe she'll give you some tips."

Lily scowled. "What does Rose know? I have to practice piano now anyway. That stupid paper can wait a while."

Gertie dropped by in the evening. They settled down in the kitchen while the girls were up in their rooms. "I've been dying to talk to you," said Mary.

"Me, too," replied Gertie. "Pete had a meeting tonight so I slipped away. There's something I want to tell you, but you'll have to promise me that it won't go any further."

Mary squinted at Gertie. "You look worried. I hope it's not bad news."

"Actually it is, hon, but it's not something that I want anybody else to know."

"If you want me to keep a secret, you know it's safe with me."

"That's true. I'm sure I can trust you." Gertie clutched her hands and bent forward, a strained look on her face. "Remember when I told you Pete dabbled in stocks?"

Mary perked up. "Yes, I remember. You said you didn't pay any attention to what he did with stocks."

"I should have paid attention." Gertie stamped on the floor. "Pete lost a whole lot of our money in the crash. I had no idea he was spending so much on stocks." She paused, a scowl soaring. "Whoosh! Every darned one of them went down the drain. Now we don't have any stocks or any of the money we spent on them."

Mary gasped. "I'm sorry. That's an awful blow. I had no idea you and Pete were having any financial problems."

Gertie eyed Mary. "I shouldn't be telling you this, but I've got to tell someone. I know you have your own problems to worry about, but you're the only friend I can trust. Pete's not telling a soul. He says it'll ruin his reputation as a savvy lawyer. His clients won't trust him to fix the jams they get in if they find out he lost money in the crash . . . so he's acting like things are fine and dandy. We're going to use what I earn teaching school to run the house. I can't save my salary anymore like I've been doing for a long time."

"How terrible, Gertie. That's not fair."

She shrugged. "It'll work out some way, Mary. He'll still have cases when he can get them. We simply have to be more careful about spending from now on."

"Money seems to be a problem whether you have too much or too little," griped Mary. "I always thought you never had any financial woes."

Gertie clicked her tongue. "We never know what we're going to meet down the road, hon. I tell my students that every blessed day. Everybody has good and bad times in life."

"I'm getting scared now, Gertie. People are losing the jobs they've held for years. I'm afraid my bridge classes will be canceled, even though they're only a part-time deal. The check I get makes it worthwhile. I hope that doesn't change. Somehow I have to find a way to send my girls to college so they'll be able to earn a living. I've found out the hard way that you can't count on always having a husband to keep you."

Gertie cleared her throat noisily. "You're smart to put your kids through college. I wish more parents could see how education affects what you do for a living. The only thing most girls think about is finding a husband and having a family. They look at graduation as a time to start looking for a man to marry."

"True," said Mary. "There ought to be a class about careers in high school. That's something we should bring up at our next PBS meeting. Maybe we can make something good happen."

"Agreed," replied Gertie. "I'm for kids learning about different kinds of jobs and the preparation that's needed."

"Lily's as determined about *not* going to college as I am that she's going," said Mary. "I keep telling her how important an education is, hoping she'll see the light. So far it hasn't worked. Any ideas about how I can bring her to accept my way of thinking?"

Gertie nibbled at her lip. "Lily couldn't have a mother who has worked any harder. You've done everything possible to be a wonderful model for your daughter."

"So what can I do?" Mary's tone was beseeching.

Gertie patted Mary on the arm. "Afraid I don't have any help to offer. I've seen how stubborn Lily can be. You know what they say. You can lead a horse to water, but you can't make him drink."

Mary wasn't sure whether or not that was true until she read Lily's theme for Miss Torino's English class.

TIPS FOR DOING HOMEWORK
by Lily Dunmore

1. *Pick a subject YOU like. Example: What's Wrong with Teachers*
2. *Rest first so you are not too tired to push the pencil.*
3. *Find two good pencils with real good erasers.*
4. *Use paper that has lines.*
5. *Think hard about what YOU WANT to write.*
6. *Look in a book or magazine for ideas.*
7. *Eat a snack to get energy for writing.*
8. *Fix a good drink for when your throat dries up.*
9. *Go to a private place where no one can disturb you.*
10. *Make a DO NOT DISTURB sign to stick on the door.*
11. *Get in a comfy position on the bed.*
12. *Write.*

Note: If you fall asleep, start over where you left off. Cats are a help if you read aloud to them what you write. They purr if they like it.

Chapter 38

Mary finished answering Andy's letter dated September 1, 1930. He was good to write her every few months. Andy was climbing up in the ranks and had his eye on becoming one of the top brass so to speak. From time to time he mentioned that he'd like to be a Colonel some day. He moved around the country now and then but was never near enough the Dunmore house to drop in. Nobody else in the family bothered to take pen in hand except Hannah and Rebecca. Occasionally Mary's sisters sent pretty picture postcards with a line or two scribbled in pencil. Hannah was having a nifty time keeping up with her husband, Matt, and Faith who seemed to be a live wire in middle school. Sometimes she was put out of class and had to stand in the hall. Rebecca still clerked at Mays Department Store but hadn't met a man that she wanted to snag for a husband. Occasionally she mentioned going to a play or movie with a friend.

Mary wished her kin lived closer so they could pay each other a visit once in a while. She could hardly believe Tom had already been gone for over six years. The loneliness that had plagued her ever since his death was eased somewhat by staying busy. The Great Depression held its grip, but she still taught a weekly bridge class in Pittsburgh. Presenting a lesson and chatting with ladies who were eager to play cards brought about a sense of accomplishment. Being elected Eastern Star Secretary also added to her well being.

During the School Board meetings, Mary kept members up-to-date about what PBS was doing to help pupils. She invited Jack Thompson and Nick Pecori to the sessions and persuaded them to schedule weekly assemblies that informed pupils about careers. Workers in West Park began appearing on the stage at Stowe High every Friday. They described their jobs and answered questions. A carpenter, bank president, fireman, secretary, electrician, nurse, and restaurant owner had talked about their duties at work.

Comments about the assemblies were positive except for Lily's. "I don't care about any of those jobs, Mother. Why don't you get a musician to talk?" Before long, Sean Foster stood on the stage and described how he had become a music teacher, band/orchestra director, and study hall manager, rolled into one. Lily hung onto every word but asked no questions.

Mary pondered about becoming a Worthy Matron in the Eastern Star. She recalled her intimidation when Principal Thompson persuaded her to take Tom's seat on the board. She was the only woman, surrounded by six men. That alone triggered a chill. Nevertheless, elation bloomed after she offered her ideas about how the schools could be improved. The board actually paid attention to what she said and posed questions.

Gertie was quick to express her thoughts about Mary's becoming Worthy Matron. "You preside at PBS. You're on the School Board. No other woman in West Park or McKees Rocks has ever done those things. By golly, Mary, you're qualified. You have to become a Worthy Matron, not only for yourself but for womanhood."

Mary's eyes danced with laughter. "Those things just happened to me."

"Baloney," declared Gertie. "Your daughters will be tickled pink when you become the leader of the Eastern Star."

Lily's June graduation was peeping 'round the corner. Her dreams centered on wearing a special dress. "I don't want one you make, Mother. I want a dress from Hornes. We have to go to town so I can find the right one."

Mary twitched. "I'd rather make it, Lily. You can pick out any pattern you want. That would be cheaper and easier than buying a dress."

Lily dug her nails into her palms and fastened her gaze on her mother. "Everybody's buying a gown for the prom. I'm not going, but I deserve an extra-special dress . . . not a homemade one. I want one from Hornes."

"You should have that dress," replied Mary, anticipating a challenge.

"Can't be like anybody else's, Mother. Can't be. Can't be," echoed Lily.

"I know, sweetie. You only graduate once from high school. You should have an extra-special dress."

"We'll walk across the stage and get our diploma. That'll be scary. I want to look my very best."

"Everybody will look alike, honey. The robes will cover up what you're wearing."

Lily jerked. "Gosh, I never thought of that." She wiggled her head. "Well, I still want an extra-special dress for my graduation."

"And you shall have it," promised Mary, patting Lily on the back. "I imagine you'll practice lining up on the stage and find out exactly what you're supposed to do."

"Um." Lily slapped her palms together. "I'm glad *I* don't have to give a speech. Caroline Huffaker is real jumpy about being valedictorian. What can she say? That she sat in a lot of boring classes and is glad she's finished now? That's what I'd say."

Mary was staunch. "Caroline will do fine. I'm certain she doesn't feel like that. It's an honor to have the highest rank in the whole class."

"She didn't do anything but study, study, study," flared Lily.

Mary gave her a pointed look. "That's what Caroline wanted to do. Now she's reaping the benefits. Gertie said two colleges have offered Caroline a scholarship."

Lily looked toward the ceiling and sniffed. "So? I heard she's going to the Prom with Billy Modarelli. Must have learned how to dance when she wasn't cramming."

"*You've* never gone to a dance," twitted Rose.

"I can still dance any time I want to." Lily whirled around the room for a second, her eyes blazing. "See?"

Rose shrank. "Hope I get to go to dances. And I wanna have dates, too. When can I have dates, Mother?"

Mary sank down on the bed. "It will be a long time before you have any dates, Rose. First, you have to be 16. Then someone has to ask you for a date. Go downstairs now, Lily. It's time for you to give Rose her piano lesson while I drum up some supper."

They hurried from the room, Mary trailing behind. She wished she was graduating from high school and had a diploma in hand, proving her completion of the required courses. That would be ecstasy beyond belief. A tear blurred her eye, and she wiped it away with the back of her hand.

Stowe High's orchestra presented its first annual concert one week before graduation. Lily's name appeared on the program. One of the orchestra's selections was *The Blue Danube*, featuring a piano solo by Lily Dunmore. She smiled after the crowd applauded generously. Sean motioned Lily to stand and take a bow. The audience clapped harder.

"That really felt good," she told her mother afterwards. "I loved it."

"You played beautifully, Lily. I hope your father was listening, even though he wasn't wild about music. I'm very proud of you. You're graduating from high school, too. That's far more than I ever accomplished."

It took two trips to Hornes before Lily found a dress that suited. Lavender taffeta with a circular skirt in walking length. The blouse was empire style, trimmed with lace. Patent leather shoes and silk stockings completed her outfit.

Back stage on the evening of graduation, Lily made a face when she donned her maroon robe. Her extra-special dress was hidden underneath from every eye. "Nobody will see how pretty it is," she complained.

Albert Moritz, the class clown, pulled open his robe and showed her his red plaid underwear. Lily gasped and turned away. She peeped from behind the curtain to spot Mary, Rose, and Gertie. They were seated in the third row of the auditorium.

"We can't stay together because we have to be in alphabetic order," Lily whispered to Nellie Wolferman. "I'll look out there and smile real big at my mother when I get my diploma."

The moment came. Lily was so scared all she could do was clutch her diploma and disappear behind the curtain.

Chapter 39

Two weeks after graduation, Mary and Lily rode the trolley to Pittsburgh Musical Institute where they met Dr. Serge Lenel, Lily's new piano teacher. With his graying hair and pale blue eyes cornered by furrows, he was a far cry from energetic Sean Foster. Dr. Lenel always wore a starched white shirt and a black bow tie as though it was a compulsory uniform. His shoes were shined to a mirror finish. He had a habit of staring at them and stroking his chin thoughtfully whenever a pupil played poorly. Lily adored him from the beginning. The highlight of her week was the day when she arrived at PMI for a lesson. It wasn't long before she started taking more pains about her appearance, powdering her face, wearing lipstick and brushing her straight hair until it glistened.

Mary insisted that Lily continue giving Rose piano lessons. "They're expensive. We need to get all we can out of them. I can't afford lessons for both of you girls. You'll have to teach Rose whatever Dr. Lenel teaches you."

Lily glared at her sister. Rose was tickled and began to giggle. "Maybe I'll learn to play good as you, Sis."

The two girls were never friends at the piano. Eyes sparked, voices tangled, and faces flushed whenever they sat side by side on the bench. The day came when Mary wasn't nearby and Lily twisted Rose's wrist because she wouldn't pay attention.

Privately, Mary asked Rose why she disliked her lessons. Rose complained in a stout voice. "Lily always tells me I ought to do better, no matter how good I play . . . and she makes me use exactly the same fingering that she does on every piece. Whoever listens never knows what fingers I use so why does it matter, Mother?"

During that summer, life at the Dunmore's home began to change. The family had oodles of time to kill. Even though the weather was warm, the root beer and ice ball business slowed down. Dave didn't want to go to the trouble of making root beer, and the Isaly's store on the corner of Broadway was turning kids onto Popsicles. Many Dunmore customers bought refrigerators instead of ice. They paid for Frigidaires on the installment plan—so much every month. Mary shook her head. She knew that she was lucky to still have some ice business. Every little bit of money counted.

One evening when Mary was getting supper, she cornered Lily. "You have to start looking for a job, sweetie. We only had a few customers today, even though it was hot. The icehouse can't keep running without customers. We need more money to live on."

Lily frowned and turned away, paying attention to setting the table. "You know I'm headed for the concert stage, Mother. I can't spare any time for a job. I've got to practice."

"You have miles to go before that can ever happen, Lily. So far you haven't even played in a recital."

"I will. I will. Don't worry. Dr. Lenel said I might be ready by this fall. All I have to do is memorize the sonata."

Rose came upstairs from the cellar and began to fill the iced tea glasses. "I meant to tell you, Mother. Mrs. Millard talked to me today when you sent me to buy bread. I think I have a sort-of job now if it's okay with you."

"What do you mean by a sort-of job?" asked Mary, giving her mashed potatoes a final whip with the big spoon.

Rose perked up. "Mrs. Millard asked if I'd accompany Tillie while she practices singing. Tillie's starting voice lessons. Her teacher says she needs someone to play the piano while she sings. Mrs. Millard wants me to start next week."

"My goodness. How did she know you could play?"

Rose rocked back and forth on her heels. "Well, Mrs. Millard heard that I played for the music teacher at school sometimes. Mrs. Millard said she'd pay me by the hour. One hour three days a week. Fifty cents an hour."

"That's wonderful, Rose. Congratulations on your sort-of job." Mary set the bowl of potatoes on the table. "I believe I'd call that a part-time job."

Lily glared at her sister. "You can't play Tillie's songs. They're too hard for you."

"I'll try," snapped Rose.

Mary untied her apron. Her eyes riveted on Rose. "I'm sure you'll be able to play anything Tillie wants, honey. Supper's ready. Let's eat."

Business at the icehouse became so tortoise-like in August that Mary knew it was time to close down for good. "I hate the thought, but I'm losing money instead of making it," she told Dave. "Please put up a sign so people know we won't be selling ice anymore after the end of this month. The icehouse opened in 1922. You've been a lifesaver for almost ten years. I truly appreciate all the help you've given me. I'd never have managed without you."

"Don't worry about me," replied Dave good-naturedly. "I understand your situation. I'll always be able to find some kind of work. I hope you'll get by okay."

Mary smiled at him. "I'll call on you whenever anything breaks down around here. You have so many talents people will always be hounding you for help."

In September, Mary became the Worthy Matron of the Eastern Star in McKees Rocks. "A couple of months ago Lily was fidgety about going through graduation," she told Gertie. "Now I've got the shivers, worrying about the installation ceremony. You have to help me pick out a dress right away, Gertie."

"I'd love to do that, hon. We'll find something that makes you look like high-class royalty."

Mary winked. "Remember, it has to be extra-special like Lily's graduation dress."

"Don't worry. We'll find one. Lily's eyes will pop when she sees you."

On the way to Hornes, Mary confided in Gertie. "I didn't tell the girls I'm Worthy Matron now. I wanted to surprise them. I feel as though being elected to the highest office is almost like a graduation."

"That's right," agreed Gertie. "You ought to be real proud. They should be, too."

Mary sighed. "I wish Lily could wear her dress again. If she plays in a recital, that dress will be like icing on a cake. Maybe it'll happen. She swears she's going to be on the concert stage, but I wonder. She has talent, but I don't see her performing in public."

"She performed at the orchestra's concert, hon."

Mary nodded. "Sean was clever the way he managed to get her in the public's eye. Her solo went very well when she was part of the orchestra. I wonder what would have happened if she had to perform without the backup of the orchestra."

"I don't know," puzzled Gertie. "I'm sure you'll find out when Lily plays in a recital at PMI."

Mary scratched her chin. "Rose is shy, too, but not like Lily. Rose makes friends on the spot. Lily hangs back. Rose likes school. Lily despises school. Rose wants to go to college. Lily says she won't go to college."

"They're different. That's perfectly normal, Mary. Don't worry about it."

"Easier said than done, Gertie."

An hour of trying on one dress after another resulted in finding the right one. "The Princess gown is the prettiest," commented Mary, standing before the mirror in the dressing room at Hornes. "It's pricey, but I'll go overboard just this once."

"You look lovely," said the sales lady, peeping in the door. "I believe this one's perfect for you."

Mary began to take off the dress. "I wish it wasn't so expensive."

"You deserve to splurge," noted Gertie. "The dress is wonderful on you. You could be a model if you wanted. The satin shimmers against your dark hair, and I love the high neck and the tucks in the bodice. Wear your gold necklace. You'll stand out in the big hall where you're being installed. Let's go home and surprise the girls."

"First we have to find the right shoes for the dress, Gertie."

"Shoes are on the third floor," offered the sales lady. "I'll see to your package."

"I'm tired," said Mary as she and Gertie arrived at the house on Broadway and got out of the car. "Let's have a nice cup of tea."

"I have to get home. Pete and I are invited to a bridge game tonight, and I've got to fix supper. I'm dying to see the reaction of the girls to your dress before I leave."

"I'll try it on then." Mary carried the large box up the porch steps while Gertie held the shoe box.

Lily was playing Beethoven's *Moonlight Sonata* from memory when they walked in. Rose was stretched out on the carpet, poring over the comic pages.

"I've got something to show you," said Mary, starting up the stairs.

Rose jumped up. "What did you bring us?"

"Nothing. I shopped for myself today." Her words were tart.

Lily kept right on memorizing while Gertie trailed Mary. "We'll call you in a few minutes. Make your mother a pot of tea, Lily. She's worn to a nub from shopping."

In the bedroom Mary unpacked the dress and hung it up. She glanced in the mirror and scowled. "I have to freshen my face. I'm as bedraggled as a wet hen."

Gertie opened the shoe box. "These white satin pumps are lovely. They match your gown like they were made for it."

"They cost too darned much, and I'll never wear them again," said Mary, putting on fresh powder and lipstick.

After finishing her make-up, Gertie helped Mary slip into the gown and fastened her gold necklace. "You look absolutely lovely. I can't wait to see the girls' faces," chimed Gertie.

Mary gave her hair a final brush. "I'm ready." She called the girls to come upstairs.

The moment they entered the room, they stopped in their tracks, eyes fixed on Mary.

"What's going on?" gasped Lily.

Rose grinned, her eyes bright. "It's a bridesmaid dress. I'll bet Mother's gonna be in a wedding."

Mary and Gertie looked at each other and broke into hearty laughs.

"Good heavens no," said Mary when she'd calmed down. "I've been elected Worthy Matron in the Eastern Star. This is my extra-special dress from Hornes that I'm wearing for my installation ceremony."

Rose reached out and smoothed her hand lovingly over the satin. "It's so pretty. Remember, I said you'd be a star some day."

Lily stood quietly, taking in her mother. "I wish Daddy could see you now. You're beautiful."

Mary reached out and gathered her girls close.

"Maybe he is seeing her now," murmured Gertie.

Chapter 40

Mary had studied the Eastern Star rituals painstakingly in preparation for being installed. Every word was memorized and spoken, over and over again. She knew for certain that Tom would want her to do well . . . imagined that he was peering down from heaven, keeping track of this important event. The thought hammered that he'd allow no mistakes. Relief abounded when the ceremony proceeded as planned.

She and Gertie left the hall in the Rocks and headed for home in the car. Mary slipped off the new pumps and gave her sore feet a healthy rub. "I can't believe it's finally over. Everything was perfect. Absolutely perfect."

"I told you not to worry, hon. The ceremony was lovely. One you'll always remember, that's for sure." Gertie pulled a rag from the car pocket and treated the windshield to a wipe while she drove with one hand.

"I can't get over my beautiful Eastern Star." Mary looked down at the pin on her dress. "The five diamonds on the points of the star sparkle. They're real diamonds, too."

A chuckle escaped Gertie. "Just wait 'til your girls see that pin. They'll swipe it if they get the chance. You may have to hide it under lock and key."

Mary put her shoes back on. "I feel like a new woman, Gertie. Truly I do. Now that the installation's over, a weight's been lifted off me." She paused, took a deep breath and let out a sigh. "I have to find a project I can undertake as Worthy Matron. It has to be something related to education. Guess I'll have to put on my thinking cap."

"Too bad you aren't a schoolteacher," replied Gertie. "I'm sure you'd be a fine one. You always work hard and make everything come out okay. Everybody I know thinks you're smart."

"Hush, Gertie. I've been thinking about what we could do for the community. Our chapter has always volunteered at Ohio Valley Hospital when they needed help with something. Maybe we could tutor the kids who are laid up there. Lend them a hand in staying up-to-date with their school work, provided they're well enough to do it."

"That sounds like a splendid idea. It would help pass the time as long as they're not too sick to do their lessons. Why don't you find out how everyone feels about that at the next meeting?"

Mary smiled. "Will do."

The day following the installation, Gertie snapped a dozen pictures of Mary wearing her gown. Some of them were made with Lily and Rose at her side. Mary was pleased. "Thanks loads for taking the pictures, Gertie. I'll buy copies and send them to the family right away."

The girls were captivated by the pin adorning Mary's dress. "I'm gonna belong to the Eastern Star so I can get a pin like that," spouted Rose.

"Silly," responded Lily. "They'd never let you in. Not in a million years, kid."

Rose made a monkey face at her sister. "I'll get in. You just wait and see, smarty."

When red roses arrived for Mary from Andy, the girls squealed with delight. Andy's card read, "Way to go, Sis!"

Lily turned ecstatic when she came home after her piano lesson. She laid her music on the piano rack and zipped her fingers up and down the keyboard several times, announcing her arrival. "Guess what, Mother. Dr. Lenel put me on the fall recital program. I played the sonata from memory and didn't foul up. Not even once. He said I was ready to perform."

Mary hurried to the parlor from the kitchen. "That's absolutely marvelous. I'm so proud of you, Lily." She hesitated and wiped her floury hands on her apron. "I'll ask Gertie to join us. She'll want to hear you play. Just think. It's your very first recital."

"I'm going to rehearse at home beforehand. Pretend like I'm in the music hall. Dr. Lenel said that was one way to overcome stage fright."

"Sounds like a smart idea to me," said Mary, happiness streaming that Lily was finally on the path to fulfilling her dream of being a concert pianist.

Recital day arrived. Lily slipped into her extra-special dress. She was pleased when she eyed herself in the full-length mirror in Mother's bedroom. The empire blouse and full skirt made her look taller and slimmer . . . a young lady ready to get a taste of a new life. She went downstairs, holding onto the banister, being careful that she didn't trip on her new high-heeled pumps.

Mary, Rose and Gertie sat on the parlor couch, waiting to become an audience. Lily walked sedately and took her place at the piano. For a second she studied the keyboard, wishing that it was a grand piano instead of an upright. Then she performed the Beethoven sonata from memory without a noticeable mistake. When Lily played the final chord, the onlookers clapped so heartily their hands blushed.

Gertie stood up and cried, "Bravo! Bravo! Bravo!"

Rose snickered and gave her sister a slap on the back.

Mary beamed and hugged Lily. "You'll be fantastic today, sweetie. No need to worry one bit. You know that piece so well you could play it in your sleep." Mary felt a quickening within. For the first time the thought comforted that Lily might really turn out to be a concert pianist some day.

The auditorium was crowded when the Dunmores and Gertie arrived. People milled around in the entrance, exchanging hellos and talking excitedly about their sons and daughters who were going to perform.

Mary squeezed her daughter's hand and whispered, "Good luck, honey." Lily hurried to the front row and took her place with seven other pupils.

As soon as they were settled, Mary focused on the program. Lily was the last one to perform. A quick scan told her that most of the pianists were probably younger than her daughter. Mary nudged Gertie. "It would have been nice if Lily had been first . . . not have to sit on pins and needles waiting for her turn."

"Don't fret, Mary. I promise you, Lily will be the best on the program. I'm sure Dr. Lenel saved the best 'til last."

Mary frowned and pointed to the list. "It'll be an hour before Lily's turn."

Gertie nodded. "You might as well get used to this if she's going to give concerts. Consider this a tryout."

In an effort to ease her jitters when the program started, Mary tried to relax and become limp like a rag doll. But when it was time to clap for someone she had to sit up straight and react. Lily's past performance with the orchestra, followed by a burst of applause, flitted through Mary's mind. Her spirit sailed. While Delia Case was playing Mendelssohn's *On the Seashore*, Mary closed her eyes and imagined that she was lying on a sandy beach where the sun warmed her skin. But as one performer after another took their place at the piano, she began to feel wrung out.

Lily's turn finally came. Mary patted her damp face with a hanky. She watched her daughter move up the steps, the taffeta skirt swishing as she approached the grand piano. Lily sat down, smoothed her skirt and eyed the keyboard. She began to play. The *Moonlight Sonata* flowed . . . familiar, melodious, dreamlike. Mary's tension ebbed. She unwound, folded her hands in her lap and let the sound sink in. Then unexpectedly, the music became garbled. The notes fought each other, battling the theme and turning into mishmash.

Mary froze. Her fingers gripped the edge of her seat. She fixed her gaze on Lily. The jumbled notes continued, on and on and on, making no musical sense whatever. The audience moved about uneasily in their seats. Abruptly the discord ceased. Silence prevailed.

Lily stood up and rushed off the stage, running down the steps and up the aisle toward the exit. An awesome quiet filled the hall except for two claps that died in the air.

Chapter 41

Mary tried everything she could think of to console her daughter after they got home. When sympathetic words failed, Mary snuggled Kitty in the bed with Lily and brought hot cocoa topped with marshmallows. Still, she could not be comforted. The tears kept coming. Finally, Mary gave Lily an aspirin, along with a kiss, and hoped it would put her to sleep.

Upon leaving the bedroom, Mary went to the kitchen. She sank down in Tom's chair to ponder the day. The memory of Lily's fleeing from the music hall cut through like a knife. Outside, Mary had found her daughter leaning up against the brick wall, sobbing about her failure. Mary offered Lily a hug and a hanky, but it was useless in drying up her tears.

"It's all right, sweetie . . . it's all right," Mary had said. "Everybody can forget when they're scared. You simply got stage fright and couldn't remember all that hard music you'd memorized. It was your first time to play in a recital. People understand. Truly they do."

"I'll never be able to perform on the stage. I can't do it," stormed Lily. "I know that now, Mother. It doesn't matter anyway. Dr. Lenel will never give me lessons after what happened."

The next day Mary sent Lily and Rose down street to buy groceries. Intent upon finding out what Dr. Lenel had to say about Lily's behavior, Mary phoned him while the girls were gone. As expected, he was very disturbed that Lily failed to perform.

"Running away has never happened to any of my students until now," he wailed. "I regret it more than I can tell you. I thought Lily was well prepared. She was supposed to be the highlight of the program. I never expected her to play Lord knows what, run off and head for the door. Everybody was flabbergasted."

His lamenting reminded Mary of a preacher's drone at a funeral. She winced and struggled to sound pleasant. "Lily rehearsed before she left home, Dr.

Lenel. We had a make-believe recital. My ten-year old daughter and I, along with a good friend, pretended we were the audience. Lily played the sonata from beginning to end without a hint of a problem. So . . . we were amazed when she lost track of the piece she'd memorized and fled. I think she was frightened. That's all it amounted to."

Mary could hear Dr. Lenel fumbling with the phone. Finally he said, "I was dumbfounded. I recall telling Lily that pretending to be in a recital might be helpful. Some of my students have done that. It worked for a couple of them . . . reduced their anxiety. However, no matter how much you've prepared, you can't be sure what will happen during a recital."

"I figured Lily would do real well, Dr. Lenel. She performed beautifully when she was featured in a solo, combined with the high school orchestra. The audience showered her with applause."

"I know," he replied. "Sean Foster told me about that. He said she was an excellent pupil."

"Lily wants to be a concert pianist, Dr. Lenel. I guess she's told you. Is this realistic for her now?"

He began to cough. "Sorry," he said when he'd cleared his throat. "The fall ragweed's getting to me. Lily never expressed that wish to me." He paused. "Certainly she has talent and plays well. She's above average, and I'm pleased to work with her. But . . . becoming a concert artist, well, for many musicians that's only a pipe dream that never comes true."

Mary gripped the phone harder. "Are you telling me that Lily should stop taking lessons, Dr. Lenel?"

"No, of course not. Talented musicians keep learning over a lifetime. As I said, Lily has considerable ability that can be used in many ways. She can enjoy playing for herself as well as for others. Perhaps after more study she might become a piano teacher. If she earned a degree in music, she could teach in the public schools. Maybe she'd like to play for church services. Libraries and music stores hire people who have a musical background. There are many possibilities, believe me."

"I'm glad to know that," replied Mary. "I want my daughter to fend for herself . . . not depend on somebody else for a livelihood. She has a high school diploma and isn't interested in college. I think Lily needs to look for a job now."

"I understand. I'm glad you called me, Mrs. Dunmore. I'll talk to Lily when she comes for her lesson and see if I can be of help."

"I'd appreciate that very much. Thank you, Dr. Lenel."

Mary hung up and reflected. Lily would be better off if she had a college education, but she didn't want it. Tom's efforts to turn her into a schoolteacher failed. Instead, Rose was the one who played teacher in the cellar because she wanted to.

Mary left the parlor and went to the kitchen. Standing at the back door window, she gazed at the icehouse, its door shut tight, red-gold leaves piling up on the porch. Once upon a time people stood in the alley, buying ice to keep their food fresh. Now, refrigerators were replacing iceboxes. The icehouse was no longer a money-maker. That put a dent in the budget, a real concern when she planned on sending Lily and Rose to college.

Mary opened the cupboard and stared at her pickle jar, stuffed with money. "Count your blessings," she shouted. "Stop worrying about Lily's tuition. Save for Rose's tuition."

She began to laugh, harder and harder until the sound bounced off the walls. Then she stopped, took a deep breath and grabbed her apron off the hook. She gasped. "The girls will think I've lost my mind if they catch me talking to myself."

At that moment Lily and Rose opened the landing door and came up the steps to the kitchen, their arms loaded with groceries. "Let's eat," they chorused, dumping the bags on the counter and beginning to empty them.

Mary searched Lily's face. No trace of tears. She seemed like herself. Relief hovered. Lily would be heartbroken if Dr. Lenel canceled her lessons. Mary took a deep breath and peered at her daughter.

"By the way, I talked to Dr. Lenel on the phone while you were gone. He's expecting you for your lesson at the regular time."

Lily flashed a bright smile at her mother. "Great."

Mary smiled right back.

Chapter 42

Winter arrived with its temperamental gales and fury. Pelting rains often turned into sleet that made the streets slick as glass. When there was snow, the wind blew flakes in whatever direction it chose, making walking and transportation treacherous. Mary and Lily had to take care not to fall when they caught the trolley on the corner. All of the Dunmores wore galoshes to keep their feet dry.

The house never became warm enough when the weather dipped close to zero. In the evenings, the family took turns sitting by the parlor register, toasting their toes. Mary had already talked to Dave about installing a stoker that would feed coal to the furnace and eliminate doing it by hand. She was worn to a frazzle from shoveling that made her back ache.

"Another thing on my to-do list that will be expensive. I'm having the furnace fixed when summer gets here," she promised her girls.

But no matter how bad the weather, Mary kept the monthly PBS meetings going strong, like Tom would have wanted. On the heels of persuading the principals to hold weekly assemblies about careers, Mary led the members in developing a program they named *Job Pursuit*. The high school pupils were allowed to spend one day with a worker of their choice, learning about a particular job. Mary presented the plan to Jack Thompson and Nick Pecori. They applauded the idea, and the board approved the program to begin in the spring.

One afternoon Mary met with Thompson and Pecori to finalize the plan. Thompson tilted his head and concentrated on Mary. "Spring is the best time to visit companies. Pupils are tired of school and look forward to getting out. This program might motivate them and decrease absences. It could improve our graduation rate, too."

"I'd appreciate having a list of the requirements for graduation," said Mary. "That information would be useful for PBS members. I'm sure they'd like to know exactly what pupils have to accomplish in order to graduate from high school."

"We'll make copies for you to hand out to your group," offered Pecori.

"Thank you." Mary hesitated. "There's another matter I need your help on."

Thompson's bushy eyebrows curled. "What's that?"

"I'm Worthy Matron in the Eastern Star now. The members have agreed to undertake a project named *Catch-Up*, provided it's approved. Volunteers from the Eastern Star will tutor children who are laid up at Ohio Valley Hospital. If the pupils are well enough to study, we'd like to help them keep up with their lessons as long as they can't attend class. Of course, we'd need the permission and cooperation of the principals, parents, and teachers at every school that has a hospitalized pupil."

Pecori slid his hands back and forth over the smooth arms of his chair. "Sounds worthwhile but seems like plenty of hard work to me. You'd have to get the assignments and the books for every child that enters the hospital. At the same time, your volunteers would need to have a real good handle on the subjects."

"Of course," responded Mary, "but that's not a problem. Some of our members are high school graduates."

Pecori straightened up, concern on his face. "Appears to me you're undertaking way too much. You'd be looking after *Catch-Up* this winter and *Job Pursuit* in the spring. That would be a ton of responsibility."

Mary nodded. "Of course, I'd have to talk to the hospital administration and get their approval. If they want the program, that'll be great. The attendance and graduation rates at the schools would probably benefit. When pupils fall behind in their lessons, they often give up. This program should keep that from happening."

"You may be biting off more than you can chew," said Thompson, getting up, signaling that the meeting was over.

"I can do it," declared Mary with a smile.

She said goodbye and hurried away with hope in her heart.

Miss Francesca Bukowski, Head Counselor at Ohio Valley Hospital, welcomed Mary. "How can I help you?"

"I want to help *you*," replied Mary pleasantly.

She described *Catch-Up* and appreciated the way Miss Bukowski seemed to be relishing every word. The counselor's dark eyes shone above her pale yellow shirtwaist. "We've never had anybody who wanted to help us like this. Undoubtedly, it will be a labor of love. Sometimes we have children who have broken a leg or an arm. Maybe they're sick with an awful case of the flu. They have to stay with us a while. Then they're lost when they return to school. That has to dash their hopes."

"For sure," said Mary. "We'd like to try this out and see how it works. If the principals, teachers, and volunteers cooperate and the pupils complete their assignments, it will be for the good. What a blessing if everyone graduated from high school."

The counselor nodded. "Having that diploma is mighty important. It's the stepping stone to employment. I'll discuss this matter with the president and get back to you as soon as I can."

"I'll appreciate it," added Mary, recalling that Lily's diploma was lying in a drawer in her bedroom. So far it hadn't been a speck of help in Lily's getting a job.

After Mary read the graduation requirements that Pecori gave her, an idea popped up. She'd pored over all the books that Thompson left for Lily when he and Pecori paid the Dunmores a visit. Every text had been studied, cover to cover. Her notebook was chock-full of information. Feeling bold, she made an appointment to meet with Thompson and Pecori again. Despite hating to admit that she lacked a diploma, Mary decided to tell the principals that her schooling was sparse. She tried to look at ease while facing them, even though a clamminess overtook her.

"I have a personal request to make," she said. "When you asked me to take Tom's place on the board, I began to learn a great deal about our education system. I grew up in the country where there was only a grade school. Still, I read every book I could get hold of. Later, I got a job at the A&P in Pittsburgh and learned a lot, especially about numbers. After I married and had children, I paid attention to what they studied at school. You handed my daughter, Lily, her Stowe High School diploma in June. Now *I* would like to earn a diploma. Is that possible in this day and age?"

Thompson scrutinized Pecori. Pecori stared right back. The room was silent while their minds churned. Then Thompson cleared his throat nervously and leaned back in his chair. "Nobody has ever asked us that question. Guess we'll have to give it some thought."

Mary clasped her hands together, seeking comfort. "I understand that seniors take tests to see if they'll graduate in June. Can I take those tests? I'd like to see my grade."

The principals gazed at each other again as though their thoughts were running from head to head.

After a minute, Pecori broke the silence. "The senior exams are given in May. Maybe we can arrange for you to take them."

Thompson grunted. "Since you're on the board, we might get by with doing that. We'll have to think about whether it could cause a problem, but . . . we couldn't give you a diploma, even if you passed those tests." He shook his head hard. "It wouldn't be on the up-and-up. You haven't attended class and you're an adult."

A glimmer lit up Mary's face. "I understand, but I'd be grateful if you'd let me take those tests and see whether I could pass."

"We'll look into the matter, Mrs. Dunmore," said Thompson, getting up abruptly.

"Thank you. Thank you very much." Mary headed to the door. She left the office, her heart pounding with expectancy.

Chapter 43

By the time daffodils began to sprout, announcing spring's arrival, Mary was alive with accomplishments. The Eastern Star volunteers had tutored five pupils who had been hospitalized. Four of them were laid up with broken bones while one was seriously ill with whooping cough. Their work was up-to-date when they returned to class, thanks to *Catch-Up*.

Twenty-one boys and fifteen girls had spent a day in April at a company, learning about a particular job. Afterwards, they wrote papers describing their experiences. The stories were printed in the Gazette, along with pictures of the pupils at the work sites. *Job Pursuit* was labeled an outstanding success that should be held every year to acquaint seniors with the workplace.

"Seems as though this venture was a smash," commented Thompson, handing the paper to Pecori. "We've never had this much favorable press before."

Pecori settled down and began to read. After finishing, he raised a quizzical brow and gave Thompson a bright look. "I believe we hit the jackpot real big this time. Guess we'll have to let Mary Dunmore take those exams after all."

Thompson's fist hit the desk. "Better hope we don't end up in a ditch. We were sure lucky that nobody raised cane about giving her Tom's seat on the Board."

Thompson and Pecori finally dredged up enough courage to approve Mary's taking the senior finals. Thompson phoned her Saturday morning and warned, "Don't advertise what you're doing. We'll keep this under our hats. No telling how the public will view this. The whole idea is risky."

Mary was ecstatic. "Wonderful. Of course, you understand that my girls will have to know what I'm doing, Mr. Thompson. There's no way I can hide it from them. Thanks for helping me." She hung up and told Lily and Rose the good news.

"I don't see why you want to take those awful exams," spat Lily. "What good will that do?"

"It will give me an idea of how much I know and don't know," retorted Mary.

Rose gave Lily a fierce stare. "You're afraid Mother will do better than you on those tests."

"Don't be a smart aleck," replied Lily.

"Simmer down," ordered Mary. "I'm going to phone Gertie."

Rose slipped off to the corner drug store while her mother was having a long-winded conversation about taking the exams. "You have to promise not to tell anyone, Gertie."

"I promise," vowed Mary's best friend. "I teach stenographic skills so I don't have anything to do with those senior exams."

Rose returned from the store and handed her mother a surprise present. "I love having money to spend." She waved her arms in the air while Lily looked askance.

"Thanks, honey, but you shouldn't have," said Mary, putting on the pretty flower pin. "I love it, but I want you to save your money. You'll need it for college."

"I have plenty of time to save money, Mother. It's fun playing the piano for Tillie. It doesn't even seem like a job. The other day Mrs. Millard asked if I could teach piano. That made me feel grown-up."

"She what?" flared Lily.

Rose grinned. "Mrs. Millard said her niece wants to take lessons."

"I hope Mrs. Millard knows that you can't teach piano," spit out Lily.

Rose cornered her sister. "I can play. Why can't I teach?"

"You're not taking lessons from Dr. Lenel like I am. You have plenty more to learn, squirt."

"You don't teach piano to anyone except me, and I don't pay you," taunted Rose.

Lily clouded up. "I can teach if I want. Dr. Lenel said the only way I'd know if I could teach was to try it."

Mary stood with hands on her hips. "So why don't you, Lily? It's almost a year since you graduated. I can't keep paying for those expensive lessons. It's high time you started teaching or found a job."

Lily was stunned. "I don't know how to find a job, Mother."

Mary's exasperation rose. "Tell Mrs. Millard you've taken piano lessons ever since grade school. Tell her you've taught Rose. Be sure to say you'd love to teach Mrs. Millard's niece. You have to hunt work, Lily. It doesn't hunt you."

The senior tests were given on four days—Monday through Thursday. Mary expected to sit in a classroom with students who'd stare at her. Knots were beginning to tie up her stomach. She planned on finding a seat in the back of the room where most of the kids wouldn't pay attention to her. Undoubtedly, she was invading what they considered to be their private space. Fortunately, after entering the school office early Monday morning, a clerk led her to a corner table in the library, usually reserved for a pupil who was isolated due to bad behavior. Mary began to breathe easier when a clerk delivered the exams. Miss Louisa Halenda, librarian, kept a watchful eye and used a timer to tell Mary when to start and stop each section.

An hour was allowed for lunch. To avoid being seen, Mary brought a peanut butter sandwich from home and depended on the hall fountain for a quick drink of water. She slipped in and out of the girls' lavatory when no one else was around. By the time Thursday arrived, her brain was numb from thinking and her fingers were numb from writing. It was then that she fathomed why Lily disliked school. After finishing the last test, Mary felt as though a great weight had been lifted off her shoulders.

"I survived," she told Gertie later. "Getting an education is like being a soldier heading into battle."

When Mary reached home, she was startled as she headed up the walk. A metal sign was propped up on the banister out front—PIANO LESSONS. The door opened before she reached it. Lily and Rose stood there, looking amused.

"Well," said Mary, "this certainly is a surprise. Where on earth did you find the sign?"

"We made it out of stuff we found in Dad's workbench," said Rose. "They didn't have a sign we could use at the hardware."

Mary entered the house, laughing to herself. "It looks great, girls. I'm glad you had the notion. I hope you get some pupils, Lily."

"I already have one," she announced in a perky tone. "I talked to Mrs. Millard. Her niece will be here tomorrow afternoon for her first lesson."

Mary broke into a smile. "Fantastic, Lily. I'm proud of you."

Rose clicked her tongue. "I told Mrs. Millard her niece could borrow my beginner books, Mother. I don't need them anymore."

Mary grinned at Lily. "Maybe I'll start taking lessons from you."

Lily snickered. "Good. You can be my second pupil. I'll even teach you for free, Mother."

Chapter 44

Mary was jubilant when Thompson called one week later. "You've passed the senior exams with flying colors. You made an A on every test, Mrs. Dunmore."

"I can't believe it," she cried. "I can't believe it." After a moment, "Gosh, wish I had something to show that I passed."

Thompson cleared his throat noisily. "You were told that there's no way we can issue a diploma. I'm sorry, but you're to be congratulated on what you've done."

"I'd really like to have my tests so I can see the grades, Mr. Thompson."

"Afraid we can't do that. The pupils don't get theirs back either. That could cause all kinds of problems."

She sighed. "I understand. Thanks for making it possible for me to take the exams."

Mary hung up, victorious, yet unfulfilled. Having a diploma in hand would be pure satisfaction.

When she told Lily and Rose that she'd passed with a high grade, they cackled but couldn't understand why she didn't get a diploma. "Remember, I wasn't a pupil," explained Mary. "The schools have to follow rules. I didn't attend classes or do homework, but now I'm educated. I just can't prove it."

She wrote to Andy and told him what she'd done. He sent her a Noah Webster dictionary. The card read, "This will last longer than flowers, Sis. Congratulations on your graduation!"

Abigail Hendrickson, a sunny-haired second-grader, arrived for her first piano lesson popping bubble gum. She thought school was a good time. Her mother gave Lily and Mary a searching look. "Abigail couldn't wait to get here. She's always wanted to learn how to play the piano."

"That's good, Mrs. Hendrickson. The lesson will take about an hour since it's her first one," explained Lily in an unusually sweet voice.

"Have fun, Abigail. I'll be back to fetch you." Mrs. Hendrickson hurried away.

Mary settled in the kitchen and edged her chair up close to the wall. She was showered with guilt but determined to eavesdrop and find out how Lily would teach Abigail. Surely Lily wouldn't be a killjoy like she was when teaching Rose. Mary listened intently while Abigail blew a bubble that burst.

Abigail snickered. "I can't wait to play a song. Will I be able to play one today?"

"I hope so. We'll have to wait and see," replied Lily. "First, get rid of your gum please."

Abigail stuck it in a wrapper. That accomplished, Lily said, "Now I want you to learn the names of the fingers. We're going to give them numbers."

Mary swallowed over the lump in her throat. She pressed her ear against the wall, trying to catch every sound in the parlor.

Fifteen minutes later, Lily and Abigail were playing *Three Blind Mice* together as though it was a duet.

"This is fun," squealed Abigail. "I love it. I love it."

The words were music to Mary's ears. Satisfied that the lesson was going well, she moved away from the wall and picked up the paper. A headline caught her eye.

AMELIA EARHART FLIES SOLO ACROSS THE ATLANTIC OCEAN

On May 20, 1932, Amelia Earhart, nicknamed "Lady Lindy" after the celebrated Charles Lindbergh, took off at 7:12 p.m. in her single-engine red Lockheed Vega from Newfoundland, Canada. She carried nothing but a thermos of hot soup. Bad weather set in with a vengeance as she flew out over the Atlantic. The plane's wings soon became coated with ice, forcing her to fly at low altitudes, sometimes only 75 feet above the waves. A broken altimeter made it impossible to tell how high she was flying. One time the plane dropped almost 3,000 feet and went into a spin. Flames shot out of the exhaust manifold. Gasoline leaked into the cockpit.

After a harrowing trip lasting 15 hours and 18 minutes, Earhart landed in a farmer's field on May 21 near Londonderry, Ireland. She had made the second solo flight across the Atlantic. The first one was done by Lindbergh in 1927. Earhart not only completed the first flight across the Atlantic by a woman. She also finished the longest nonstop flight by a woman—2,026 miles.

As a child, Earhart's parents encouraged her to play sports, including baseball and football. She enjoyed fishing with the boys. After her first 10-minute airplane ride, there was no doubt in her mind that she wanted to fly.

Earhart served as a nurse for wounded soldiers in the World War. Later, she studied at Columbia University but dropped out and worked in California to pay for her flying lessons. During 1921-1922, Earhart took lessons from Neta Snook, the first female graduate from the Curtiss School of Aviation. The Federation Aeronatique Internationale awarded Earhart a pilot's license in 1922. She co-founded the Ninety-Niners in 1929, an organization composed of 99 charter members who promoted women's participation and opportunities in aviation.

Crossing the Atlantic solo plunges Earhart into the celebrity world. No doubt she will receive many prestigious awards in the coming days. Her independent spirit, determination, and courage are bound to encourage women to explore and travel new roads.

Mary read the story over and over again. How could a woman do such daring things? Be a nurse in the World War . . . fly a plane solo over the Atlantic Ocean. Such daring!

Thoughts whirled. Mary shook her head and muttered, "I'm 42 and don't even have a high school diploma. I've got to do more with my life."

Chapter 45

Gertie dropped by for a visit. They settled on the front porch swing where they could enjoy the daffodils that were beginning to bloom in the flower boxes Tom had made. "Congratulations, Mary! I know how excited you are about passing those senior tests. You can't complain anymore about not having an education."

Mary looked doubtful. "I'm thankful I took those exams and made a good grade, but I still don't have a diploma, Gertie. Nothing to prove that I passed. If I tried to get a job, who'd ever believe that I took those tests?"

"It's a rotten shame, that's what it is," said Gertie. "I wish there was some way you could get that darned piece of paper you earned. You've taught classes, even if they weren't in a high school. Nobody ever asked if you had a diploma, did they?"

"No. Not even once." Mary leaned back and slapped her thighs. "But if I wanted some kind of job—like teaching school for instance—it would be impossible."

Gertie clicked her tongue. "I'm afraid you'd need a college diploma to do that, Mary."

"No college would admit me. I don't have a high-school diploma."

Gertie was surprised. "I had no idea you wanted to teach in high school."

Mary brightened. "I've been thinking about it lately. I'd love to teach English. I got that notion when I studied those books Mr. Thompson left here for Lily. I remember how she hated the writing assignments in English class." Mary gripped her hands together and gave them a shake. "If I taught, by darn I'd make the subject entertaining."

"Now exactly how on earth would you do that?"

Mary gave the swing a hard push with her feet. "If I taught English, I'd turn the class into a company. Each pupil would have a title, something like President, Treasurer, Secretary, or Assistant. Instead of writing those paragraphs and themes that kids hate, they'd compose memos, letters, or rough drafts.

Then they'd be delivered to the proper person in the business. I'd oversee the pupils as they worked and offer help when it was needed. After the allotted time arrived, the company employees would read their mail aloud. The class would offer comments—good or bad. Finally, I'd give everybody's work a grade . . . privately, of course."

Gertie's eyebrows arched. "Wow, that sounds first-rate."

Mary shrugged. "I'll never get to try it so my dream is worthless."

"Keep on dreaming." Gertie pushed a stray curl away from her face. "You've already accomplished more than any other woman I know." She hesitated. "By the way, I like that sign you've put out. It's good that Lily's started teaching piano now."

"The sign was Lily and Rose's idea. It's about time Lily got a job. If she's not headed for college, I want her to go to work. Earn her own way and learn how to take care of herself. Maybe she'll make teaching piano her career. I'd like to know she can manage if she never marries."

"Good thinking, Mary. I'll spread the word that she's teaching. Lots of people want to learn how to play the piano."

Mary pointed to the newspaper on the nearby end table. "Did you read that story about Amelia Earhart?"

"Sure did. Wasn't that something? She's one smart woman who can do anything she sets her mind on."

"Right-o," replied Mary. "Seems nothing stops her. She even dropped out of college. Then, to beat all, she went on to become famous."

Gertie snickered. "I don't think that happens very often."

Mary turned to Gertie and gave her a searching look. "I'd never have the nerve to attempt what Amelia did. How'd you feel when you started college?"

Gertie threw up her hands. "Scared stiff. It was so different from high school. There were only a few girls, and I didn't know a soul. The guys stared holes in me like I was invading their territory . . . had no right to be there. And the professors were strict, some of them standoffish. I worked my tail off, trying to keep up with the assignments and studying for exams. No matter how bad the weather was, I still made it to class on the streetcar. I was never late, never missed a class either."

"How'd it go when you had to start teaching, Gertie?"

She groaned. "I taught two classes for a whole term. Believe me, I had the willies, but I made up my mind I'd get through it no matter what. After all the hills I'd climbed, I wasn't giving up. I went in that room where a supervisor gawked at me, listened to every word that came out of my mouth and watched every move I made. I finally got my degree."

"Are you glad you're a teacher, Gertie?"

She grinned. "Sure. I've never been sorry I became a teacher. It won't make me rich, but I think I've been able to help some people."

Mary sighed. "Gosh, college sounds real tough. I've always heard you're a fine teacher. You should be proud."

"You, too, Mary. Everybody around here thinks you're outstanding. No other woman in this town is on the School Board. You're President of PBS and a Worthy Matron. Besides all that, you look after two girls and run a house by yourself since your husband passed."

"I still don't have a diploma," groaned Mary.

Chapter 46

Mary got off the trolley and headed up the walk to Triangle University in Pittsburgh. It was a sunny July day with wispy clouds nesting in the blue sky. Students streamed by, headed for class or a quick bite at the Keystone Grill across the street. They were wearing shorts and shirts, relieved to be rid of the cumbersome sweaters and coats they bundled up in when the weather was bitter cold. She gripped her handbag tighter for reassurance and glanced down at her blue cotton dress, copied from a manikin in a window at Hornes. The neckline was draped and accented with a pretty bow. She wore high-heeled Vitality shoes, her gold wedding ring and a Hamilton wristwatch fastened by a velvet strap. Her chestnut brown hair was short now and easier to manage. She hated having it cut, but women were bent on making their lives simpler in 1932.

Mary approached the brick archway, her heart fluttering with excitement. For a scant moment relief wafted. Nobody appeared to be paying her any mind. She had expected that college students would gawk at a 42-year-old lady from West Park, a melting pot where people of many nationalities lived, learned, and worked. Women that age didn't set foot in a college.

A tall, slim man leaving the building headed toward her. He carried a black leather briefcase and wore gold-rimmed glasses that caught the sunshine. He gave her a glance and a broad smile. Probably one of those professors she'd read about. An air of importance swirled around him as he passed, prompting her to walk faster. She swept through the doorway and took a deep breath, amazed that she was actually entering a university.

The overhead lights were dazzling. She stood still and glanced around, collecting her thoughts and figuring which way to go. Her eyes settled on an Admissions sign accented with a red arrow. She walked in that direction for a short distance and came to an office where young people waited at a counter. She got in line, sensing that they were paying attention to her because she looked different from everybody else. When her turn came, Mary told the clerk that she wished to speak to someone about enrolling.

"First, you need to submit an application, along with your high school transcript," directed Anna Persutti, a tow-headed girl with a nametag pinned on her white eyelet blouse. She slid a form through the opening in the window.

Mary clasped the paper and hurried to a section of the room where young people, mostly fellows, sat in armchairs, filling out papers. She spied a seat in the back row, sat down and concentrated on reading. In a matter of moments she realized that it was impossible to write even one word. Grade point average, courses taken and grades, and class rank were questions for which she had no answers. It rankled that she had no high school transcript and no diploma. Mary nibbled anxiously at her lip and put on her thinking cap.

Half an hour later, she headed to the administrative offices on the other side of the building. Standing before the entrance labeled Administration in bold brass letters, she murmured a prayer.

"Stay the course," she whispered and opened the door. A lemony aroma from a large potted plant on the floor brought a welcome breath of relief. The only person in the room was the receptionist. With head held high, Mary approached the desk.

The girl with flamingo rose fingernails and lips to match stopped typing and looked up. "May I help you?"

Mary smiled. "I'd like to talk to the director of curriculum please."

The receptionist frowned and puzzled for a second. "Dr. Walter McNeese is the Curriculum Director. You don't have an appointment, do you?"

"No."

"Dr. McNeese can't see you now. Do you want to make an appointment?" The girl's voice was needle sharp.

"No. I had business to take care of in Admissions and got through sooner than I expected. I thought it might be possible to finish my work while I'm here and not have to make another trip."

The receptionist flipped a page of her July 1932 desk calendar. "He can see you tomorrow afternoon at half-past two. Your name?"

Mary stiffened. "Mrs. Mary Dunmore. I can't come tomorrow." She watched while the receptionist hurriedly scanned pages in her calendar.

"Dr. McNeese has some time next week—Monday afternoon at half-past two."

Mary edged closer and spoke firmly. "I'm on the School Board at Stowe High in West Park. I want to talk to Dr. McNeese about setting up workshops for our teachers."

Momentarily the receptionist became flustered, then recovered. "Please wait while I find out if Dr. McNeese has time to see you." She hurried down the hallway behind her station, her high heels clicking a tune on the tiles. Several minutes later she returned with a satisfied look on her face.

"He'll talk to you now, Mrs. Dunmore." She pointed. "It's the second door on the right."

Dr. McNeese was a heavy-set man with a sparkle in his gray eyes and a pale moustache that hid most of his upper lip. He rose from his executive chair behind the mahogany desk and motioned. "Have a seat, Mrs. Dunmore. What can I do for you?"

"It was good of you to see me, Dr. McNeese. I know you're a very busy man." She took the chair he offered and briefly described her accomplishments. He listened with silent, watchful eyes.

When finished, Mary added, "Since those projects were a success, I've asked the board to hold university workshops for our teachers. They liked my suggestion. I believe our students will enjoy their classes more and make better grades if they're exposed to newer methods. A change of pace always refreshes."

His gaze flickered. "Of course we can provide workshops. We also offer summer courses that keep teachers current on methods. I think some members of your faculty are enrolled right now."

He stroked his chin for a moment. "Sounds like you've been managing a yeoman's job in West Park. I hope the community appreciates your efforts."

"I enjoy helping, Dr. McNeese, especially when I can interest people in improving the schools. I'd relish taking college classes. If I had a degree in education, I'd like to teach in high school."

He tapped the desk rhythmically with his manicured nails. "Why don't you work toward a degree? You seem to have the attitude and feel for teaching."

"I've taught flower-making classes in McKees Rocks. Now I'm giving bridge lessons at the Women's Club of Pittsburgh. I love teaching."

"Um, that's invigorating to hear," he commented.

She edged closer to his desk. "This spring I took the senior exams at Stowe High to get a better understanding of the graduation requirements. The information I gained will be useful in developing sessions that can enable our teachers to do even better."

His eyes opened wide in surprise.

Quickly she added. "Unfortunately, since I wasn't able to go to high school and don't have a diploma, Triangle University won't admit me, Dr. McNeese."

Baffled, he wagged his head back and forth. "First time I ever heard a story like that."

He turned and stared out the window at a yard man, mowing the lush lawn into neat, evenly spaced rows. After several minutes he moved around in his chair and faced Mary. "I'll have to get together with my staff. That will take a while. They're covered up with summer classes and registering students for fall semester. Most of our applicants have no idea what path they want to follow, even though it's one of the most important decisions they'll ever make. It takes considerable time to steer them in the right direction."

"That's why I developed *Job Pursuit*, Dr. McNeese. I wanted students to learn about different jobs. We need classes where young people explore careers and think about what they would like to do after they graduate from high school."

He nodded. "I agree, Mrs. Dunmore. My secretary will be in touch with you when I have something to report."

"Splendid, Dr. McNeese. I appreciate your taking the time to talk to me." She hesitated before getting up and quickly opened her handbag. "In case you have questions about the projects I've developed, I brought some references that might be helpful."

She handed him three envelopes. "These letters are from the two principals at Stowe High and the president at Ohio Valley Hospital."

He got out of his chair hurriedly. "Thank you, Mrs. Dunmore. I must say that you seem to have left no stone unturned."

When she headed down the hallway, she whispered, "Will I ever hear from him again?"

Chapter 47

Mary and Gertie sat at the kitchen table where they unscrambled their thoughts and spit out whatever words they wanted. The sound coming from the piano crept under the door that had been shut while Lily was giving Karen Deegan a lesson in the parlor. It was the first week in August, and Mary still hadn't heard from Dr. McNeese.

"I was afraid he wouldn't bother with me," she told Gertie. "I'll never hear from him. It'll be awfully embarrassing when I have to tell the board he hasn't gotten back to me about the workshops."

Gertie perked up. "I'm sure you'll hear, Mary. You don't understand. Things that need to get done always take longer in big institutions. They have to go through a lot of rigamarole from one office to another. Don't worry. Dr. McNeese will set up workshops for Stowe's teachers. That's the university's business."

"It's wonderful to have a friend like you," confided Mary. "I can tell you anything and know you'll understand."

Gertie seemed pleased. "The best thing about summer is that I can spend time with you and not have to rush home to fix supper for Pete."

"Be thankful you have a husband to look after," said Mary.

"I am." Gertie snickered. "It's just that I'm feeling cantankerous. Pretty soon I'll be back in the harness. School starts in September. It takes extra pep to get going again."

"I'm grateful to you," said Mary. "Lily has six pupils now, thanks to your word-of-mouth advertising. I'm wondering what to do if she gets more pupils than she can manage."

"Don't worry." Gertie reached over and gave Mary a pat on the hand. "If that happens, Lily can double her fees for new pupils. Then she can teach half as many and make as much money as she's making now."

"You're crazy," said Mary.

Gertie began to laugh. "Considering all you've been through, it's time Lily shaped up."

Sadness flitted over Mary. "Tom never wanted Lily to teach piano. I wonder what he's thinking now."

Gertie sniffled. "I'll bet he's real proud that she's doing something worthwhile."

Mary got up to let Kitty out the back door to sun herself on the banister. "I'll admit that I was getting afraid that all Lily was ever going to do was study piano and never make a living. Now she seems to like teaching, and I'm thankful."

Gertie brushed her bangs away from her forehead with a flip of her wrist. "I'm happy for both of you. I know how much you wanted Lily to go to college, but her grades would be a stumbling block. They'd never accept a girl with a C average. If it was a guy, they'd grab him in a minute."

Mary sat down again. "I hope she'll do something with what she learned in high school. All that education she suffered through is going to waste."

"Somebody told me that education is hanging around until you've caught on." Gertie giggled. "Kids change when they grow up. Lily's no exception. Some day she may surprise you and start college."

Mary snapped her fingers. "I'd love to start right this minute. I could use the money I've saved for Lily and graduate before Rose starts college. I'd be the first person in the McGuffy family and the Dunmore family to be a college student."

"You'd be the first *woman* in the family to be a college student," chimed Gertie.

Mary scowled. "I can't be. I don't have a diploma. Rose will be the first one in the family who becomes a schoolteacher. That's what Tom wanted."

Gertie gave Mary a hard look. "Don't you expect your girls to marry and have a family?"

"Sure. Nothing's more important than family. That comes first in my book. Since Tom's gone, our family circle's been broken. I can't even imagine life without my girls. But I won't be around forever. I want Lily and Rose to know enough to hold a decent job and take care of themselves. Not have to depend on a man to keep them."

"That's smart thinking," agreed Gertie.

"Rose hasn't started high school, and she's getting paid to accompany Tillie Millard while she practices singing. I'm real pleased about that."

Gertie took a deep breath. "Is Lily still taking lessons at PMI?"

"Sure. In fact, she started paying for her piano lessons this week."

"You can't beat that," declared Gertie.

Soon after Gertie left the house, Mary got a phone call from Dr. McNeese's secretary, inviting her to a meeting regarding the workshops for Stowe's teachers.

Mary waved her arms willy-nilly in the air. "I finally heard. I was beginning to think he'd given up on me," she told Lily and Rose.

"Nobody would ever do that," spurted Rose.

Lily cast a devilish look. "We'd shoot him if he gave up on you, Mother."

A glow spread over Mary's face. "I hope they're going to have some workshops that will help our teachers. Maybe I've done some good after all."

Chapter 48

Mary had no argument with the receptionist when she arrived at Triangle University the next afternoon. The girl welcomed her with "Good day. Dr. McNeese is expecting you. I'll tell him you're here, Mrs. Dunmore."

Her heart pounded as she reached his office. Dr. McNeese stood up when she entered. A tall, slim man wearing gold-rimmed glasses also rose, the same gentleman she had passed the first day she arrived at Triangle University.

Dr. McNeese made the introductions. Mary was pleased to meet Dr. Allen Masters, Trinity Workshop Director. She took the chair that was offered, trying to appear composed even though her head was in a flutter.

After sitting down and pushing aside the stack of papers on his desk, Dr. McNeese leaned forward and rested his arms on the blotter. He focused on Mary. "Dr. Masters will direct Stowe High's workshops, Mrs. Dunmore. He'll present the topics and explain the activities that have to be accomplished. Miss Madelaine Proust, the Workshop Supervisor, will assist him. I'm sorry she couldn't be here to meet you. She's teaching today."

He cleared his throat. "We've planned a workshop for fall, winter, and spring. Dates are suggested, but your board must decide on those. Each session will last six hours—three in the morning and three in the afternoon. Most of the time will be spent in the teachers pursuing activities instead of listening to lectures."

"That's great," said Mary, feeling pleased. "I'm looking forward to your workshops."

Dr. Masters handed her a notebook. "This is an outline of the sessions that you can use when talking to the board. Dr. McNeese and I will meet with you after you've reviewed the plan and discussed it with them. We'd like to have your comments and suggestions."

"Of course. I'm really excited about being involved."

Dr. McNeese leaned closer, his gaze on Mary. "Dr. Masters and I want to offer you the opportunity to assist Miss Proust. I'm sure she'll have plenty of tasks to keep you busy. I believe that helping in the workshop will be a worthwhile experience for you." He paused. "Of course, you'll receive compensation if you accept."

Mary gulped. "I'd be delighted, Dr. McNeese."

He smiled. "I appreciated the references you gave me. I sent them to Dr. Jon Stokowski, Director of Admissions, along with your Senior exam grades that I requested from Jack Thompson. I'm pleased to tell you that Dr. Stokowski has made special arrangements for you to bypass the diploma requirement. You can register for classes whenever you wish."

Mary was speechless. She hunted for words. "I can't believe what you're telling me, Dr. McNeese. It's the best news I ever heard in my life. Thank you. Thank you from the bottom of my heart."

Both men broke into big grins and shook her hand as she prepared to leave.

"I'm looking forward to working with you, Mrs. Dunmore," said Dr. Masters.

Out in the hall, Mary stopped long enough to take a deep breath. Then, with head held high, she swept past the receptionist and headed straight for Admissions. Her time had finally arrived. She welcomed it with open arms.

THE END